Shemnara turned to Davyn, regarding him solemnly. Davyn always found it eerie how she seemed to know where he was even though she couldn't see him.

"You must journey back over the mountains," she told him. "In the far north, past the ruins of Vingaard Keep, you will find the village of Kentrel . . . Outside Kentrel is the cursed house of Viranesh, the residence of the Dragon Knight."

"This Dragon Knight is the one who can break the bond?" Davyn asked.

Shemnara nodded. "If you have the aid of the Dragon Knight, you have a chance to save Nearra."

DragonLance

THE NEW ADVENTURES

SPELLBINDER QUARTET

Volume 1
TEMPLE OF THE DRAGONSLAYER
Tim Waggoner

Volume 2
THE DYING KINGDOM
Stephen D. Sullivan

Volume 3
THE DRAGON WELL
Dan Willis

Volume 4
RETURN OF THE SORCERESS
Tim Waggoner

DRAGON QUARTET

Volume 5
DRAGON SWORD
Ree Soesbee

Volume 6
DRAGON DAY
Stan Brown

Volume 7
DRAGON KNIGHT
Dan Willis

Volume 8
DRAGON SPELL
Jeff Sampson
(July 2005)

DragonLance

THE NEW ADVENTURES
VOLUME 7

Dragon Knight

Dan Willis

COVER & INTERIOR ART
Vinod Rams

MIRROR STONE

DRAGON KNIGHT
©2005 Wizards of the Coast, Inc.

All characters in this book are fictitious. Any resemblance to actual persons, living or dead, is purely coincidental.

This book is protected under the copyright laws of the United States of America. Any reproduction or unauthorized use of the material or artwork contained herein is prohibited without the express written permission of Wizards of the Coast, Inc.

Distributed in the United States by Holtzbrinck Publishing. Distributed in Canada by Fenn Ltd.

Distributed to the hobby, toy, and comic trade in the United States and Canada by regional distributors.

Distributed worldwide by Wizards of the Coast, Inc. and regional distributors.

Dragonlance, Mirrorstone, Wizards of the Coast, and their respective logos are trademarks of Wizards of the Coast, Inc., in the U.S.A. and other countries.

All Wizards of the Coast characters, character names, and the distinctive likenesses thereof are property of Wizards of the Coast, Inc.

Printed in the U.S.A.

The sale of this book without its cover has not been authorized by the publisher. If you purchased this book without a cover, you should be aware that neither the author nor the publisher has received payment for this "stripped book."

Art by Vinod Rams
Cartography by Dennis Kauth
First Printing: May 2005
Library of Congress Catalog Card Number: 2004116896

9 8 7 6 5 4 3 2 1

US ISBN: 0-7869-3735-1
ISBN-13: 978-0-7869-3735-6

620-88599000-001-EN

U.S., CANADA,	EUROPEAN HEADQUARTERS
ASIA, PACIFIC, & LATIN AMERICA	Wizards of the Coast, Belgium
Wizards of the Coast, Inc.	T Hofveld 6d
P.O. Box 707	702 Groot-Bijgaarden
Renton, WA 98057-0707	Belgium
+1-800-324-6496	+322 457 3350

Visit our web site at **www.mirrorstonebooks.com**

To my dear wife, Cherstine.
Without your love, your patience, and
your unwavering support,
this book never would have happened.

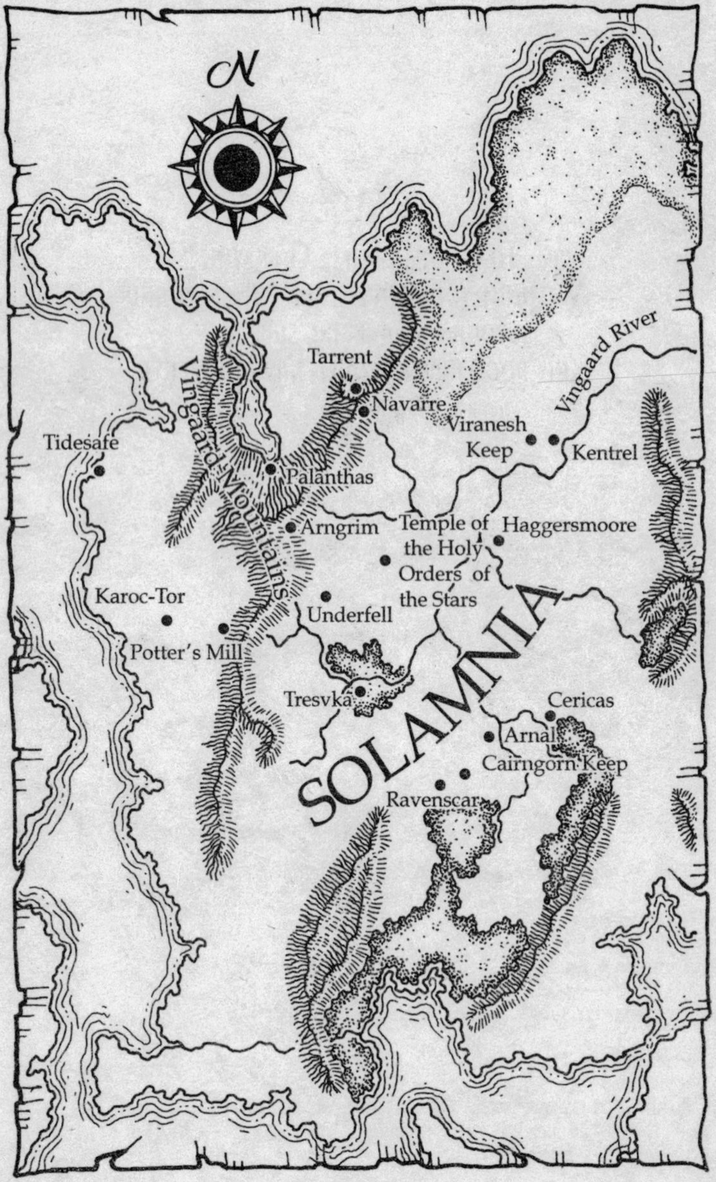
N
Tarrent
Navarre
Viranesh
Keep
Kentrel
Vingaard River
Vingaard Mountains
Tidesafe
Palanthas
Arngrim
Temple of
the Holy
Orders of
the Stars
Haggersmoore
Karoc-Tor
Underfell
Potter's Mill
SOLAMNIA
Tresvka
Cericas
Arnal
Cairngorn Keep
Ravenscar

Contents

1. Dreams and Despair 1
2. Second Chances 9
3. Back in the Dog House 14
4. Return to Potter's Mill 25
5. A Knight Quest 38
6. Arnal 44
7. The Archer 54
8. The House of Wheels 64
9. Motives 74
10. Kentrel 85
11. The Cursed House of Viranesh 91
12. Blades in the Dark 104
13. Heir to the House of Viranesh 117
14. The Pit 129
15. The Others 139
16. Exhuming the Crypt 147
17. Reunion 158
18. The Escape Plan 170
19. Fire in the House 181
20. Redemption 193
21. Dragon Knight 203
22. Aftermath 213
23. Heir to the Dragon 225
24. Paths 235
25. City of the Dead 242

CHAPTER 1

Dreams and Despair

Davyn was running.

There was no sound aside from the clamor of his boots in the long, dark corridor. He could barely see the stone floor. From somewhere ahead came a light. Somewhere in the darkness, the tunnel ended in a golden chamber. Davyn knew from experience that the light came from there.

A tortured scream echoed in the blackness. Davyn began to sprint. His lungs burned and he could barely feel his legs. But he didn't care. All that mattered was reaching the room before the screaming stopped. If he could only reach them in time, things would be different.

At last, he raced through the doorway. He stumbled in the piles of gold and jewels littering the floor. On his hands and knees, he scrambled through the treasures, his focus on the throne at the center of the room.

He was two steps from the dais when the screaming peaked in a shriek of agony and then suddenly stopped. Davyn leaped desperately, but he knew he was too late. Even as he cleared the edge and scrambled up on the dais he could hear the sound of the body falling.

Elidor.

Davyn had his sword out, but he knew there was nothing he could do. There never was. Elidor lay beside the throne, his lifeless eyes staring accusingly at Davyn. His body was impossibly thin, his life force having been ripped away by Asvoria's magic.

Beside the throne stood Nearra. She looked at him, pleading, her eyes as quiet and blue as the summer sky. For a moment he thought he might have a chance. But then the irises flashed purple and he knew she was gone. No longer the vulnerable girl Davyn remembered, the sorceress Asvoria now stood before him. Gone was Nearra's innocence and kindness. Asvoria's face was a mask of disdain and haughty pride.

Without hesitation, Davyn raised his sword and charged. He had been unable to save Nearra, unable to save Elidor, but this time . . . he might not be too late to prevent the rest.

Asvoria laughed. She raised her hands and a blue light began to shine out from beneath her palm. Her fingers morphed into claws, piercing Davyn's chest. Davyn collapsed to the platform, choking for breath. His chest tightened.

He was going to die.

Davyn sat up with a gasp. Something was holding him, restricting his movement, and he flailed against it.

A moment later, he fought his way free of his covers and leaped out of bed. He stood there in the dark of his room, panting like a racehorse and drenched with sweat.

It was the dream again. For almost six months now, this same dream had haunted him. Nearra and Elidor gazed out at Davyn with their accusing eyes.

Why could you not save us? Why were you so weak?

Davyn went to the dressing table and bent over the washbasin. Without hesitation, he poured the water from the pitcher over his head. But even the shock of the icy water on his head could not bring him back from where the dream had taken him.

As he scrubbed his hair with a towel, he stared vacantly at the peeling paint on the wall. The room was a bit run-down, but at least it was clean—unlike so many of the other places he'd stayed in since leaving his friends. In the last six months, Davyn had been all over Solamnia, trying to find some way of getting on with his life. He'd worked as a scout, a woodcutter, and even a gamekeeper. Wherever he went, though, the nightmares caught up with him. They'd keep him up nights, and only strong ale would let him sleep.

So far he'd been fired from every job he'd had.

Davyn looked in the mirror above the washbasin. He barely recognized the sunken eyes that stared back at him.

The low buzz of patrons talking drifted up from the inn's taproom on the floor below. Davyn considered his unkempt bed for a moment, before deciding he'd never be able to get to sleep now.

He threw the towel on the floor, pulled on his clothes, and made his way wearily downstairs.

The Silver Bough's taproom was a long, narrow room running along the building's south side. The hearth filled the west wall and the bar ran along the north side.

Davyn inhaled the smell of the place as he tromped down the staircase. Like most taprooms, this one smelled of simmering ale, of roasting mutton, and of the hay strewn on the floor.

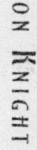

The room was filled with benches and tables where a handful of patrons were enjoying drinks as the few remaining hours of the day slipped away. A tall, rotund man with a thick moustache stood behind the bar, wiping its shiny oak surface with a towel.

"You look like you just crawled out of the Abyss," the man called as Davyn approached the bar.

Davyn grinned. Tom, the barkeep and owner of the Silver Bough, was a master of the art of conversation, like most in his profession. In the few weeks Davyn had been here in the city of Cericas, he'd taken to telling his troubles to the man in the hopes of off-loading some of them. To date, it hadn't worked.

Tom handed him a tankard of ale.

"Thanks." Davyn sipped the drink. It was strong, just the way Davyn liked it. "And if I ask for another one, give it to me."

"Do you think that's a good idea?" Tom said. "After what happened last time . . ."

"Let me worry about that," Davyn said, slapping a copper coin on the bar. The nightmares were already ruining his life. What difference did it make how much ale he drank?

Tom quickly snatched up the coin and tucked it into the pocket of his apron. "Nightmares again?" he asked, sympathy on his face.

"Well, Tom, what's a few nights' rest without them?" Davyn asked sarcastically.

"Why don't you go see the apothecary on Devon Street? She's got some roots that'll make you sleep like the dead."

"I've been." Davyn shook his head. "They don't help. They just make my head feel like it's stuffed with wool." He took a long drink. "No. This is something I've just got to live with. Until it kills me." Davyn tapped his tankard on the bar. "Another one."

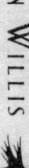

Tom rolled his eyes, but refilled Davyn's tankard. While Davyn took a swig, the barkeep ladled a thick stew into a wooden bowl.

"If you don't take better care of yourself, the nightmares won't get the chance to kill you," Tom said, putting the bowl in front of Davyn. "When was the last time you ate?"

"What day is it?" Davyn joked. He didn't really feel hungry, but he picked out a small potato with his spoon and slid it into his mouth. The spicy stew tasted better than he thought it would. His stomach grumbled, and soon he was shoveling spoonfuls into his mouth.

"These nightmares," Tom said, "what are they about?"

Davyn looked down and quickly took another bite of stewed mutton.

"Don't worry, boy." Tom chuckled. "I've been a barkeep for twenty years. Believe me, I've heard it all."

"I see my friends," Davyn answered quietly, setting his spoon aside. "They're in trouble. I try to save them, but I'm too late." His voice fell to a whisper. "I'm always too late."

"Yeah, but it's just a dream, right?"

"Yes—" Davyn looked down again and shook his head. "But they really died. They trusted me to keep them safe, and I let them die."

"I see." Tom picked up a cup and began polishing it with his rag. "Did you do everything you could to help them?"

"Yes, but it wasn't enough. They died anyway."

"Davyn," Tom sighed, putting aside the cup, "I've seen all kinds of things in this job over the years and let me tell you something. Sometimes we do everything we can and things still turn out bad. Life ain't fair."

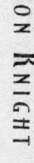

Davyn felt the buzz of anger in his ears. "Don't tell me about life, Tom. What do you know? You live your whole life hiding behind this bar, hearing other people's stories. Let me tell *you* something, Tom. It's a lot easier to sit here, dishing out stew and advice, than it is to fight for your friends. To fight and to fail."

Tom recoiled, surprised by Davyn's anger. He grabbed the tankard. "I think you've had enough."

"I was finished anyway." Davyn pushed back his stool and slapped down a coin for the stew on the bar. "I think I'll try to get some sleep now."

As Davyn stumbled up the stairs to the second floor, he wondered how he would ever get to sleep. But when he entered his room, the answer came. No sooner had he shut his door than something heavy struck him on the back of the head.

He spiraled down into darkness.

For the second time that night, Davyn startled awake. He was lying on his bed, his hands wedged behind his back. His fingers tingled and his head throbbed. At first he thought it was just the effects of too much ale. Then he remembered getting knocked out. He tried to tug his hands out from beneath himself, but they were bound tightly with rope.

The room was dark, with only a sliver of moonlight seeping in through a crack in the shutters. In the dim light, Davyn could see his sword, hanging where he'd left it on a peg on the far side of the room. He struggled to sit up.

Immediately, the cold steel of a knife pressed against his throat.

"Don't move," a voice whispered in his ear.

Davyn felt hot breath on his neck. Whoever was holding the knife was breathing quickly . . . in excitement? Or in fear?

"Your name is Davyn?" the voice hissed.

"Who wants to know?"

The knife pressed harder against his throat.

"Answer me," the voice hissed again.

"Yes," Davyn said. "Who—"

"Quiet," the voice demanded. "You passed through Trevska more than a year ago with a girl who had lost her memory?"

"That's right," Davyn admitted. "You want to tell me what this is about?" Carefully, Davyn began tugging on his bonds with his fingers. It was a risk, but he'd rather try than just sit there and let someone cut his throat.

"What was her name?" the voice whispered intently.

"Nearra."

There was a long pause, and Davyn wondered if the knife-wielder was debating whether or not to cut his throat.

"Where is she now?" the voice came again.

"She's dead," Davyn said.

At that moment, Davyn's hands came free. He drove his elbow backward into the gut of the person behind him. The knife wavered as his captor gasped, and Davyn dived forward, out of the blade's reach. He lunged across the room, grabbing his sword off the peg.

But the aftereffects of two tankards of ale made him clumsy. He stumbled, and before he could draw his sword from its scabbard, his captor charged out of the darkness.

The naked blade of the captor's dagger glinted in the moonlight. Davyn used his sheathed sword to catch the knife, forcing it aside. The hooded figure lashed out with his free hand.

Davyn caught the man's wrist and drove forward, forcing his assailant back. The hooded figure slashed with the knife, forcing Davyn to let go, and jumped back, holding the knife out defensively.

Davyn took the opportunity to draw his sword. "Drop the knife, and you might live through this."

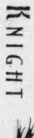

Davyn smiled. Only a fool would face a sword with a small dagger.

But to Davyn's great surprise, the hooded man did not heed his warning. He threw the dagger.

Davyn jumped aside, and the dagger spun into the darkness. He stepped forward, pinning the hooded man to the wall.

Davyn brought his sword up, ready to drive it through the man's chest. He yanked the hood back—and almost dropped his sword.

"Nearra?"

CHAPTER 2

SECOND CHANCES

The girl's deep blue eyes sparkled with anger. Her face was twisted into a sneer of rage. Her face was so much like Nearra's, and yet, as Davyn recovered from his shock, he began to see some differences. Instead of honey-blond, this girl's hair was raven-black. She looked to be about thirteen, younger than Nearra had been when Davyn had first met her.

"Where is she?" the girl demanded, tensing to continue the fight. "Where is Nearra?"

"I told you," Davyn said. He released her hood and stepped back, but he kept his sword pointed at the center of the girl's chest.

"You lie!" she cried. "If she were dead, I would know."

"In all ways that matter, she *is* dead," Davyn said. "Now tell me what this is about!"

Davyn used his sword to direct the girl to the room's single chair. Once she was seated, he sheathed his sword and lit the lamp on the table.

In the warm glow of the lamp, Davyn could see the

dark-haired girl better. She was so like Nearra. He had to keep reminding himself that it wasn't her. The girl was dressed in plain brown traveling clothes and she had the look of someone who'd been on the road a while. Everything about her seemed normal, except the fact that she'd tried to kill him.

"Who are you?" Davyn asked, picking the girl's dagger off the floor. "What do you want with Nearra?"

"My name is Jirah," the girl replied defiantly. "Nearra is my sister."

"What?" Davyn took in a quick breath. "I didn't know she had a sister."

"You said she was dead," Jirah said, her voice strong, "but that's not possible. If she were dead, then it would fall to me to break the curse. I'd know if she were dead."

"Look, I don't know about any curse, but—" Davyn stopped when the girl stood up suddenly.

"Tell me what happened to my sister." She stood there, fists clenched, exactly as Nearra would have in her place.

Davyn took a deep breath. He couldn't tell her the truth, but he had to tell her something.

"Her body is still alive," he said, "but it's been taken over by the spirit of a powerful sorceress named Asvoria."

"What? How?"

Davyn grimaced. "It's a long story . . . " He went on from there, giving Jirah a brief history of his time with Nearra. He told her about the wizard Maddoc and his schemes to revive Asvoria's spirit. He described Catriona, Sindri, and Elidor and their journeys together across the Vingaard Mountains from Arngrim to Potter's Mill, where they'd met the seeress Shemnara, then back again to Maddoc's keep, where Asvoria's spirit had finally taken over Nearra's body. They'd made one last desperate attempt to stop Asvoria in Navarre, where everything had gone so horribly wrong. He explained how the guilt over Elidor's death was eating him alive. So he'd left Catriona and Sindri on the boat to Southern Ergoth, angry with them and with himself. After months of wandering, he'd ended up here.

When he was done, Jirah just stood there, staring at him, tears in her bright blue eyes. "You promised you'd protect Nearra." Jirah's voice rose an octave. "And you let that witch take her body anyway? You just gave up?"

"I tried to stop it. Catriona, Sindri, Elidor . . . we all tried to save her." Davyn took a step back. "But in the end, I failed them all. I wasn't good enough." His voice cracked. "And now, Nearra . . . Elidor . . . they're gone because of me. They depended on me to take care of them and I failed."

Jirah moved toward him. "But it's not too late, right? You said her body still lives. That means there's hope. We can still save her."

Davyn hung his head. "I don't think Nearra even exists anymore." And before he could stop himself, he began to cry.

"What are you doing?" Jirah grabbed Davyn's shoulders and shook him hard. "Do you think Nearra would want this? Do you think she'd want you to be standing here, half-drunk and feeling sorry for yourself?"

Davyn wiped his eyes.

"Look," Jirah said. "I can see that you're a fighter. A moment ago, you weren't going to give up until you had me pinned. Now you're telling me you don't have it in you to keep fighting for my sister?"

Davyn looked up at her, his cheeks sticky with tears. He gritted his teeth. "You don't understand. I've been to the Abyss and back trying to save your sister. But tangling with Asvoria has only brought death to everyone I love. I'm a failure. Even my friends think so." Davyn glanced at the floor. "My former friends."

"Everyone deserves a second chance." Jirah crossed her arms. "And after everything, you owe it to Nearra to help me find her."

Davyn didn't want to, but he met her eyes and nodded a little.

"That's better." She smiled.

Davyn felt a sudden pang in his chest. She looked so much like Nearra.

Jirah turned and began to pace the room. "You said the last time you saw Asvoria was in Navarre. So, all we need to do is return there and find her."

"You make it sound so easy," Davyn said, laughing a little. The girl was so determined that he felt a tiny wave of hope washing over him. But it quickly passed. He frowned. "Even if we go back to Navarre, there's no guarantee we'll find Asvoria. And even if we do find her, how are we going to force the sorceress out of Nearra's body? It's impossible."

"Nothing's impossible," Jirah declared, passion in her voice. She stopped her pacing and looked out the window. "There must be someone, somewhere who can tell us how to save Nearra."

Davyn was about to remind Jirah just how big the world really was when she suddenly whirled around to face him.

"The seeress!" she said. "The one in Potter's Mill. You said she foresaw everything that happened to you. Maybe she'll be able to predict how we'll rescue Nearra!"

Davyn shrugged. "She might be able to help *you*."

"Oh, no," Jirah said, gripping his shoulder. "You're not going to get off that easy. You're going to take me to Potter's Mill.

You made this mess and you have to clean it up. It's time for you to stop running."

Davyn wanted to tell her to go straight to the Abyss, but her words stung more than he would care to admit. She was right. If there really was a way to fix all this, he owed it to Nearra to try. No, he owed it to himself. Maybe then the nightmares would stop.

"All right," he said. "I'll take you to Shemnara. We'll get you a room for tonight and start for the mountains in the morning."

CHAPTER 3

BACK IN THE DOG HOUSE

After two weeks on the road, Jirah was just as much a mystery to Davyn as when he first met her. She was Nearra's sister, Davyn was absolutely sure of that. Quite apart from the family resemblance, there was a certain innocence about her that reminded Davyn of Nearra. It was hard not to trust her.

"Can we rest for a minute?" Jirah panted, slumped under the weight of the pack on her back.

"We're almost there." Davyn tugged at Hegga's reins. The mule and the small cart she pulled behind her weren't quite as sturdy as he would have liked, but it was all they could afford for now. Davyn did have a fair amount of steel saved up from his series of failed jobs, but he knew they'd need many supplies for the long journey to Potter's Mill. So he'd bought a cheap cart and mule and kept the rest of his coins locked in a strongbox in the back of Hegga's cart.

Davyn tipped his head toward the rickety cart and called out, "Why don't you throw off your pack? It will make it easier to walk. I bought this old thing to carry our gear, after all."

Jirah looked down and suddenly began walking briskly. "That's all right. I'll manage."

"Have it your way." Davyn shrugged. "The trading post is just up ahead. It's run by a dwarf named Dog."

"Dog?" Jirah said.

"Don't ask," Davyn said. "We're going to stop there and buy the equipment we'll need to go over the mountain. Then, in the morning, we'll follow this road up and over and on to the town of Potter's Mill."

Jirah took a breath to ask more questions, but just then they rounded a bend and Dog's trading post came into view. It was much as Davyn remembered it: a squat, stone building appearing far too small to be a business. Davyn knew that most of the building was, in fact, underground. The slate roof seemed to have been replaced with red clay tiles, and a good portion of the porch seemed to be new.

Davyn stopped the little cart next to the porch. He set the brake and dumped the last of their oats into Hegga's feedbag.

"Just a minute," Davyn said as Jirah mounted the steps up to the porch. He turned and rummaged in his pack for a moment before coming out with a scroll case.

"What's that?" Jirah asked.

"An old debt," Davyn replied, climbing up to the porch.

Unlike the last time he'd been here, the door was ajar. It was only just noon, and Dog's place was open for business. Davyn pushed the door open and a bell above it jingled.

Inside, the trading post was exactly as Davyn remembered it. Cupboards full of goods for sale lined the walls and a large, round table took up the bulk of the middle of the room. On the far wall was an iron stove with a kettle on it. The door that led to the rooms below stood slightly ajar.

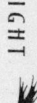

"Well, lightning strike me," a guttural voice called from the table. "I never thought I'd clap eyes on you again." Dog got up and shook Davyn's hand vigorously.

"It's good to see you, too," Davyn said.

Dog was dressed in linen breeches with a fine shirt and an embroidered vest with brass buttons. His beard was braided and combed and he had silver clips holding the tips of his mustache. To Davyn, the dwarf appeared to be doing very well for himself.

"I see you managed to avoid that dwarf feller," Dog said, still shaking Davyn's hand.

"Dwarf?" Davyn asked.

Dog spit into a brass spittoon. "The Theiwar."

"Oddvar." Davyn nodded. "He came here?"

"Oh, yes," Dog said. "Tried to threaten me into revealing which way you went. Said he'd use his magic on me."

"I hope he didn't cause too much trouble," Davyn said. He knew Oddvar didn't have any magic to speak of, but the dark dwarf was cunning, resourceful, and more than a little vindictive.

"I knowed he was a fraud when I saw them goblins with him," Dog said. "No self-respecting dwarf would take up with goblins, wizard or no. I told him I didn't care a whit for his magic and shooed him off. If I'd known what he had up his sleeve, I would've shot him, though."

"What happened?" Davyn asked.

"First he tried to skewer me with a tainted knife, then he had his little helpers set fire to my place." Dog shrugged. "Lucky it's mostly stone, but he burned off a perfectly good porch."

Davyn was about to ask if anyone was hurt when the dwarf's eyes narrowed and he leaned around Davyn.

"Hello," he said, staring at Jirah. "Who's this now?"

"This is Jirah," Davyn said.

The girl smiled weakly.

"You look downright tuckered, dearie. Why don't you have a seat?" Dog gestured to one of the hard chairs. "And let me take your cloaks and that heavy pack. I'll hang them up where they'll be safe."

Davyn gratefully handed over his cloak but Jirah pulled back reflexively. "That's all right. I like to keep my things . . . with me."

"All right." Dog shrugged. "Let me get you something warm to drink." Dog tottered over to the stove pot and began fixing tea.

As Dog poured steaming water into a yellow teapot, he hollered, "That's not the same girl you came through with last time. I thought you were rather taken with that other gal."

Davyn blushed a deep shade of pink. "Jirah is Nearra's little sister."

"Good," Dog said, handing Davyn a cracked cup. "I'd hate to think a nice young feller like you would play with a lady's affection."

Davyn blushed even more. He set the scroll case on the table without looking up. He couldn't bear to meet Jirah's eyes.

"What's this?" Dog asked, unlatching the case and pulling out a roll of parchment.

"And you call yourself a dwarf," Davyn said, as the color in his face returned to normal. "This is what I owe you."

Dog unrolled the scroll and leaned over the weathered parchment, squinting to read the writing. "Ah," Dog said, his eyes alight. "This map is accurate?"

Davyn nodded. "I bought it in Cericas. The cartographer swore it was perfect."

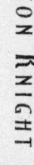

"I've always wondered what's at the other end of this road," the dwarf said. "And here's my place." He beamed.

Davyn was about to point out Potter's Mill when he saw Jirah suddenly perk up and look at the map intently.

"Maybe we'd better get down to business," Davyn said.

"Right," Dog said, rolling up the map and slipping it back in its case. "What do you need? You caught me early enough in the year this time. I'm fully stocked."

The remainder of the afternoon was taken up with provisioning the little cart for their journey. This time Davyn bought thick cloaks, a tent, and a full set of cooking gear. Dog threw in some fresh food and cavern root, and Davyn even bought a small sack of dwarven hardtack for old time's sake. By the time he was done assembling the gear and packing his cart, the sun was hovering over the horizon.

"I trust you'll stay the night," Dog said.

It was more of a command than a question, but Davyn didn't mind. He'd never intended to leave before morning.

Like the last time, Davyn and Jirah stayed in the big common room downstairs. This time the dwarf-sized bunks didn't bother Davyn so much, though he would swear he was two inches taller than last time. He lay in the bed for a long time just thinking. Finally, unable to sleep, he reached into his pack and pulled out an intricately carved flute. Davyn stared at it in the dim glow of the dying fire.

The flute had been Elidor's. Davyn hadn't even known the elf could play, but they'd found it tucked into his belt after . . .

Davyn shook his head, trying to shake the vision of Elidor's death out of his mind.

He got up quietly. The kitchen was on the other end of the underground chambers. If he shut the door, Davyn could probably practice the flute without disturbing anyone.

He was almost to the kitchen door when he heard the sound of talking. A wave of déjà vu washed over him as he remembered finding Nearra awake in the middle of the night in that very same kitchen.

As Davyn came silently through the door, he saw Jirah sitting at the table. A large cup of what Davyn assumed to be tea rested in front of her, but instead of drinking, she was hunched over her lap, staring at a mirror and muttering to herself.

He glanced down and saw her pack resting beneath the chair. He cleared his throat, and said, "Hi."

Jirah nearly jumped out of her seat. "I didn't hear you come in." Blushing furiously, she leaned over and stuffed the mirror into her pack.

"You're up late," Davyn said, still unable to get the image of Nearra out of his head.

"I couldn't sleep," Jirah stammered. "Tea calms my nerves."

"I was looking for somewhere to practice." Davyn held up the flute.

"What's that?" Jirah asked.

Davyn sat down opposite Jirah and handed her the long, slim instrument. It was made of some dark wood and stained with years of handling. Beautiful carvings of vines ran around the body of the flute, roses surrounded the finger holes, and an intricate family crest was carved just below the mouthpiece.

"It's beautiful," Jirah said, turning the instrument over in her hands. "Why haven't you played for me?"

Davyn blushed, taking the instrument back as Jirah offered it to him.

"I don't play very well," he admitted.

"You have an awful nice flute for someone who doesn't play well," Jirah said.

"It . . . it's not mine," Davyn said after a pause. "It belonged to Elidor."

"The elf?" Jirah asked.

Davyn nodded. "After his death, I vowed to learn to play it. I haven't made much progress, though."

Jirah reached out and put her hand on his.

"You must have been great friends," she said.

Her hand was soft, smooth, and warm, and her dark hair shimmered in the dim light. With a shiver, Davyn remembered the last time he'd sat with a girl in Dog's kitchen in the middle of the night. His chest tightened at the memory of that moment and he forced his mind back to the conversation. "Yes, Elidor and I were close. As close as if we had been from the same family. Like you and Nearra."

A strange look of anger and pain flickered across Jirah's face and she withdrew her hand.

"Nearra and I weren't like that," she said, looking away. "She was the perfect child, while I was nothing but a disappointment." She sighed deeply, a faraway look in her eyes. "It's not important. Why don't you play me something?"

Davyn wanted to know more, but he could tell Jirah didn't want to say anything more.

So instead, he placed the flute to his lips and managed to squeak his way through a folk tune a bard had taught him. Jirah smiled and applauded like it was the most amazing thing she'd ever heard. "That was wonderful!"

"Liar." Davyn grinned. "But thanks anyway."

Three days out from Dog's trading post found Davyn and Jirah in the heart of the mountains. Davyn was amazed at how quickly the trip was going. Last time it had taken almost two weeks to get to this part of the mountains. Of course this time he knew where he was going, and he had Hegga to pull all the heavy gear. That plus decent food, cooking gear, and a tent made the trip downright enjoyable. They still had to stop early each night to make camp. Although there was no snow, the nights were decidedly cold. Shelter and a good fire were essential.

While Davyn set up the tent, Jirah insisted on chopping firewood. Davyn tried to help her, but she pushed him away. "My father's a woodcutter. I've been doing this for as long as I can remember."

As Davyn watched, Jirah sunk the axe into the stump she'd been using to split the wood. Even as she chopped wood, she still wore the heavy pack on her back. She wore it everywhere. She slung a few of the split pieces at Davyn for him to build a fire, then went back to chopping wood without a word.

After a good half hour of chopping, Jirah gathered up the rest of the split pieces and trudged to the fire where Davyn sat minding dinner.

"I think that will be enough to keep us warm through the night," she said, dumping the pieces on their ample woodpile. She struggled out of her pack and sat down, holding the bag in her lap.

Davyn poured her a cup of tea and passed it to her. Jirah mumbled her thanks and sat, staring at the fire and sipping her drink.

"Dinner's almost done," Davyn reported, checking the iron pot. "Now why don't you tell me what you've got in the pack?"

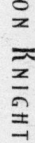

The question took Jirah by surprise. She reflexively clutched the bag to her chest.

"What do you mean?" She sounded scared.

"You go everywhere with that bag," Davyn said, leaning back against a fallen log. "You even wear it while you're chopping wood."

"I don't know what you mean." Jirah set the bag aside as if it didn't mean anything.

"Look, if I wanted to steal whatever you've got in there, I could have done it by now," Davyn said. "If you want my help, you're going to have to start trusting me."

Jirah sighed and nodded slowly. "I suppose you're right." Slowly, she picked up the pack and withdrew a long wooden box from inside. With a practiced move, she slid one of the side panels out, revealing a padded lining. Cradled in the lining was an intricately carved statue of a dragon.

Davyn let out a low whistle. The dragon statue seemed to call to him. It wasn't steel or covered in jewels, just a simple black statue, yet he wanted to move around the fire to examine it more closely. The prospect of falling under its magic, however, kept him where he was.

"This is the Trinistyr," she said. "I've been carrying it with me, in the hope that when we find Nearra—"

"If we find Nearra," Davyn interrupted.

Jirah gulped and nodded, and then continued. "One of my ancestors, a wizard named Anselm, found it after receiving a vision from Paladine. Ever since then, a curse has lingered over my family."

"What kind of curse?" Davyn asked.

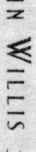

Jirah looked him in the eye. "Anselm was a wizard, as was every member of our family who came before him. Powerful magic-users. His descendants—my family—should have had the talent to use magic as well. But the curse has robbed all of us of power."

"So how can you break this curse?"

"No one knows. All I know is that when it is broken, the power of the gods will flow through Nearra—"

"But if that happens while Asvoria inhabits Nearra's body . . ."

Jirah nodded. "Asvoria will have access to the power of the gods themselves." She looked down at her hands, and tears suddenly blossomed in her eyes. "If you and your stupid father hadn't kidnapped—"

"He's not my father," Davyn said softly.

"I don't care!" Jirah yelled. "If all of you hadn't interfered in our lives, Nearra would be home safe now. She'd break the curse, and my family would be free. Instead, you've put the whole world in danger."

Jirah clutched the Trinistyr to her chest and wept. Davyn got up slowly and knelt in front of her, gently lifting her face until her eyes met his.

"I'm sorry for all the trouble I've caused," he said. "And I promise you that I'll make it right or die trying."

Jirah suddenly threw her arms around Davyn and buried her face in his shoulder, still crying. Davyn patted her shoulder and let her cry. After a long, awkward moment, she withdrew.

"I'm sorry," she said. "I know you're doing your best to help. I'm just scared."

Davyn took the lid off the iron pot and scooped hot stew into a bowl.

"Eat something," he said, handing the bowl to Jirah. "We'll get an early start in the morning. If we push a bit, we'll be in Potter's Mill by tomorrow."

Jirah wiped her tears away and began to eat. Davyn had lost his appetite so he sat down to play Elidor's intricately carved flute.

The sound seemed to fill their little campsite and echo off the trees. A second, more distant echo accompanied Davyn from the granite peaks. The sound was somehow soothing and seemed to relax the knots in Davyn's stomach. He didn't know if his practicing was paying off, but in the quiet glens of the mountains, even his unskilled playing sounded like music.

CHAPTER 4

RETURN TO POTTER'S MILL

The sun was low in the western sky when Hegga pulled the little cart off the dirt road and onto the cobbled main street of Potter's Mill. The last time Davyn entered Potter's Mill it had been dusk, and the houses had all been shuttered. The only lights in town had been the torches that lit up the town square to ward off the Beast.

Now, as Davyn stepped onto the cobbled streets, he could almost feel the energy of the town. Everywhere he looked, shutters were open and people were moving about. Children played in the streets, and the smells of cooking suppers filled the air. Davyn felt both happiness and regret as they strolled down the street. He knew the town's freedom had come at the expense of his own father's life.

There was a line of horses and carts outside of the town's single tavern, and the last few customers were still loading their wagons out in front of the trading post. One of the clerks at the trading post noticed the new cart rattling down the street. After a moment, he broke into a wide smile and waved.

"Davyn!" the man called. "Welcome back! Are you staying?"

"For a few days," Davyn said. "We'll be at the inn."

"Does everyone here know you?" Jirah asked.

Davyn grinned. "Maybe we should have waited and come in after dark," he said. They brought the cart to a halt at the end of the row of horses. By the time Davyn had tied up Hegga, word of his presence had spread through most of the town. The innkeeper, a woman named Kirian, came hustling out of the tavern with a group of townsfolk in tow.

"You're back," she gushed, sweeping Davyn into a massive hug. She released Davyn and turned to Jirah. "Someone said you had Nearra with you," Kirian said, looking disappointed.

"Not this time." Davyn shook his head, wondering how anyone could mistake the dark-haired Jirah for her blonde sister. "This is Jirah, Nearra's little sister."

Kirian brightened and the smile returned to her face. "Well, Nearra's sister is certainly welcome as well. Come inside and get something to eat. You both look traveled."

Davyn self-consciously tried to brush the road dirt from his clothes. Jirah chuckled.

"I'll have a room prepared for each of you," Kirian said as she swept back into the tavern. "How long will you be staying?"

Davyn wanted to answer but he was stopped by the sea of townsfolk crowding around him.

"You look like you could use a drink," the blacksmith said. "Let me buy you something to wet your whistle."

"Is Cat coming too?" the baker called.

"What about Elidor and the others?" someone else said.

Davyn got a cold knot in the pit of his stomach when he thought of his friends. He held up his hands for quiet. "Let me get settled," he said, "then I'll answer all your questions."

It took Davyn and Jirah almost five minutes to reach the tavern door. Before they could go in, however, Davyn heard a familiar voice from behind him.

"You're in town five minutes and you don't look up your friends?"

"Set-ai!" Davyn cried, pushing his way back through the crowd.

The grizzled woodsman was just as Davyn remembered him: tall and broad in his green armor, dragon claws hanging from his belt. His face was wrinkled and his hair was white over a salt-and-pepper beard, but his eyes sparkled with a youthful spirit.

Set-ai pulled him into a bear hug.

"How you been, boy-o?" he asked, thumping Davyn on the back. "Where's the rest of you?"

Davyn couldn't meet Set-ai's eyes. Set-ai had trained him, had prepared him to lead, and he'd let the man down. In the end, he hadn't been up to the challenge.

Davyn wrinkled his brow but didn't get to reply.

"Hey!" a chipper voice called out. "Where'd you get all that steel! And who's this with you?"

"Mudd," Davyn cried out, shaking hands with the young man. He was taller and lankier than Davyn remembered, but it was Mudd all the same. "What do you mean, steel?"

"I just looked in your strongbox," Mudd declared, as if it were the most natural thing in the world to do.

"How—" Davyn started, but Set-ai cut him off.

"The boy's picked up bad habits recently," he growled. "I keep tellin' him not to go through other people's things, but he just doesn't seem to learn."

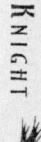

"It's not my fault Solamnic locks are so easy to open," Mudd said with a shrug, though he did take a step away from Set-ai's glowering form. "Dwarven ones are the toughest," he went on, "though some gnome ones, the ones that work, are really tricky. They've got all these little pieces—"

"Since you're so familiar with my strongbox," Davyn turned to Mudd, "bring it in and have Kirian put it in the strongroom for me."

Mudd smiled enthusiastically and darted off toward the cart.

"Don't mind him. He's harmless." Set-ai sighed. "Ever since you left Potter's Mill, I've been stayin' with him and his sister Hiera. Their parents were killed by the Beast and they needed someone to bring 'em up right." Set-ai shook his head. "But I don't know if I've been much use. I've tried to interest Mudd in the fightin' arts but he's obsessed with takin' things apart and findin' out how they work. I tell you, the boy should've been a gnome."

Kirian had a table ready once Davyn and the others finally made it inside. She'd pulled it off into one corner so Davyn and his friends would have some privacy.

Davyn waited for the cider to arrive, then started in. He related the whole story: how they'd gone against Maddoc, and how Asvoria had taken control of Nearra and killed Elidor. He told them about his leaving Cat and Sindri and then being found by Jirah. When he was done, there was silence at the table.

"Sometimes I forget you're just a kid, yourself," Set-ai said at last.

"Thanks," Davyn grumbled, feeling lower than ever.

"I didn't mean it that way, lad." Set-ai put a hand on Davyn's shoulder. "I mean that there are things you learn about life when you get older."

"Like what?" Mudd piped up.

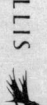

"Like there are things you just can't control," Set-ai explained. "And you're a fool if you think you can. Sometimes bad things happen and it don't matter how good you are or how smart or how strong."

"I wish I could believe that," Davyn said, gritting his teeth. "But I was there."

Set-ai looked like he wanted to say more but he thought better of it. "Someday, you'll understand."

"So, why did you come back to Potter's Mill?" Mudd asked.

"Shemnara didn't tell you?" Davyn asked. The first time he'd been to Potter's Mill, the seeress had known everything about him long before he had arrived.

"She doesn't tell me anything about you anymore," Mudd said, a grumpy look on his face.

"She didn't want to worry him," Set-ai confessed.

"Did she tell *you* why Davyn's here?" Mudd demanded.

Set-ai blushed. "Well, no," he admitted. "She seems to like her secrets." Set-ai turned back to Davyn. "All she told me was that you'd be here tonight."

"So she's had visions of us already?" Jirah asked.

Set-ai grinned mischievously. "Well," he said, giving Davyn a conspiratorial wink. "She doesn't see much of anything these days, but for Davyn she makes an exception."

Mudd stood up suddenly. The boy was so full of nervous energy that every move seemed sudden.

"I'll go tell her that you're coming," he said as he darted out of the room.

"Come on," Set-ai said, getting to his feet. "The speed that boy moves, he's probably there already, and we don't want to keep the lady waiting."

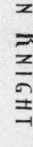

Set-ai led them out of the tavern and up the street to the end where Shemnara's house stood. Davyn could feel his heart beating more quickly as the large house came into view. He'd first seen the house the night the Beast attacked Potter's Mill. As they drew closer, Davyn saw the new section of railing on Shemnara's porch. It had weathered considerably in the time he'd been gone, but it was still visible. Mudd replaced it the day after the Beast had smashed through it in a vain attempt to eat Elidor. Davyn could almost see the elf leaping out of the way of those razor-sharp claws.

Davyn sighed as he followed Set-ai up the stairs and onto the porch. So much had happened since his last visit, and very little of it was good.

Mudd met them at the door and ushered them into the parlor. The emblem of Mishakal stood in its usual place over the mantle, and several comfortable chairs were gathered around the hearth.

Davyn kicked the dust off his boots before entering. Inside, he found Shemnara waiting for him in the chair nearest the fire. She was clad in a plain, blue dress and her white hair was bound behind her head with a silver clip. Her face was lined but not so much as to suggest great age. For the first time, Davyn realized he had no idea how old Shemnara actually was. The white cloth she wore around her blind eyes obscured much of her face, making it impossible to guess.

"Welcome back," Shemnara said, carefully putting the teacup back on the saucer.

"It's good to see you again," Davyn said.

Shemnara smiled and stood. She reached out her hand and Davyn took it.

"You're very kind," she said, "but I know young people. You've come because you need my help."

Davyn turned to Mudd but the boy just shrugged.

"One doesn't have to be a seer to know that." Shemnara laughed, then suddenly her face turned serious.

"I'm sorry about Elidor," she said. "I saw that he fell into shadow several months back."

"You've been watching us?" Davyn asked, genuinely shocked.

"Should you be doin' that?" Set-ai said in a concerned voice.

"I shall use the time left to me in the manner I see fit," Shemnara said, then she turned to Davyn and smiled. "He's as bad as a nursemaid."

Set-ai snorted indignantly.

"Take me back to my chamber," Shemnara said, squeezing Davyn's hand.

Davyn knew very well that Shemnara could walk the corridors of her house without aid, but he put her hand on his arm and led the way.

In the chamber, there was a comfortable, padded chair for Shemnara directly behind a small table. Hard chairs stood around the outside of the room for those seeking visions. Davyn suspected that these chairs were so hard in part to prevent the seekers from overstaying their welcome.

Davyn led Shemnara to her chair and then took the seat next to her. The seeress reached out and clutched the sides of the round table. Shemnara paused, waiting for the others to take a seat. Once they were all inside, Mudd started to leave.

"Stay, Mudd," Shemnara said. "My visions may be dwindling, but I can see that you are tied up in this."

Mudd shut the door and took a seat next to Set-ai.

"Set-ai said you weren't having visions as much as you used to," Davyn said. "Is something wrong?"

In answer, Shemnara lifted the wooden tabletop from the basin. Pale light streamed out from the basin, but it was not as bright as Davyn remembered it. As he looked in, he could see that the thick liquid sloshing restlessly in the basin was barely half of what he remembered.

"You see?" Shemnara asked. "Ever since the Dragon Well was destroyed, my basin has been dwindling. Every time I seek a vision, a little more is used up."

Shemnara set the tabletop cover aside. With a practiced hand, she untied the white cloth that bound her eyes, folded it, and set it in her lap. The white scar across Shemnara's face seemed to shimmer silver in the pale light.

Davyn watched all this in silence. When he'd seen Shemnara use the basin on previous occasions, an undulating mist had reached up from the liquid, as if attempting to escape. Now Shemnara had to lean down to entice the magic to rise.

A long, misty tendril crept up above the level of the basin. It wavered there for a moment, then suddenly transformed itself, becoming a ghostly dragon before rushing forward to strike Shemnara in her sightless eyes.

For a moment, Shemnara's eyes glowed with the same pale light as the liquid in the basin. Another tendril rose out of the well and struck the seeress's eyes, then another and another. Some of them formed shapes in the air as they rose. Davyn saw images of swords, castles, human forms, and several more dragons.

Those images worried Davyn more than a little bit.

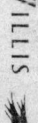

At last, Shemnara sat back in her chair and closed her still faintly glowing eyes. She sighed and then motioned for Davyn to put the tabletop on the basin. She bound her eyes again with the white cloth and, once Davyn was finished with the table, she sat up formally in her chair. Everyone in the room seemed to be holding their breath.

"Nearra is not beyond our reach," she began.

There were sighs of relief around the room.

"When Nearra was exposed to the Dragon Well, its magic formed a bond between her soul and that of Asvoria. As long as this bond exists, Asvoria will never be able to completely destroy Nearra, nor will Nearra ever be free of Asvoria."

"How does that help us?" Jirah interrupted, desperation in her voice.

"It gives us hope," Shemnara explained. "While Nearra survives, it is within your power to save her."

"Are you saying that she's in danger?" Davyn asked.

"Asvoria is moving forward with her plans," Shemnara said. "Soon she will discover the bond that links her to Nearra. When that happens, she will use all her magic to break the bond. Eventually, she will succeed."

"Then I've got to get to her before that happens," Davyn declared.

"What about me?" Jirah protested. "I'm coming with you."

"Me too," Mudd piped up. "Shemnara said I've got a part in this. You're not leaving me behind."

"Absolutely not," Davyn said. "Asvoria is evil and cruel. She'd kill you in a second if she got the chance."

"We'll just have to take her by surprise then," Jirah said.

"It's too dangerous," Davyn said. "I've already got one friend's death on my conscience. I'm not risking any more."

"I'm afraid you have no choice," Shemnara said softly. In the heat of the argument the seeress's presence had been forgotten.

"You cannot break the Dragon Well's bond easily," she explained. "Only one living person can break that bond."

"Who?" Mudd gasped when Shemnara did not immediately continue. The poor boy was squirming so hard in his chair, Davyn worried he'd wear a hole in the wood.

Shemnara turned to Davyn, regarding him solemnly. Davyn always found it eerie how she seemed to know where he was even though she couldn't see him.

"You must journey back over the mountains," she told him. "In the far north, past the ruins of Vingaard Keep, you will find the village of Kentrel." Shemnara turned to Mudd. "Don't eat the fish when you're there, dear." Then she turned back to Davyn. "Outside Kentrel is the cursed house of Viranesh, the residence of the Dragon Knight."

"This Dragon Knight is the one who can break the bond?" Davyn asked.

Shemnara nodded. "If you have the aid of the Dragon Knight, you have a chance to save Nearra."

"You still haven't explained why I can't go alone," Davyn said.

"Because, dear boy, there are things that even someone as talented as you cannot accomplish alone," Shemnara said. "You will need the aid of your friends and of others if you are to succeed."

Davyn slumped back in his chair, rubbing his temples.

Jirah smiled. "Ha," she said. "I told you that you'd need me."

"It is true that you must go," Shemnara said, "but you must leave your relic behind."

Jirah gasped. "How did you—"

Shemnara held up her hand. "Just as Davyn will fail if he leaves you behind, you will fail if you take the Trinistyr."

Jirah folded her arms, a defiant look on her face.

"Well," Set-ai spoke for the first time, "it sounds like you're going to need all the friends you can get, boy-o. Count me in."

Davyn flashed his friend a grateful smile, but Shemnara's face darkened.

"Are you sure?" she asked, concern plain in her voice.

"I am," Set-ai said without hesitation. "Even if it means I won't come back."

Shemnara smiled, but Davyn thought the expression looked forced. She placed her hand gently on Set-ai's massive hand.

"It won't be easy for you," she said. Her voice was so quiet it was almost a whisper.

Set-ai reached out with his other hand and placed it atop Shemnara's.

"I'll be all right," he said. There was no trace of fear or doubt in his voice.

"Thanks," Davyn said, after a pause. "I'll feel a lot better with you in charge."

"No," Shemnara countered. "Set-ai may go, but it is you who must lead. Only you have the power to succeed, Davyn."

"Shemnara's right," Set-ai interjected before Davyn could protest. "This is your task, lad. You've got to see it through on your own terms."

Davyn took a deep breath to tell Shemnara and Set-ai what they could do with *his* task, but thought better of insulting his friends. He didn't want Mudd and Jirah along, but he had to admit that with Set-ai there, the chances of them staying safe were greater.

"All right." Davyn turned to Shemnara. "You mentioned that we'd need others to help us. Where do we find them?"

"The archer will find you," Shemnara said. "The rest you must seek out. Set-ai will take you to the gnome—"

Set-ai cleared his throat. "I only ever knowed one gnome, and that's Bloody Bob. He lives in Haggersmoore, a little town on the Vingaard River."

Shemnara nodded. "But first you shall seek out the dark dwarf in Arnal."

"Dark dwarf?" Davyn asked, an ugly suspicion growing in his mind. "What dark dwarf?"

"The one who worked for the wizard," Shemnara said. "For Maddoc."

"What?" Davyn slammed his fist on the arm of his chair. "Have you gone completely mad? Oddvar spent the better part of the last two years trying to get me killed! I can't ask him for help!"

Shemnara recoiled as if she'd been slapped.

"Easy there, boy-o," Set-ai said, rising out of his chair.

Davyn lowered his eyes and took a deep breath, forcing himself to calm down. "I'm sorry," he said. "I shouldn't have yelled. But I don't understand. Why Oddvar? Why is he so important?"

Shemnara leaned forward. "Viranesh is cursed. Oddvar is the only person to ever enter the keep and live to tell about it."

"Ever?" Mudd squeaked.

Shemnara nodded. "Other than the dwarf, no one has escaped Viranesh Keep in the twenty years since its cursing."

Davyn's heart sunk. This trip was sounding more and more dangerous by the minute. It was one thing to do it on his own, but with all these others depending him? With Oddvar? Davyn shook his head. "I don't know—"

"Know this, my child." Shemnara gripped Davyn's arm. "If you do not make this journey, Nearra will be lost. Forever."

"This is just great," Davyn said, shrugging off Shemnara's grip and standing up. "As if I don't have enough to deal with, now I have to make a trip to a cursed keep, risking the lives of two kids, an old man, some archer I've never even met, a bloody gnome, and my own worst enemy!" Davyn's voice rose to a crescendo. "And if I don't, Nearra will die?" Davyn whirled around to face Set-ai. "Is this what you meant by life being out of my control, Set-ai? Well, I'm sick of it! I'm sick of this responsibility. I've already failed once at this, and I'm not going to do it again!"

With that, Davyn stormed out, slamming the door behind him.

There was a long silence, then Jirah nervously cleared her throat.

"So," she whispered. "What do we do now?"

CHAPTER 5

A Knight Quest

"This is insane!"

Davyn knew he was ranting but there didn't seem to be anything else to do. He paced back and forth on the soft ground of the forest, bathed in the pale moonlight. He had paced so much in the short time he'd been there that his boots were already beginning to wear a track in the soft earth.

"How many people does Shemnara want me to kill?" Davyn shouted at the little wooden marker that stuck up from the ground. The marker was a flat board with the name "Senwyr" carved on it.

"I can't do this." Davyn slumped against a nearby tree. "I won't do this. I won't lead any more people to their deaths." His voice dropped to a whisper. "I won't let anyone else pay for my mistakes."

"Is that what you think you're doin'?"

Davyn whirled, half-drawing his sword. Set-ai stood at the far side of the little clearing, regarding Davyn coolly.

"How did you find me?" Davyn grumbled, slamming his sword back in its sheath.

"Wasn't hard," Set-ai said. He stepped out of the trees into the little clearing and sat down with his back to a tree. "I figured you'd want to talk to your dad."

Set-ai nodded to the wooden marker. Now that Elidor was dead, Set-ai was the only one alive who knew where Davyn had buried his father's ashes.

"You realize you're makin' a fool of yourself?" Set-ai said with no trace of humor.

"Because I don't want any more people to get killed on my account?" Davyn almost laughed. "I guess I'm a fool then."

"So, what happens to Nearra if we all stay here where it's safe?"

Davyn looked away. He didn't have any answer for that.

"And what about this Asvoria?" Set-ai continued. "What's going to happen to the world if no one stops her? How many people will die then?"

"Cat will stop her," Davyn said, not believing it.

"You heard Shemnara," Set-ai countered. "You're the only one who can do this. Even if Cat kills Asvoria, if she's still bound to Nearra, then Nearra will die too."

Set-ai paused until Davyn turned to look at him. "You're the only chance that girl has."

Davyn slammed his head back into the tree. He just stared up at the stars. Set-ai was right. Davyn knew it. He just couldn't get Shemnara's words out of his head. No one had escaped Viranesh Keep in twenty years.

Viranesh Keep was a deathtrap and Shemnara expected him to just lead people right into it.

Hot tears burned in Davyn's eyes. Normally he wouldn't have let Set-ai see him cry, but he was so overwhelmed he didn't care.

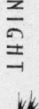

"What am I going to do?" he pleaded. "You heard Shemnara—this quest is dangerous. There's a good chance that none of us will make it back. I can't be responsible for that."

"Don't worry so much, lad. Shemnara wouldn't be sending us to Viranesh Keep if she thought we were all goin' to die. She sent us there because the Dragon Knight is the best chance to save Nearra."

"What if he won't help us?" Davyn asked.

"We'll cross that bridge when we come to it—if we come to it."

Davyn sighed and looked back at Set-ai. The big warrior sat opposite him in the little clearing with Senwyr's marker between them. In many ways Set-ai was more of a father to Davyn than Maddoc had ever been. The kind of father Davyn imagined Senwyr had wanted to be. Davyn was grateful that Set-ai cared enough to play the role, even if it was unofficial.

"We can't trust Oddvar," Davyn said. "He's a bottom-feeder who'd sell his own mother for steel."

"We'll keep an eye on him," Set-ai said.

Davyn shook his head. "It's too dangerous. Mudd and Jirah are just kids. We can't expose them to someone like Oddvar."

"They're stronger than you think, lad," Set-ai said. "Besides, if this dwarf makes that much trouble when you're not watchin' him, maybe it's good to have him close by where we can keep an eye on him."

Set-ai grinned in the darkness. Davyn thought about what he'd said. Set-ai's argument made sense in a strange way. It would be difficult for Oddvar to make trouble right under Davyn's nose. On the other hand, Oddvar hadn't bothered him in months, and he was absolutely sure he didn't want the dwarf back in his life. There didn't seem to be any way around it, though.

Davyn sighed.

"I guess I don't have a choice," he said at last. "I got Nearra into this mess and it's up to me to get her out. I won't succeed unless I have all of you to help me, so I guess that's it."

Set-ai grinned, his teeth lit up by the moonlight.

"That's the spirit, lad," he said. "When there's nothin' you can do about somethin', you might as well get on with it."

"You'll be there to help?" Davyn said, pushing himself to his feet.

"You bet." Set-ai nodded. "Now," he said, extending his hand, "help an old man up."

Davyn took Set-ai's arm and pulled him to his feet. Together they began the long walk back to Potter's Mill.

Davyn was about to enter his room in the inn when a soft sound caught his ear. As Davyn concentrated, he could just barely make out Jirah's voice. Jirah's room was the only one with light showing beneath the door. Davyn crept silently forward and pressed his ear against the door.

"We're going to be picking up some people first," she was saying. "A dark dwarf named Oddvar in Arnal and then north to Haggersmoore. There's a gnome there that the woodsman knows. He's supposed to come along too."

Davyn silently cursed himself for a fool. Jirah was telling someone the details of their plans. He should never have trusted her! He drew his sword quietly and then rapped on the door.

There was a long pause, then Jirah's voice came from behind the door.

"Who is it?" she called.

"It's me," he said. "Davyn."

"Just a minute," came the reply.

He heard the scrape of a chair as Jirah got up, and a second later the sound of her door being unbolted. Jirah opened the door a crack and peeked out. As soon as she did, Davyn shouldered the door open and charged into the room.

"What are you doing?" Jirah shouted.

The room was small, just a bed, a table with a single chair, and a wardrobe. The chair where Jirah had been sitting stood beside the table, and the table was empty except for Jirah's washbasin.

"Where are they?" Davyn asked, throwing open the doors to the wardrobe.

No one was inside.

"Where are who?" Jirah asked, blushing, as Davyn went to check the window.

"I heard you telling our plans to someone," Davyn said, lowering his sword at Jirah. "Where are they?"

Jirah backed up and flattened herself against the door.

"There's no one here," she squeaked, her eyes on the point of Davyn's sword. "You can see that."

"Then why were you repeating our plans out loud?" Davyn said, his sword still pointed at Jirah.

"It . . ." Jirah started. "It's how I remember things. I repeat them out loud to fix them in my mind."

Davyn didn't lower his sword.

"I swear," Jirah pleaded.

Davyn felt stupid. He'd looked everywhere and there certainly wasn't anyone hiding in Jirah's room. On top of that, the girl was looking at him as if he were insane.

"I'm sorry," Davyn said, lowering his weapon.

"Why don't you trust me?" Jirah said, relaxing. "Why do you always think I'm up to something?"

"Because you haven't been completely honest with me," Davyn answered, sheathing his sword.

"It's true," Jirah said without shame. "I haven't told you every sordid detail of my life. But all I want to do is find my sister and help her break our curse," Jirah finished. "Believe that."

There was a tone in Jirah's voice that made Davyn look at her. She was standing by the door in her nightdress, shivering, but there was defiance in her eyes. She reminded him so much of Nearra that he kept forgetting she was still thirteen, far from home, and all alone.

"I'm sorry," Davyn said. "My life hasn't been very stable lately. It's just safer if I assume everyone's out to get me."

"But you do believe me?" Jirah said, hope in her voice.

Davyn nodded. "I believe you," he said.

Jirah suddenly rushed forward and threw her arms around Davyn, burying her face in his chest.

"Thank you," she said.

Davyn could hear her crying softly. He rolled his eyes.

Congratulations, Davyn, he thought, you made a girl cry.

CHAPTER 6

ARNAL

Sweat rolled down Oddvar's face and into his beard as he pulled a piece of metal from the forge. All around him, the ring of hammers on steel filled the cramped quarters of the smithy. The weather was cool in anticipation of winter so the smithy doors had been thrown open to dissipate some of the heat from the forge. From his place in the back of the smithy, Oddvar wasn't sure it made any difference.

Oddvar placed his work on the anvil and began striking it smartly as the smithy's owner lumbered over. The owner, one Master Tuggens, was an enormously fat man with bushy brown hair and a bulbous nose with so many veins in it that it looked like a roadmap. He had the annoying habit of inspecting the work being done by his four apprentices, commenting on each piece before moving on.

"Be sure not to shape it too much," Tuggens said, looking over Oddvar's shoulder. "We don't want the steel to be soft."

Oddvar rolled his eyes and went on hammering just as before. Tuggens nodded sagely, then moved on. He was a clever businessman, but he wasn't a smith. The more like an armed camp Arnal became, the more need for weapons and armor there would be, and Tuggens had hired all the talent necessary to fill that need. Even though the man didn't know a shaping hammer from an anvil, he was making a fortune.

That was what Oddvar found particularly galling.

The dwarf had made his way to Arnal after leaving Maddoc's service. He had intended to just pass through, but thanks to a little misunderstanding he'd had with a pack of mercenaries on a drunken night of gambling, he didn't have the funds to continue. So he'd taken the job as Tuggens's fourth apprentice. Oddvar wasn't trained as a smith specifically but all dwarves receive some training in the shaping of metal. Despite his position as fourth apprentice, Oddvar probably knew more about smithing than all the rest put together.

That galled Oddvar as well.

Oddvar struck the steel on his anvil with an especially violent blow and instantly regretted it. He was putting the finishing touches on a slim little dagger, the kind some sneak thief would keep in his boot, and he'd bent it.

"Now Oddvar," Tuggens said in his simpering, superior voice, "you must be more careful. See here, you've bent your dagger."

Oddvar resisted the urge to slam his hammer into Tuggens's face and began pounding the little dagger straight again. While Oddvar finished the dagger, he contemplated his life.

There was a time when he'd had some self-respect, but that was long ago. He had entered the service of the wizard Maddoc and, when Maddoc was brought down, Oddvar fell with him.

Now all that was left to him was basic survival. As he tossed the finished blade on the workbench, he decided life just couldn't get any worse.

"Hello, Oddvar." The voice from Oddvar's past sent chills through him.

He turned, holding his hammer tightly in case he had to use it as a weapon. To his great relief, he did not find himself facing a sword.

Maddoc's brat, Davyn, stood in the middle of the smithy. His hand rested on the hilt of his sword and he was regarding Oddvar with a hard look on his face. The other smiths took no notice of a customer talking to one of their number and went on about their work.

Oddvar ground his teeth. He was forced to admit to himself that his life could, in fact, get worse.

"Hello, Davyn," Oddvar said, keeping his voice neutral. "What brings you to Arnal?"

"I came looking for you."

"You need a sword made?" he asked, hopefully.

Davyn shook his head—and he wasn't smiling. Oddvar had a sinking feeling in the pit of his stomach. Whatever Davyn wanted, the dwarf was sure he wasn't going to like it. He momentarily considered using the hammer on Davyn. But he'd seen what the young man could do with a weapon. If Oddvar's first blow didn't take the boy out, it would get ugly.

"I'm going after Nearra," Davyn said.

"What's that got to do with me?" Oddvar asked. "I don't know where she is."

"You helped Asvoria emerge," Davyn said, "and now you're going to help me kill her."

Oddvar could hear the faint tremble in the boy's voice. He laughed a short, ugly laugh.

"If you want to get yourself killed, kid, that's your business, but don't expect me to help you. Your family's already cost me too much."

An angry look flashed across Davyn's face, and Oddvar tensed in case the boy drew his sword. A moment later Davyn's face softened.

"Shemnara tells me that, not only will you help me, but I've got to take you with me."

Oddvar remembered the name; it was the seer woman in Potter's Mill.

"So you need me." Oddvar almost relaxed. Things might just be looking up. "My help," he went on, "it's worth something to you?"

"No," Davyn said flatly. "As far as I'm concerned, you can rot in this stinking smithy for the rest of your life. Unfortunately, my destiny seems to be tied up with yours again."

Oddvar laughed at that. Imagine! One of the brats who ruined his life now needed his help. "I guess your destiny will just have to wait," he spat. "I'm not doing you any favors."

Davyn actually smiled. It made Oddvar's skin crawl.

"I know you better than that, dwarf," he said. "You're a steel-grubbing weasel. I'm not asking for your help. I'm offering to buy it."

Oddvar was so shocked he almost dropped his hammer. He wanted to spit in Davyn's face, but the prospect of picking up enough steel to get out of Arnal was tempting. Davyn had even said something about coming with him. If the boy had enough steel to get him somewhere better and pay him for the privilege, he'd be a fool not to go along.

"What's your offer?" he asked.

Davyn shook his head. "Not here. There's a tavern on the west side of town. The Hangman's Noose. Be there." Davyn turned and left.

Oddvar was about to relax when he saw an enormous shadow detach itself from the darkness outside and join the boy. Oddvar didn't know who the big warrior was, but he was obviously with Davyn, and Oddvar could see the silhouette of a crossbow in his hand. As Oddvar hurriedly put his hammer away, he was very grateful he hadn't attacked the boy.

Oddvar hung up his apron and brushed the soot from his beard. He knew the Hangman's Noose. That was where he'd met that pack of mercenaries. Oddvar shook his head. Not the sort of place he'd expect Davyn to frequent. But maybe the boy was more like Maddoc than Oddvar thought. He smiled and picked up his axe and thrust it into his belt—no sense going unprepared. Last of all, he picked up the sack of arrowheads he'd been making for a private client.

He hurried out into the dark street and turned east. The Hangman's Noose was north from the smithy, but Oddvar had a stop to make first. If he played his cards right, he might just get out of town with enough steel to live comfortably.

He pushed open the rickety door of the boarding house and was greeted with a howl. As usual, the woman who ran the place was most displeased to find a sooty dwarf in her parlor.

"What do you want, dwarf?" the old woman demanded.

"You know why I'm here, Hudsen," Oddvar said. He passed the old woman the bag of arrowheads. "These are for the boarder in number three."

"I know who they're for," Hudsen said, taking the bag. "If there's nothing else, I suggest you leave."

Oddvar smiled as sweetly as he could. "There's the small matter of my fee," he said.

Hudsen wrinkled up her nose in disgust at the thought of leaving the dwarf alone in her parlor, but she went just the same. A moment later she returned with a bag of coins.

"One more thing," Oddvar said, tucking the bag into his belt without counting it. "Tell number three that I'll be at the

Hangman's Noose tonight with an old friend of mine named Davyn."

"What am I?" Hudsen demanded, "a messenger service?"

Oddvar handed the woman a coin, which disappeared so quickly Oddvar thought it had vanished into thin air.

"Just deliver the message," he said, then he turned to leave.

Davyn selected a table in the back of the Hangman's Noose taproom as the best place to do business. It was big enough for everyone to sit down, and Davyn and Set-ai could keep their backs to the wall. In a place like the Hangman's Noose, that was a very important thing.

Mudd, fidgety as usual, was having trouble waiting. He leaned over to Davyn and whispered, "Are you sure he's coming?"

"He'll be here," Davyn said. "His type can't resist the chance to get some steel."

Mudd looked as if he were about to launch into a litany of things that could go wrong, but, at that exact moment, Oddvar entered the grubby taproom. He stopped at the bar to pick up a drink, then made his way back to the rear table and sat down.

"All right, I'm here," he said, coming right to the point. "What's this about?"

"We need your help," Davyn replied, as Oddvar sipped his drink, "to find a place called Viranesh Keep."

Oddvar spit out a mouthful of his drink and began coughing uncontrollably. Set-ai thumped him on the back, perhaps more forcefully than was necessary.

"Viranesh," Oddvar gasped once he was able to breathe again. "You're mad."

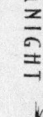

"The only way for me to save Nearra is to petition the aid of the Dragon Knight," Davyn explained, "and he lives in Viranesh Keep. So, I have to go there."

"No one lives in Viranesh Keep, boy," Oddvar said. The dwarf's eyes were as wide as saucers. "Leastways not anymore."

"What do you mean?" Jirah asked.

"Who's the kid?" Oddvar jerked his thumb at Jirah.

"Jirah is Nearra's sister," Davyn said. "This is Set-ai and Mudd," he continued around the table.

Oddvar shook his head, a nasty look on his face. "Quite the pack of fools," he laughed. "An old man and a couple of kids. Is that the best you could do?"

Mudd and Jirah bristled. Before they could say anything, however, Set-ai simply crushed the pewter mug in his hand.

"I'm beginnin' to take a dislike to you," Set-ai said in a measured voice.

Oddvar swallowed his mouthful of ale but kept up a belligerent face.

"Well, if you're going to Viranesh Keep, I don't have to worry about your good opinion," he said, "because you won't be coming back."

Davyn slammed his tankard down on the table.

"I'm going to Viranesh Keep," he told Oddvar, "and I need you to show me how to get there."

Oddvar sat back in his chair and gave Davyn a patronizing smile.

"Well, if that's all you need, maybe I can help you," he said. "Just go up the Vingaard River until you find a little pile of dirt and mud called Kentrel. From there it's straight west to Viranesh Keep. You can't miss it, it's the only cursed ruin for miles."

Davyn smiled but there was no humor in it.

"I need you to take me there," he said slowly. "I need you to get me inside."

Oddvar laughed. "You couldn't get me to go back to Viranesh for all the steel in Ansalon. People go in there but they never come out."

"You got out," Mudd said.

"I was lucky," Oddvar admitted. "But I'm telling you, there's no treasure in that place, only death."

"Treasure?" Mudd asked.

"Legend says the place is full of steel." Oddvar snorted. "That's why people go there."

"And that's why you went there," Davyn said.

Oddvar nodded. "I fell in with this human named Cirill. He said he had it all figured out. Once we got inside the keep, though, we couldn't find our way out again. I got separated from the others. That's when I escaped."

Davyn wondered exactly how Oddvar came to be separated from his friends, but decided to let that slide.

"So, Cirill never got out?" Mudd asked, his eyes wide.

"No," Oddvar said, "and neither will you."

"Shemnara says we will," Davyn said.

"She's the woman who predicted you kids would destroy Gadion?" Oddvar asked after a pause.

"She's a seer," Jirah said. "She can see the future."

The dwarf began stroking his beard. Davyn could tell he was mentally calculating the odds. He feared Viranesh, but the chance of getting in and then back out, maybe with all that treasure, was tempting.

"If Shemnara says we'll make it out, I believe her," Davyn said. "All I want is to talk to the Dragon Knight. If there's any treasure, you can have all you want."

"Less our expenses," Set-ai added quickly.

"All right," Oddvar said at last. "I'll take you to the keep."

"And show us how to get inside," Davyn said.

"But I get all the treasure I want," the dwarf said.

Davyn extended his hand to the dwarf.

Oddvar grinned and seized Davyn's hand. "Done," he said, shaking hands vigorously. He stood up and drained his cup. "This calls for a drink," he said. "Anyone else?" When there were no takers he shrugged, muttered something about humans, and stalked off to the bar.

"Does he know we aren't going to be looking for treasure while we're there?" Jirah asked.

"Nope." Set-ai grinned like a wolf.

"I suggest we don't tell him," Davyn said. He didn't return Set-ai's grin. He still wasn't sure that taking Oddvar with them was a good idea. It was too late to worry about it now, though. Oddvar was in. At least he didn't have to spend any of his dwindling funds bribing the dwarf.

"Can we go now?" Jirah asked. "The smell in here is making me sick."

Set-ai nodded agreement. "We'll go as soon as the dwarf finishes his drink."

While they waited for Oddvar to get his cup refilled, Davyn pulled Elidor's flute from his bag and began to play it softly. There were still a few scratchy notes but he felt he was beginning to get better.

"Here comes the dwarf," Jirah said in a grateful voice as Oddvar approached their table.

Davyn was about to put the flute away when someone seized his arm. A girl in a heavy cloak had come up beside him. Her golden hair curled around the pointed ears of an elf.

"Where did you get that?" she demanded.

"It belonged to my brother," Davyn said, jerking his arm free from the stranger's grasp.

"Liar," she accused. "That flute is elf-made."

"He was my blood brother," Davyn said, wondering why he was explaining himself to the raving woman, "and—"

He was cut off by a sudden commotion at the bar.

A dozen armed men stood there looking right at Oddvar. The dwarf swore and regular patrons scrambled out the door. Without a word, the men drew their swords and charged.

CHAPTER 7

The Archer

Davyn leaped to his feet, sending his chair crashing to the floor. He jerked his sword free of its scabbard and stepped between Jirah and the onrushing mob.

Mudd had drawn a pair of daggers, but that didn't seem like much against a dozen men. Almost casually, Set-ai stood and threw the table directly into the three lead ruffians. The men went down in a tangle of arms, legs, and bits of table.

There was no sign of Oddvar. Davyn wasn't sure whether he hoped the dwarf was safe or not, but he didn't have time to make a decision.

"Get out of here," he thundered to Mudd. "And take Jirah with you!"

"I can fight!" Jirah protested. "Don't you remember back at Cericas?"

But there wasn't time to answer her. Two of the remaining ruffians rushed Davyn.

Davyn kicked Mudd's chair into the first man to reach him. The chair caught him in the knees and he tumbled to the floor.

Stepping around him, Davyn brought his sword up to parry the second man. The ruffian was bigger and older than Davyn, but he had no real skill with his weapon. Davyn turned the blow aside and used the ruffian's momentum to throw him into the wall.

As the second man went down, the first one got up. This one wielded a wicked hand axe. He chopped at Davyn with all the force needed to fell a tree. Davyn dodged back, waiting for the swing to pass. Then while his opponent tried to reverse his blow, Davyn deftly stabbed him in the leg. Howling in pain and clutching his leg, the ruffian went down.

The three men Set-ai had taken out with the table were struggling to their feet. Davyn charged into them, driving his shoulder into the nearest man and slamming him backward into his companions. He lifted his sword for a killing blow when something hit him from behind.

A sharp pain shot through Davyn's shoulder as he realized what had happened. The ruffian he'd knocked into the wall had recovered and tried to stab Davyn from behind. His armor had taken the brunt of the blow, but the blade had still penetrated.

Bellowing in pain, Davyn turned and lashed out with his sword. The ruffian wrenched his knife free of Davyn's armor and lunged again for Davyn's unprotected throat. Davyn brought his sword up to deflect the blow but it never landed. The ruffian's eyes went wide, he gurgled, and then he pitched forward onto the floor. A long, white-shafted arrow protruded from the center of the man's back.

Davyn scrambled to his feet. The raving elf girl who had accosted him about Elidor's flute stood in the corner of the room. She had cast aside her cloak and Davyn could see she wore the armored leather tunic of an archer. A quiver of white-shafted arrows hung from her belt and she carried a curving elven war bow. She wore a long fighting knife strapped to each thigh and long leather gloves to protect her hands and arms from the snap of her bowstring. The woman's hair was a cascade of golden curls and her green eyes sparkled in the lamplight.

Davyn knew elves could be incredibly beautiful, but this was the most exquisite girl he'd ever seen. He stood there, mesmerized by the sight. It almost cost him his life.

As Davyn watched, the woman nocked an arrow, drew a bead on him, and shot in one smooth motion. The arrow flew by Davyn's head so closely he felt the wind from its passing.

Behind him someone bellowed in pain and the spell was broken.

"Are you trying to get yourself killed?" the elf demanded.

Davyn turned to find the three men he'd knocked down were back up. The one closest to him had an arrow in his shoulder and was rapidly scrambling backward. The other two, however, rushed him as one. Davyn chopped the sword out of the first man's hand, sending it spinning into the crowd of other patrons. The second man swung at Davyn. The sword slammed into Davyn's side, but it wasn't sharp enough to penetrate his armor.

Davyn was about to respond when he heard Jirah scream. At the far end of the tavern, Mudd was standing on the bar, kicking at one of the men who'd pursued him. Jirah was trying desperately not to be pulled over the bar by a ruffian who had her by the hair. A third man had climbed onto the bar and was waiting to attack Mudd.

Davyn pushed at his remaining opponent, intending to run to the bar. The ruffian dodged and brought his sword around, aiming a chopping blow at Davyn's head.

"Set-ai," Davyn called, barely managing to bring his sword up to deflect the blow.

The big warrior was busy fighting four others at once, but he looked up long enough to take in the scene at the bar. At that precise moment, one of his opponents swung at him with a hand axe. The weapon struck Set-ai in the left arm and stuck into his armor with a solid-sounding thunk. Set-ai bellowed in pain and dropped the dragon claw he held in that hand.

Davyn dodged another blow, determined to reach the bar. His opponent had other ideas, slashing at Davyn with a hail of blows. As Davyn struggled to parry and keep the bar in view, the ruffian pulling at Jirah managed to get her away from the bar. At that same moment, a white-shafted arrow struck the man on the bar in the leg. With a scream of pain, he toppled behind the bar and out of sight. A second arrow caught the man holding Jirah in the shoulder. As the man howled, Jirah scrambled free.

Davyn refocused on his opponent, hoping that Mudd could keep the other man at bay long enough. It didn't matter, however. Responding to some signal Davyn wasn't aware of, the remaining ruffians broke and ran, stopping only long enough to pick up their wounded.

They were gone in an instant.

"Set-ai," Davyn called, rushing to his old friend's side.

The hand axe was still there, stuck in Set-ai's armor. From the angle of the blade, Davyn could tell the wound was deep. "This looks bad."

"I've had worse," Set-ai grimaced. "Pick up my dragon claw. I don't want it left here."

"What was that about?" Jirah said, as she and Mudd arrived.

"It doesn't matter." Davyn picked up Set-ai's dragon claw. "Right now we need to take care of Set-ai."

"We need a healer," Mudd said.

"You won't find one in this town." It was the elf archer. She'd put her cloak back on and was now standing a few paces off.

"A surgeon then," Mudd said, starting to panic. "Anyone with a knowledge of wounds."

"Take it easy, lad," Set-ai said. "I'm fine."

"I might be able to help you," the elf said. "But first we'll need to get him somewhere clean. There's an innkeeper nearby who doesn't ask questions."

"Who are you?" Davyn asked. He wasn't sure he was ready to trust this girl, beautiful or not. "Why did you . . . why are you helping us?"

"My name is Rina," the elf replied. "Now I suggest we get your friend out of here."

Davyn sheathed his sword and turned to Rina. "Lead the way."

"Better make sure it's safe," Set-ai advised when they reached the door.

Davyn drew his sword and peeked outside. There were several people in the street, but they all seemed to be minding their own business.

He was about to step out when a voice made him turn. "Glad to see you're still in one piece."

Davyn turned to find Oddvar emerging from behind a stack of kegs.

"No thanks to you," Davyn said, motioning Set-ai and the others out into the street. As Rina took the lead, Oddvar fell into step beside Davyn.

"Would you care to explain who those men were?" Davyn asked, sheathing his sword.

Oddvar looked down. "I might have owed them some steel."

"You could have mentioned that we might run into trouble on your account," Davyn said.

"I thought they'd left town," the dwarf said. "It's been months since I've seen any of them."

"Just how many are there?" Davyn asked, knowing he wouldn't like the answer.

"A few," Oddvar muttered. "Four less after tonight."

"Are the others likely to be close by?"

"Could be," Oddvar said. "We should probably leave town as soon as possible."

"Great," Davyn said through clenched teeth. He stopped suddenly, grabbing Oddvar by the arm.

"Know this, dwarf," he said, leaning down to look Oddvar in the eye. "The next time we run into trouble you'd better help out . . . or I'll kill you myself."

A hard look passed over Oddvar's face but then, unexpectedly, he smiled. "I shall endeavor to take your safety more seriously in the future," he said with mock contrition. "I see you met the elf." Oddvar nodded toward Rina.

"Rina?" Davyn asked. "What do you know about her?"

"Ah . . . I'm afraid that information will cost you a lot more than you'd care to pay." Oddvar smiled wickedly and scurried on ahead.

Rina led them away from the Hangman's Noose and down an alley to a side street. From there it was only a few blocks to a small inn.

Rina knocked and a few moments later an elderly man appeared at the door. After a whispered conversation, he admitted them into a small common room. The old man charged Davyn an outrageous sum for a room, then left them alone in an empty chamber at the back of the inn.

"First thing," Rina said when they were alone, "you've got to get this out." The small axe was firmly stuck in Set-ai's armor.

She put Set-ai's arm on the room's small table and had Oddvar and Mudd hold his wrist.

"All right," she told Davyn. "One good pull should get it out."

Davyn's hands were suddenly sweating and he wiped them on his pants. He grabbed the axe carefully, took a deep breath, and pulled. The axe was buried deep but it came away after a second. Set-ai groaned, his teeth clenched tightly.

As the axe came free, Set-ai's wound began to bleed freely.

"Get his armor off," Rina said, taking the axe from Davyn and setting it aside. "Someone cut a piece of cloak for a bandage."

"I've got some clean linen in my bag," Jirah said, unslinging her pack.

With great effort, Davyn and Mudd got Set-ai's armor off. The wound was still bleeding, but the flow had slowed somewhat. Rina packed the wound and tied the bandage around his arm. Half an hour later Set-ai was lounging on the bed, his arm hanging from a sling and the majority of the blood cleaned from his armor.

"Your turn," Rina said, turning to Davyn.

At first Davyn had no idea what she was talking about, but then he remembered being stabbed in the back.

"Just a scratch," Rina declared once he had removed his armor and his shirt—though she seemed to take a long time to reach that conclusion. "Just clean it and pack it. It'll be all right in a day or two."

Davyn bellowed like a branded calf when Rina poured wine into his wound, then sat there patiently as she tied a bandage over his shoulder. To distract himself from his stinging shoulder, he picked up Set-ai's armor.

"I'll have to find someone in town to repair it," Set-ai grumbled.

"It can wait," Rina said. "You won't be wearing your armor until that wound closes anyway."

"She's right." Davyn gingerly pulled his shirt back on. "Besides, those mercenaries who attacked us probably have friends."

"I vote we leave town tonight," Oddvar said.

Set-ai nodded. "That's not a bad idea."

"Will you be okay to travel?" Davyn asked, sitting next to the woodsman on the bed.

"It's my arm, lad, not my leg," Set-ai said with a grin.

"All right," Davyn said, standing up. "I left Hegga and the cart at the stables on the north side of town. We'll pack her up and head out tonight. Everyone stay together and stay alert."

Mudd and Jirah helped Set-ai up and they all began moving to the door.

"What about me?"

Davyn turned to Rina. He'd completely forgotten she was there.

"Thanks for your help," Davyn offered.

Rina put her hands on her hips. "Thanks indeed," she said.

Davyn could tell she was angry, but he wasn't sure why.

"Just what am I supposed to do if those men do have friends looking for you?" she asked. "Remember? I shot a couple of them. They probably think I'm one of you."

"She'd better come with us," Mudd said, bouncing with excitement.

"Which way are you going?" Rina asked, hands still on her hips.

"North." Davyn didn't mind Rina's company, but he didn't want to let her in on more than he had to.

"I'm heading north, too," Rina said. "Maybe I'll travel with you for a while."

"How convenient," Oddvar sneered.

"We've got to get goin'," Set-ai said. "Do you need to collect anything, lass?"

Rina nodded. "I've got my gear at a boarding house on the east side. Where can I meet you?"

"We'll meet you at the north bridge in half an hour," Davyn said.

"I'll be there," Rina said as she opened the door.

"Do you want someone to go with you?" Oddvar asked, uncharacteristically concerned.

"No." Rina narrowed her eyes. "I can take care of myself . . . and anyone else who might get in my way," she added.

"Don't be late," Davyn cautioned her. "I'm not going to take chances waiting around for someone to find us. If you're not there on time, we go without you."

"I understand," Rina assured him. She pulled her cloak about her and slipped out of the room.

"Do you think it's wise to bring her?" Jirah asked once she was sure Rina had gone. "We don't know anything about her."

"The girl's right," Oddvar said. "How do you know you can trust her?"

"She helped us in the fight," Mudd said. "She didn't have to do that."

"It's because she helped us that she's got to leave," Davyn said.

"A convenient situation," said Oddvar, smiling. "Don't you think?"

Set-ai interrupted them. "I think we're all forgettin' somethin'.

Shemnara said that an archer would find us. It shouldn't come as any surprise that one did."

Davyn nodded. It was too much of a coincidence to ignore.

"I think Set-ai's right," Mudd said. "Rina is our archer."

"We don't know that," said Jirah, throwing up her hands.

"Well, I do know one thing," Davyn said. "If we don't stop arguing and get out of here, we'll miss Rina at the bridge."

Jirah flashed Davyn a look, but the others agreed it was time to go.

CHAPTER 8

THE HOUSE OF WHEELS

It was a good week's journey from Arnal to the upper tributaries of the Vingaard River. From there they hitched a ride on a river barge, and passed the next three days in the small cabin onboard, in relative comfort, until they reached Haggersmoore.

Warehouses, taverns, and businesses lined the streets near Haggersmoore Harbor, with homes and shops farther in. The town itself reflected the order of the Solamnic mind, with straight, parallel streets laid out in an oversized grid pattern. The houses and shops were neat and clean, and the streets were swept.

This far north, the winter lingered longer than it did in Arnal. Davyn shivered as he stepped off the dock. An arctic blast tore at his cloak and he tightened his grip on the front.

"How come you always want to travel in the winter?" Oddvar grumbled from the far side of their little cart. The dwarf was in a foul mood. To Davyn it seemed as if his mood had been bad since they'd left Arnal—since they'd picked up Rina.

"You cold?" Davyn said, trying not to let his teeth chatter.

"Not me," the dwarf chuckled. "You don't seem as hearty, though."

Davyn wanted to punch Oddvar but he resisted the impulse. He turned around and surveyed his little group. Mudd led Hegga dutifully off the dock while Set-ai brought up the rear. Rina and Jirah were huddled together on the cart's narrow seat, trying to keep warm.

"Where to now, boss?" Rina called.

Davyn winced. No one had called him "boss" since Elidor's death. He answered Rina without looking at her. "We've got to find Set-ai's friend, Bloody Bob." Davyn turned to Set-ai. "Lead the way."

Set-ai cleared his throat uncomfortably. "Truth is . . . I never did visit ol' Bloody Bob on his stomping ground. I only know the name of his hometown from stories he told durin' the war. But I would assume he lives somewhere over there." Set-ai gestured vaguely toward the easternmost edge of Haggersmoore, the only part of town that wasn't eminently Solamnic. "That looks like Gnometown."

Gnometown was a sprawling mess of houses and shops all thrown together with no rhyme or reason at all. The streets were more like established paths through the chaos than actual roads. A river ran through the middle of Gnometown, and a dozen waterwheels churned in the current, turning shafts and driving belts that ran to nearby buildings. Strange pipes that snorted and hissed snaked their way out of some buildings and into others, sometimes running across the streets in overhead trestles. Wheels, gears, and other bits of metal littered the yards and alleys, and the sounds of hammers and wrenches were everywhere.

Davyn stopped a passing gnome riding a vehicle with

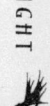

three wheels—mounted one on top of the other—and asked for directions.

"Oh, you want the House of Wheels," the gnome said once Davyn had explained their quest. "It's over on the far side of Gnometown by the bend in the river. You can't miss it." He bounced away over the road.

Davyn turned to survey the area where the gnome had pointed, wondering how he would find a single house in the cluttered mass of misshapen buildings. Before he'd even finished the thought, he had his answer. Rising out of the hodgepodge of buildings was a house that was massive by gnome standards. It was at least four stories high. Surrounding the entire structure, mounted on the side and protruding from rectangular openings in the walls, were all different kinds of wheels. Some were wood and had belts mounted on them. Others were metal with grooves or teeth, like gears. The biggest wheel, however, was an enormous waterwheel, nearly as tall as the house, that was powered by the nearby river. Davyn had never seen anything like it in all his life.

"The House of Wheels indeed," Davyn said before leading the others off in its direction.

It only took a few minutes to reach the house. As they got closer and more of the house became visible, Davyn realized that the entire house was covered with rails and levers and wires and pulleys. The waterwheel wasn't the only wheel turning—all of them were. From the big to the small, the wood to the metal, all the wheels on Bloody Bob's house turned. Some of them turned quickly, others clanked around slowly. To Davyn it seemed like the house was thrashing about, as if it were trying to get up and walk away.

As amazing as the wheels were, the rest of the house was equally impressive. The metal rails that encircled the house vanished into the building and reappeared through little shuttered doors. Wires with weights on them hung from the eaves, and to top it all off, the entire house was painted a sickening shade of green.

A rounded archway was nestled into the center of the enormous building. Davyn passed under the arch and followed a passageway a few paces until he came to a bright red door.

"I guess I should knock," Davyn said, once everyone had crowded into the alcove.

Davyn reached out but Mudd grabbed his arm.

"The sign says to pull the cord," Mudd said, gesturing to the hand-painted board hanging above the door.

Davyn looked around a moment before spotting a brightly striped cord hanging from one of the many holes in the wall.

"I guess this is it?" He shrugged and pulled the cord. From somewhere inside the house there was a loud click and a twang like a bowstring snapping. The clanking and rattling of the machinery in the house seemed to get louder and suddenly there was the sound of something moving along the metal tracks.

Davyn looked up. A pair of shuttered doors opened and a polished stone ball rolled out. The ball traveled down the track, gaining speed. Davyn couldn't help but notice that the track ended mere feet from his own head.

"Watch out!" he yelled.

Everyone dropped. The ball hit the end of the track. There was a slight upward curve to the rails at the end and, much to Davyn's amazement, the ball flew over the door and into a barrel on the far side of the alcove. The barrel tipped over under the impact of the ball and dumped the ball onto another track that took it back into the house. There was a loud crash from inside.

The noise was followed by a string of curses.

"Someone's at the door, Pop," a muffled voice came from inside.

Davyn and the others hurriedly stood up, brushing the dirt from their clothes. A moment later a slot in the door that Davyn hadn't noticed before was opened and a pair of gold eyes looked out.

"Uh," Davyn stammered, surprised by the sudden appearance of the eyes. "Does Bloody Bob live here?"

"Who wants to know?"

Davyn was about to reply when Set-ai stepped up.

"Just tell him it's an old friend," he said.

The owner of the gold eyes seemed to consider this for a moment, then shut the covering of the slot.

A moment later they could hear the sounds of several locks being disengaged, and the door swung open.

The owner of the gold eyes turned out to be a young gnome. He wasn't a child but he could hardly be the gnome Set-ai had fought with in the war. The young gnome wore a heavy work shirt under a grease-stained apron covered with pockets. Tools of all shapes and descriptions were stuffed into the pockets.

"Come on in," the gnome said, stepping back from the door. "My name's Hector. My dad will be here in a minute."

Hector ushered the little group through a cramped hallway into an equally cramped room. There was a large hole in the center of the floor around which half-finished contraptions lay in piles, along with what appeared to be all the parts necessary to complete them. Hector hastily cleared off enough chairs for everyone to sit down, then moved to the hole in the floor and yelled down.

"They're here. I don't think they're with the knights."

"I'll be right up," a voice called from far below. "Set the mechanism."

Hector ran over to a large lever beside the hole and pulled it vigorously. There was an earsplitting whistle and Davyn could hear something moving below.

"It'll just be a minute," Hector said, moving back to where everyone was sitting. "Dad's in his workshop."

"What did you mean when you said we didn't look like knights?" Mudd asked.

"You aren't knights, are you?" Hector sounded worried.

Everyone shook their head and Hector turned back to Mudd.

"Sometimes the Knights of Solamnia come to ask my father to make things for them," Hector said sadly. "His collapsible lance was a big hit until they realized it wouldn't skewer anything. It just collapses."

Rina and Davyn were trying hard not to laugh and Set-ai threw them a dirty look.

"I fought with your father in the war," he said to Hector.

The gnome's face lit up and he was about to ask Set-ai to go on when there was a tremendous sound from down below. It reminded Davyn of the twang of an enormous bowstring.

"Here comes Pop," Hector yelled over the sound.

Davyn watched the hole, wondering what to expect. An instant later a gnome shot out of the hole and up to the ceiling. Davyn hadn't noticed it earlier, but a stuffed feather mattress was strapped to the ceiling in the exact spot where the gnome hit. Feathers went everywhere and there was a loud click. As the gnome fell back from the mattress, an overstuffed couch slid out from the wall and covered the hole in the floor. The gnome landed on the couch in a heap.

"Tremendous!" he cried, sitting up. "Simply tremendous! I didn't think it would work so well the first time."

This new gnome was older than Hector but dressed much the same. His hair was long and white and was gathered behind his head in a ponytail. A black patch covered his left eye and two fingers on his right hand were missing.

"Is that the first time you tried that?" Jirah asked in disbelief.

"Oh, it's not all that dangerous." The gnome shrugged. "I've got another mattress at the bottom of the hole if the couch doesn't deploy in time."

"What if you miss the mattress on the ceiling?" Rina asked.

"That's not the dangerous part." The gnome laughed. "Missing the hole, that's the dangerous part."

Davyn hadn't said anything. He was still staring at the mattress on the ceiling that was now leaking feathers. If this was Bloody Bob, Davyn wasn't sure he wanted the gnome along. He was obviously dangerously insane.

"Well, you got me up here," the gnome continued. "What can I do—"

The old gnome's eyes suddenly came to rest on Set-ai. His face lit up, he let out a yell, and he threw himself at the big warrior, embracing him in a fierce bear hug.

"Set-ai, you old wolf," Bob said once he'd turned loose of the big man. "How've you been? What brings you here?"

Set-ai nodded at Davyn. "This lad here."

"Great flywheels!" Bob exclaimed. "You found your son?"

Set-ai's face suddenly fell. Davyn knew he had been looking for his wife and son ever since the end of the war.

"You didn't find . . ." Bob left the sentence hanging.

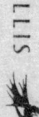

Set-ai shook his head slightly and the gnome gracefully let the subject drop.

He turned to face Davyn. "Well, what can I do for you, young fella?"

Davyn told the gnome the whole story from the beginning. When it was over, Bob sat back on his couch and rubbed his balding head.

"Well, it sure sounds to me like you could use a good gnome on this trip," he said sagely. "But then I reckon there's no trip that couldn't be helped by a good gnome."

"You'll come then?" Jirah smiled.

"No, my girl," Bob said. "I'm afraid I can't."

"What?" Set-ai sounded genuinely surprised. "Bloody Bob never backed down from a fight in his life."

Bob laughed and threw Set-ai a wry smile. "We're a long way from those times, old wolf. I'm too old to go running around cursed keeps."

"Didn't you just crash into the ceiling?" Mudd asked.

"Yes," Bob said, nodding, "but that was in the comfort of my own home. If I tried that in some drafty old keep I'd probably break something important. I might even get killed. Then one of you would have to carry me back here to be buried. No, my adventuring days are over."

"But you can't say no!" Jirah protested. "What about Shemnara's prophecy? We'll fail without you."

"If he's not going, neither am I," Oddvar piped up. "That seeress said he'd come along. If he doesn't, it means she's losing her touch and that might mean that none of us will get out of Viranesh Keep alive."

Davyn was about to tell Oddvar exactly what he'd do to him if the dwarf tried to back out, but Hector cut him off.

"I'll go," the young gnome said.

Davyn shook his head. When Set-ai had suggested Bloody Bob, Davyn assumed he'd be getting a seasoned warrior, not another wet-behind-the-ears kid. There were already too many kids on this trip for Davyn's tastes.

"I think it's a great idea," Bob thundered. "It's about time you got out into the world."

"No!" Davyn shouted. "Absolutely not. I won't—"

Set-ai held up his hands. "Give Hector a chance to speak, boy-o." Set-ai turned to Hector. "Now what can you do for us, lad? Your dad is one of the best warriors and weapon makers I've ever known, but you're not him."

"Hector designed most of this house," Bob roared indignantly. "You can't insult my son like this!"

"It's all right, Pop," Hector said. "I understand. This is a dangerous job and they don't want anyone along that they aren't completely sure of."

The young gnome leaned over and rummaged around in one of the piles by the couch. When he stood back up, he held the strangest crossbow Davyn had ever seen. It was shaped like a crossbow but without the bow arms. Where the bolt would have rested there was a large wooden box and a metal cylinder.

"This is a repeating crossbow," the gnome said. "I invented it and built it myself."

He indicated the metal cylinder where Davyn could see a small lever.

"Once I pump it about two hundred times, I get five shots in a row," he said.

Without any further explanation Hector shouldered the weapon, aimed at the ceiling, and pulled the trigger. A tiny metal dart shot out and shattered a ceramic jug that hung from one of the metal tracks. A second pull yielded another bolt that stuck into a wooden beam. Hector shot three more times before he had to stop.

"I can handle myself," Hector said.

Davyn was speechless. He'd never seen anything so impressive that wasn't magical.

He cleared his throat. "Well, in that case, welcome aboard."

Chapter 9

Motives

Davyn was running.

Running through a seemingly endless black tunnel while the screams came from somewhere ahead of him.

Davyn knew it was a dream, and yet it seemed so real. His heart pounded, his lungs strained, and his legs burned.

This time, however, something *was* different.

The screaming was higher—shriller. He heard someone yell, but it wasn't Elidor's voice.

Davyn redoubled his efforts, sprinting through the treasure-filled chamber. His sword was in his hand, though he didn't remember drawing it.

The screaming suddenly stopped.

The dais was right in front of him. Davyn lunged over the edge, ready to drive his sword into Asvoria's chest, but the sorceress wasn't there. Standing in the center of the platform, a white bandage over her eyes, was Jirah. There was blood on her hands and she was flailing about as if she couldn't understand why she couldn't see.

Davyn skidded to a halt. He'd had this dream dozens of

times but it had always been the same until now. His heart pounded with hope. Maybe this meant that he could change things after all.

He started forward to help Jirah with her blindfold, but his foot hit something soft. Down at his feet where Elidor's body usually lay was a cloaked figure. Davyn didn't have to move the body to recognize it. The mass of golden curls could only belong to one person: Rina.

Davyn sat up in bed, gasping for air and drenched in sweat. For a frightening moment he didn't know where he was. The tiny room was packed with all kinds of strange contraptions. In the darkness it appeared as if Davyn had fallen into a trash pit. As he tried to will his heart to slow down, Davyn remembered. He was sleeping in one of the many rooms in Bloody Bob's house.

It was the dream that woke him. He wasn't sure why he'd seen Jirah and Rina this time, but with his luck, it couldn't be good. Shemnara's vision had given him hope that he might yet be able to save Nearra and defeat Asvoria. His dreams seemed to be warning him that, even if he managed it, more people would suffer. The thought of Rina dead and Jirah crippled caused Davyn to shudder in the cold night air.

Pale moonlight filtered in and cast Davyn's room in shades of silver. He knew from experience that he wouldn't be able to sleep for some time, so he got up and tugged on his boots. He took a long pull from his water bag and emptied it. Since he had nothing better to do, he decided to refill it. If he remembered correctly, Bloody Bob's kitchen was just down the stairs to the left.

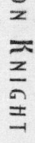

Since the house was sized for gnomes, Davyn had to duck under the doorways. It wasn't until he straightened up in the kitchen that he realized he wasn't alone. Hector was loading gear into a traveling pack. On the table in front of him, rows of weapons and tools were neatly laid out.

"You're up late." Hector grinned.

Davyn wasn't in much of a mood to talk and he still wasn't thrilled at having Hector along.

"I needed some water," he said, shaking his empty water bag.

Hector pointed over to the corner where a pipe came in from outside the house. It looked like a pump but there was no handle, just a key on top.

"The waterwheel powers a pump that brings the water up from a natural spring deep under the house," Hector explained. "Just turn the key to let some out of the holding tank."

Soon Davyn's water bag was full of sweet spring water.

"Thanks," Davyn said, sitting down at the table. He glanced at the piles of gear littering the table. "What's all this stuff?"

Hector shrugged. "I can't decide what to bring."

Davyn surveyed the table. There were all kinds of strange-looking things laid out in organized piles. There were small glass vials with different colored liquids in them, metal tubes with different colored bands around them, something that looked like a brass backscratcher with three extra hands, and lots and lots of tools. Even the gnome's backpack was strange. It had an extra wooden frame with canvas attached to it. To Davyn it looked as if the pack had its own awning.

"What's this?" Davyn asked, picking up a heavy glass ball with a silver cap and a thick liquid inside.

"It's a lamp," Hector said, taking the ball from Davyn. The gnome gave the silver cap a twist. With a click, part of the cap pivoted up, exposing a burning wick.

Davyn was impressed. The lamp was small, but it gave off more light than the single candle Hector had on the table. Davyn picked it up to examine more closely but Hector snatched it back.

"Sorry," he said, snapping the cap shut and extinguishing the flame. "You have to be really careful. If you twist the cap the wrong way it ignites the oil inside."

"You should fix that," Davyn said.

"Oh, it's not a flaw," Hector said. "It does that so you can throw it at something you want to burn. The glass breaks and the burning oil goes everywhere."

Davyn shivered at the prospect of being splashed with burning oil but Hector's smile never wavered. "Neat, huh?" he asked.

"Uh, yeah," Davyn managed. "So," he continued, trying to change the subject, "how come you're so eager to come with us?"

Hector's easy smile vanished, and he looked away. Davyn had somehow managed to pick the wrong thing to say—as usual.

"I'm sorry," he told the gnome. "I didn't mean—"

"No, it's okay," Hector cut him off. "It's mostly my pop. He's a really great inventor; almost everything he makes works. It's just that our friends all think he's a failure."

"I don't understand," Davyn said.

"You don't know gnomes," Hector said. "Any gnome inventor worth his salt would have blown himself up by now. My pop's still around so he must be a failure."

"So he's not a good inventor because he's still alive?" Davyn asked, not sure he'd heard right.

Hector nodded and continued stuffing tools in his pack.

"That's crazy," Davyn said. "So how does you going with us fix that?"

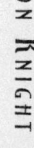

"If I have lots of adventures or maybe even get killed, it will restore the family honor."

"But your dad had lots of adventures," Davyn pointed out. "Set-ai says he was the best weapon designer ever."

Hector closed the top of his pack. "Most of the gnomes who knew what my pop did died in the war. Everyone thinks . . ." Hector paused, fighting back tears. "They think he's just some crazy old liar."

Hector slung the pack on his back and made his way to the door. "I'm going to get some sleep," he said. "Put out the candle when you go."

Davyn sat in the glow of the candle and hoped he was doing the right thing. Hector was enthusiastic and obviously a good inventor, but he'd never seen a battle. Add to that Jirah and Mudd, neither of whom were much in the fighting department. The chances of someone getting seriously hurt were pretty high.

In the past few weeks, Davyn had convinced himself that he was doing the right thing. Any chance to undo some of the damage he'd caused was worth the risk. Here in Bloody Bob's kitchen, however, he wondered if it was worth the risks he was taking. Part of him screamed that it was. But the more nightmares he had, the weaker that voice became. Every time he tried to picture Nearra in his mind, she always had those glowing hands. Hands that had sucked the life from his blood brother. With a sigh, Davyn wondered if he'd ever be able to look at Nearra again without seeing Elidor's murderer instead.

"Why so melancholy, boss?"

Davyn jumped at the sound.

A moment later, Rina melted out of the darkness into the warm circle of the candlelight.

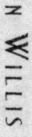

"Do all elves do that?" Davyn growled, annoyed at being taken by surprise.

"Walk quietly?" Rina asked.

"No, call people 'boss.'"

"You don't like it?"

Davyn hesitated. "My blood brother called me that all the time. He thought it was funny."

"Have you never had a brother before him?" Rina asked. "They always find things that annoy you to be funny. You just have to ignore him and he'll stop."

Davyn pressed his lips together in a humorless smile. "If I could, I would."

"What do you mean?" Rina sat down across the table. "Won't you see him again some day? After our journey ends?"

Davyn shook his head and looked down at his hands. He wasn't sure he wanted to talk about Elidor. "He's dead," Davyn said at last. "He was killed by an evil sorceress, while trying to help Jirah's sister. But it was too late. For both of them."

"And now this sorceress possesses the body of Jirah's sister," Rina said. She'd heard most of the story the previous day when they'd told it to Bloody Bob and Hector.

"I don't want to talk about it," Davyn declared, taking another drink from his water bag.

"Is that what your nightmares are about?" the elf asked.

"How do you know about my nightmares?"

She shrugged. "The first night on the barge you were tossing and turning in your sleep. When you woke up you were covered in sweat and panting like you'd run ten miles."

Davyn looked down, unable to meet those perfect green eyes.

"All right," Rina said, getting up. "I can take a hint." She moved to the pipe in the wall and, after fiddling with the key for a moment, managed to pour herself a drink.

"It's always the same dream," Davyn said as Rina sipped her water. "I'm trying to save Elidor and Nearra but I'm too late."

"You think what happened was your fault?" Rina sat back down.

"Who else's fault could it be?" Davyn slammed his fist on the table. "They trusted me and I let them down."

"So now you're worried that you'll lose some of us." It wasn't a question, just a simple statement of fact.

Davyn didn't answer; he was having trouble looking at Rina again.

"You can't plan for everything," she said when he didn't speak. "There's an old Elvish saying: 'No amount of planning can predict the outcome of a battle.'"

"What's that supposed to mean?" Davyn grumbled.

Rina pulled Davyn's chin up until his eyes met hers.

"It means that most of the time, control is just an illusion. Sometimes things happen and there isn't a thing we can do about it."

Davyn could feel his guts twisting inside him. He wanted to believe her, but he didn't know if he dared. Rina smiled and stood.

"Why are you helping us?" Davyn asked. "You could've left once we got here."

Rina smiled. "I guess I'm curious," she said.

"About what?" Davyn wondered.

"What kind of human could entice an elf to become his blood brother," Rina said.

Davyn didn't know what to say to that.

"Get some sleep," she said, moving back to the door. "We've got a big day ahead of us . . . boss."

With that Rina disappeared back into the darkness.

Davyn ground his teeth. What was it with elves and their twisted sense of humor?

The following morning came too early for Davyn's taste. He'd gone back to bed right after Rina left but his sleep was fitful. When Mudd finally shook him awake it was well after dawn and everyone was ready but him. He quickly scrambled into his armor and stuffed his nightshirt into his pack before going down to the kitchen.

Set-ai had already gone to look for a barge going north but the others were still eating breakfast when Davyn arrived. Jirah called something to him but he couldn't hear her over the incredible din in the kitchen. Bob and Hector were working on some machine that seemed to be built around the fireplace. When Hector saw Davyn come in he whistled to Bob, who pulled a lever that silenced the contraption.

"Sorry," Hector yelled as if the noise were still going on. "Boiler's a bit temperamental this morning."

"What—" Davyn started to ask, but Bob cut him off.

"How'd you like two soft-boiled eggs with bacon and toast?" he called excitedly.

"Uh, sure," Davyn replied. Then he whispered to Mudd, "What's 'toast'?"

"Singed bread." The boy held up a slice. "It's not bad with jam and—"

Whatever Mudd was going to say was lost as Bob cranked up his machine. Rina and Jirah clapped their hands over their ears as the noise level rose. Mudd was ignoring his breakfast, his eyes fixed on the machine. As Bob pulled levers and turned cranks, Hector hustled over to Davyn with a pair of heavy gloves and an empty plate.

"Put these on!" he yelled, pressing the gloves into Davyn's hands.

Hector put the plate on a little trolley that ran on one of the metal rails. The machine over the fire gave an ear-splitting whistle and Bob held up his thumb. Hector released the trolley and turned to Davyn.

"Get ready!" he yelled.

The trolley rolled down the track toward the clanking machine. As it passed under it, it tripped a rod that opened a door in the machine's belly. Two pieces of the singed bread were dumped unceremoniously onto the plate. A second rod triggered a chute that spat three strips of bacon and a wad of grease onto the toast.

"Heads up," Hector shouted as the trolley tripped a final rod.

A moveable section of track dropped down onto the table. The little trolley slid neatly down the rail and rolled onto the table, careening all the way to the far end where Davyn was still standing. Jirah and Mudd had to scramble to get their plates out of the way. Davyn was so mesmerized by the whole thing that he almost missed the eggs.

With a noise that sounded like the honking of a sick goose, the machine spat a soft-boiled egg directly at Davyn's head. He reacted out of instinct, catching it with his gloved hand. Even through the leather, Davyn could feel the heat from the newly cooked egg. He tossed the egg on his plate and started to sit down.

"Two eggs!" Hector cried.

Davyn was just in time to intercept the second missile before it slammed into his head. He tossed it onto his plate alongside its twin.

"Pretty neat, huh?" Hector said, as Davyn sat down. "Pop and I invented it after Mother..." Hector let the sentence trail off. "It's the only reason we get anything to eat. We're both too busy to cook."

Having observed the process Davyn wondered whether it wouldn't be easier to cook the food by hand. Still, the eggs were just the way he liked them and the bacon wasn't burned. The toast had sopped up most of the bacon grease, which made it delicious. All in all, it was a pretty good breakfast.

"Ain't you done yet?" Set-ai's voice called from the front door. "I got us a boat, but it leaves in half an hour."

There was a mad scramble at the table, with everyone shoveling in the remainders of their breakfast and shouldering their packs. Bob embraced Hector and wished him a good journey, and the group proceeded outside. Set-ai already had Hegga hitched up but even with that help, they still almost missed their boat. When they finally got Hegga settled and the cart lashed down on the foredeck, they were already a mile from Haggersmoore.

Davyn climbed up on the low roof of the cabin and lay down. The warm sun felt good on his skin and he was soon dozing. He heard someone climb up and sit beside him.

"You need to set a better example, lad," Set-ai said.

Davyn sighed and sat up.

"Your troops need to train," Set-ai continued. "They've got to stay sharp and that's hard to do when their leader is taking a nap."

Davyn wanted to argue but he knew Set-ai was right. Besides, it had been a long time since he had practiced with either his sword or his bow.

"All right," Davyn said, sliding off the roof onto the deck. "Let's whip this crew into shape."

Set-ai grinned, sliding down beside him. "That's the spirit," he said.

"At least there's no rush," Davyn said as they made their way back to the cabin for their weapons. "It's almost a week to Kentrel."

Set-ai put his hand on Davyn's shoulder and pulled him back.

"I didn't want to say nothin' before," he whispered, "but there might be a bit of trouble along the way."

Davyn shot Set-ai a questioning look and the woodsman continued.

"The captain told me that there's a lot of activity around the ruins of Vingaard Keep," he said. "The river's real wide there, but there's talk of pirates. We need to be on our toes when we pass there."

Davyn rubbed his weary eyes with the palms of his hands.

"Okay," he sighed. "Let's start with archery practice."

Set-ai clapped him on the shoulder and headed aft to round up the others. Davyn hesitated long enough to string his bow.

"Just once," he muttered as he followed Set-ai. "Just once I'd like for things to be easy."

CHAPTER 10

KENTREL

Davyn sat on the roof of the barge's cabins so as to be out of the way of the crew and watched the countryside slip lazily by. He'd spent the last few days training with Rina, Jirah, Hector, and Mudd in case they ran into trouble around Vingaard Keep. Rina was a superb archer, better even than he was, and Hector was pretty good with his repeating crossbow.

But as it turned out, all their preparation was unnecessary. When they reached the great bend in the river where Vingaard Keep stood, the sun was still high in the sky.

"Stand down, my boy," the captain told him. "Pirates won't risk a daylight attack."

"Well, that's that," Rina said from the other side of the roof. "All that practice for nothing."

Davyn raised an eyebrow and turned to look at the elf. "You sound disappointed," he said.

Rina strode over the peak of the roof and sat down next to Davyn.

"Maybe a little," she admitted. "A girl's got to test her skills every now and again to stay sharp."

Davyn snorted. Rina's attitude was getting under his skin.

"I don't enjoy killing people," he said, "even pirates."

"How dare you!" Rina shouted. "Are you suggesting that I do enjoy killing?" Rina slugged him in the arm—hard.

"All right," Davyn protested, rubbing his arm. "You just seemed a little bloodthirsty there."

"You'd prefer to let pirates have the ship?" she asked.

Davyn sighed. "No, of course not. Let's just forget it."

A long moment of silence passed as the barge sailed slowly down the river. For some reason, Davyn found that he couldn't relax with the elf girl sitting right next to him. Rina seemed to make Davyn nervous.

"Tell me about your family," Davyn said, trying desperately to break the heavy silence. He realized that he knew almost nothing about Rina other than that she was an especially good archer.

Rina gave Davyn a funny look, as if she were gauging whether or not he was up to something. After a moment, she spoke.

"I don't have much of a family. My mother is a Silvanesti stateswoman and she's always been too busy to spend much time with my family. My father died a few years ago. In the war." Rina paused for a moment, then added, "I have a half-brother, too. But I don't know him very well. He and my parents didn't . . . didn't get along."

"So you never saw him?"

Rina stared off in the distance. "He left home when I was young. I wish I could have known him better, but my father forbade us to spend time together." Rina laughed, and the sound reminded Davyn of a bell ringing. "As I grew older, my father's disapproval only made me more curious about my half-brother. I was determined to get to know him. But then . . ." Her voice trailed off.

"Then what?" Davyn asked.

Rina smiled but it seemed strained. "I'm getting cold," she said, picking up her bow. "I think I'll go inside."

With that, Rina hopped down on the deck and disappeared below.

It was several days later when the village of Kentrel came into view along the riverbank. Davyn was up on the roof of the barge again, a position he'd come to enjoy. From his vantage point, he could see that Kentrel was a small village with simple wooden buildings and dirt streets. The signs on the shops were so weathered as to be unreadable. Trash littered the shore and weeds had sprung up in the walkways. It was clear to Davyn, even at a distance, that Kentrel had seen better times.

A gang of seedy dockworkers slouched forward to tie off the barge and unload some of the cargo bound for various businesses in town. As Davyn watched them he was determined not to let their cart out of his sight with the dockworkers around. As it turned out, he spent most of the next hour helping Set-ai and Mudd manhandle the cart off the barge and onto the dock. Oddvar would have been a help, but the dwarf was nowhere to be found until it was time to go.

"Where were you?" Davyn grumbled as he led Hegga down the dock and onto the shore. Oddvar, for some reason, had donned his hooded cloak.

"The sun's a bit too bright today," the dwarf said, pulling his hood down. "My eyes are sensitive."

Davyn looked at the sky and didn't see how today was any different than yesterday, but he wasn't in the mood to argue.

"How far away is the house of Viranesh?" he asked.

The dwarf shrugged, which did nothing to bolster Davyn's confidence.

"Five, maybe six hours' walk," he said.

"You do remember the way?" Davyn pressed.

"Straight west," Oddvar replied. "It's pretty much the only thing out there so it's not hard to find."

"In that case, we'll stay in town tonight," Davyn said.

"There's only one inn in town, and it's a rathole," Oddvar said, his voice straining. "We'd be much better off heading for the keep now."

Rina glanced up at the sky. "But it's nearly dark and we're all tired. I think we should stay and head out in the morning when we're all rested."

Oddvar rolled his eyes. "Fine. But the elf won't like the accommodations."

"It doesn't look like anything's been built here in twenty years," Davyn said. "I guess we'll just take what we can get."

Kentrel's only inn was a ramshackle building on the north edge of town. Its name had worn off the sign.

"I'll go in and get a room," Davyn said, heading back to the stairs. "You wait here for a minute, then come in as a group."

As Davyn entered, he found the inside of the inn just as shabby and disheveled as the outside. There was a small tavern on the main floor with a few rough-hewn tables and benches and a bar polished by years of patron's hands. A large hearth filled the far end of the room, and a smoky fire smoldered there, giving off only token warmth. A bored-looking woman stood behind the bar polishing a pewter mug with a dirty rag.

"I haven't seen you around before," she drawled as Davyn stepped up to the bar.

"We're passing through," Davyn said, smiling. "We just arrived on a barge."

"We?" the woman prodded.

"There are seven of us," Davyn explained. "We'll need rooms."

"There's just a common room upstairs," the woman said. "There're enough beds for all of you, though."

"We'll take it."

Davyn settled on the price, then arranged for Hegga to be stabled and fed and for their cart to be put in the inn's barn. Davyn was a trusting person, but Kentrel struck him as the kind of town where you didn't want to leave anything unattended.

With the exception of Oddvar, who spent the evening in the room, everyone ate in the tavern. The food was bad, but there was plenty of it and everyone ate heartily.

Miruel, the woman who owned the bar, kept trying to find out what Davyn and his friends were doing in town, but everyone dodged her questions. Davyn wondered if she was just nosy or if there were something else at work. His suspicions were kindled when a group of locals came in and began an intense, whispered conversation. Some of the group cast dark looks at Davyn's table as the others talked.

"I think it's time to go to bed, lad," Set-ai said without looking up from his plate.

"I was just thinking the same thing," Davyn agreed.

As one, they all got up and made their way past the glaring crowd and up to the common room.

"Friendly sort of place," Rina said once they were inside.

"You'd better bolt the door," Set-ai said. "I have a feeling the people here don't like us for some reason."

"I'll get it," Hector said eagerly. He dug in his pack and pulled out what appeared to be a three-armed backscratcher. After setting the bolt, he attached the arms to the handle and the side of the doorframe. There was a click and the arms snapped in place. The last arm seemed to be balanced between the two.

"What's that for?" Mudd asked, fascinated by the contraption.

"It's perfectly balanced," Hector explained in a whisper. "If someone puts so much as an ear on the other side of the door, the center arm will fall."

"And then what?" Jirah asked.

"Then we know someone's outside the door," Hector said with a wide grin, "spying on us."

"I reckon it would be better to just get some shut-eye," Set-ai said. "I've a feelin' we'll be wantin' to leave pretty early tomorrow mornin'."

"Right," Davyn agreed. "I'll take the first watch. The rest of you, get some sleep."

With Hector's spy detector in place, everyone settled down for the night. Davyn took his sword out of its sheath and then sat in one of the room's two chairs with the sword across his lap. He lit a small candle and settled down right across from the door.

It wasn't thirty minutes later that the balanced arm on the spy detector tipped over.

Chapter 11

The Cursed House of Viranesh

Davyn slipped off the chair, sword at the ready. He could hear the roar of conversation from the tavern down below. From the sound of it, Davyn guessed that half the town was downstairs. He dropped down to peer under the door. Several pairs of feet were standing outside.

"Open up!" the innkeeper's voice called, pounding on the door.

"What does she want?" Jirah hissed from her bed. She was sitting up with a confused and frightened look.

Davyn crept over to Jirah, motioning her to be silent.

"Get everyone up," he whispered. "Tell them to get dressed as quietly as possible."

"Why?" Jirah asked. "What's going on?"

"Who knows?" Set-ai said, pulling on his boots. "But I think we best get out of here before we find out."

"Oddvar!" The doorknob twisted and the pounding continued. "We know you're in there!"

"I see you've made your usual good impression," Davyn growled at the dwarf.

Oddvar just glared back at Davyn.

The innkeeper pounded on the door again. "Open up!"

"It sounds like an awful lot of people out there," Rina said. "If they break down the door it could get ugly in here."

"That's why we're leaving," Davyn said, as Jirah helped him buckle the straps on his armor.

"And just how are we going to do that?" Oddvar growled.

Davyn smiled and turned to their second youngest member. "Mudd?"

Mudd returned Davyn's smile and opened the room's single window. A moment later he had the shutters open and was leaning outside.

"There's a porch roof just below," he said, keeping his voice low. "It's not much farther from there to the ground."

"Get going and hitch up Hegga," Davyn instructed.

Davyn finished getting his armor on, tightening the many straps that kept it in place. He had just finished packing up his gear when there was a loud pounding on the door.

"Oddvar!" a man's voice called among renewed pounding. Davyn recognized it as belonging to one of the men who'd been down at the tavern while they'd been eating. "Open the door! You owe us answers and we'll have them if we have to come in there and get you ourselves."

"I'm ready," Rina declared. She had donned her armored tunic and slung her pack on her back.

"Get on that porch roof and cover Mudd," Set-ai instructed.

"And don't kill anyone," Davyn said as the elf stepped out the window. "We may have to come back here."

Rina flashed Davyn a mischievous smile that didn't reassure him, and then dropped lightly to the roof below.

The door strained on its hinges. "If you don't open this door right now," the man called, "we're breaking it down."

"Get going," Davyn told Oddvar.

"I don't know whether you've noticed," Oddvar said, "but dwarves aren't good jumpers and we don't bounce."

Hector, who had been frantically pumping up his repeating crossbow finally finished and scrambled out the window. Jirah had gone first, so that left only Set-ai, Davyn, and Oddvar.

Davyn nodded after Hector. "If he can do it, you can."

Oddvar hefted his axe. "Look," he said, "there's no way I can make that jump to the ground. Just go ahead without me."

Something heavy hit the door, causing it to buckle.

"Can we hold this conversation somewhere else?" Set-ai hissed.

"I'm in charge," Davyn growled, "and I say we're not leaving you behind. Now, get going."

Oddvar hesitated, and Davyn turned to Set-ai. "Go down first and catch this fool," he instructed.

Set-ai looked like he wanted to argue but just then the door was hit again. It cracked and splintered, but it still held shut.

Set-ai climbed out onto the windowsill and dropped down to the porch roof, which splintered a bit on its own, then onto the ground. Without any prodding, Oddvar followed Set-ai out onto the porch roof. After a pause, the dwarf closed his eyes and jumped. Set-ai managed to break the dwarf's fall but both of them went down in the attempt.

Davyn gave a last look at the barred door before jumping out the window. As he landed on the porch roof, he heard the door in the room above give way.

"Get going," he called to Mudd, who was just pulling Hegga and their cart out of the barn. Mudd slapped Hegga's rump and, with a bray of indignation, the mule trotted off toward the edge of town with Mudd and the others running beside.

Davyn nodded for Rina, who was still covering the street with her bow, to get down. Then he reached up and grabbed one of the open shutters beside the window.

"They went this wa—" The innkeeper's head popped out the window and Davyn slammed the shutter closed, knocking her back into the room.

With that, Davyn figured he'd pushed his luck about as far as it would go. He dropped heavily off the porch and felt a searing pain in his ankle. Before he could even stumble, Rina grabbed his arm to steady him.

"Are you hurt?"

Davyn took a step and grimaced. His ankle was turned, but at least he hadn't broken it. He gritted his teeth and started after Mudd and the cart. Rina pulled his arm over her head and helped him along.

"I really hate that dwarf," Davyn growled as the cries from the mob behind them increased. They quickened their pace as an arrow whizzed over their heads.

"Who doesn't hate dwarves, boss?" Rina smirked.

By the time Rina and Davyn hit the edge of town, the mob was spilling out of the inn, into the street. Mudd and Set-ai had stopped on the road just beyond the town. As Davyn came hobbling up, leaning on Rina, Set-ai motioned for him to get in the cart.

"Go," Davyn said, hopping into the cart's open bed next to Hector.

Mudd snapped the reins and Hegga started forward at a quick walk.

"Can't we go any faster?" Davyn asked. "At this pace, they're bound to catch up with us."

"Don't worry, lad," Set-ai told him. "Mobs take a while to organize."

Davyn didn't know if he believed that, but he couldn't remember the last time Set-ai was wrong.

The road west of Kentrel was in remarkably good shape for one that was never used. It was heavily overgrown and the ruts were beginning to fill in with grass, but it was still easy to follow. The country was mostly open rolling grasslands, and every once in a while they saw herds of cows and sheep grazing in the distance.

Set-ai was sure that the more determined townsfolk would follow them, but the shortage of horses in the town meant they'd have to do it on foot. To stay ahead of any possible pursuit, Davyn decided that they'd push on to the keep.

As they hurried down the road, Oddvar seemed to be avoiding Davyn. He stayed at the head of the group, walking faster than all of them, which was unusual for a dwarf. Davyn was furious. He hopped off the cart, limped up to the front of their group, and confronted the dwarf.

"You want to tell me why the entire town of Kentrel wanted to get their hands on you?"

Oddvar shrugged noncommittally. "I've been there before. The people there don't like dwarves."

Davyn eyed him suspiciously. "Obviously. But why you? What did you do the last time you were there?"

Oddvar sighed. "The legend of the treasure of Viranesh Keep has been around for decades. The only reason the town exists is because of the treasure hunters. People came from miles around to try their luck. Most of the locals have lost friends and loved ones in there. They figure that, since I got out . . . "

"Then maybe their people can get out too," Davyn finished.

Oddvar nodded.

"They couldn't be sure it was you," Davyn said. "What if they'd broken down that door and been wrong?"

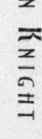

"It wouldn't have mattered," the dwarf said. "These people came to Kentrel looking for treasure. Some of them were greedy, some of them were desperate, but all of them lost someone in there." Oddvar pointed to the gray stone building that was gradually growing in the distance.

"I guess they figure that, if there's treasure in there, they've earned it," he finished.

Davyn nodded. "And they don't want anyone else beating them to it."

It made perfect sense. The people of Kentrel spent their blood in Viranesh Keep and they thought of the treasure as being rightfully theirs. Davyn felt sorry for them. He wondered how many of them lost husbands or fathers, daughters or sons. How many of them had lived in Kentrel all their lives, hoping against hope for their loved ones to someday return.

Davyn had a sudden flash of insight, "That innkeeper, Miruel. She's the one who recognized you."

Oddvar's face turned more sour than usual and he nodded.

"The man I went into the keep with—Cirill—she's his daughter," the dwarf confirmed. "She was only a teenager when we left."

There was a tone of regret in Oddvar's voice. Davyn didn't quite know what to make of it. He'd always known Oddvar to be the kind of dwarf who would sell his own mother if he could make a decent profit on the transaction. Davyn was about to ask the dwarf why he cared when Oddvar went on.

"She deserved better than to spend all these years not knowing what happened to her father."

"What did happen?" Davyn asked.

"Same thing that happened to everyone else," Oddvar said. "We went in and we couldn't get back out again."

"You got out."

"I was lucky." Oddvar sighed. "I guess I found a loophole in the curse. When I got out I ran as far away from Viranesh as I could get."

"What happened to Cirill?" Davyn pressed.

"Starved to death, I imagine," Oddvar growled. "He deserved better too."

Davyn was surprised by the dwarf's candor. He'd known Oddvar most of his life, but he'd never heard the dwarf express regard for anyone. Oddvar caught Davyn's skeptical look and bristled.

"I know what you're thinking," he fumed, "Cirill was a thief and all, but he was decent for a human. He never stole from anyone who needed it more than him."

"He was my friend," Oddvar added after an awkward pause.

"I'm sorry," Davyn said. He had thought Oddvar too self-interested to be capable of having any friends. Maybe there was more to the dwarf than simple greed.

"Count yourself lucky, boy," Oddvar said. "You seem to be able to make friends everywhere you go."

Davyn wasn't sure how to respond so he walked along in silence. He'd been against bringing Oddvar in the first place. Of course, Davyn had good reason not to trust him, but he wondered if Oddvar deserved a second chance? After all, Davyn had been responsible for Asvoria's return and Elidor's death, yet he was getting a second chance—a chance to make things right. Didn't Oddvar deserve as much?

"We're almost there," Oddvar said, interrupting Davyn's thoughts.

While they'd been talking, the keep had been getting gradually closer. Now Davyn could see that it was more like a fortified house than a keep. It was surrounded by low walls and what must have, at one time, been gardens. Scrubby trees and brush had grown up around the house, but Davyn could see where decorative arches, benches, and pleasant paths still remained.

The building itself was enormous, bigger than any house Davyn had ever seen. It was almost as big as Cairngorn Keep, Maddoc's elaborate home. There was a massive central turret from which four wings radiated out in the form of a cross. Each wing was at least five stories high and the central turret had to be eight. The roof was covered in wooden shingles. There were windows in the walls but only on the topmost floor; below were only narrow slits for archers to shoot through. The front gate was on the second floor and a long wooden ramp led up to it. In spite of its obvious age, the wood on the roof and on the ramp appeared to be brand-new.

"The magic of the curse keeps it from falling apart," Oddvar said, pointing to the roof. "The last time I was here we just marched right up to those doors and went in."

"How come you couldn't just use them to get out?" Davyn asked.

"They won't open from the inside," Oddvar answered. "We tried everything: chopping them down, burning them. They actually burned real good but the heat and the smoke drove us underground. By the time it had cleared, the doors were as good as new again."

"Underground?" Davyn said.

"Sure, most of the keep is underground," Oddvar explained. "It goes out for hundreds of feet in all directions. See there?"

Oddvar pointed to the grounds where now Davyn could see a large sinkhole nearly twenty feet around.

"Must've been a cave-in there," Oddvar said. "Some poor soul probably tried to dig his way out."

"Is that how you got out?"

Oddvar grinned and tapped his nose.

"Viranesh Keep is riddled with tunnels and secret passages," he said. "Dwarves are especially good at spotting them. I found a room that had a hole in the floor. The hole led to a sewer drain."

"Why didn't you go back for your friends?" Davyn asked.

"Because as I was making my way through it, the darn thing collapsed. I barely made it out alive."

"Then how are we supposed to get out?" Davyn asked.

Oddvar grinned again.

"With enough people you can dig through the cave-in," he said. "You go in the way I came out. That way, you know how to get back out once you find this Dragon Knight."

"You never saw anyone like that when you were inside?" Davyn asked. "Like the Dragon Knight, I mean."

Oddvar shook his head.

"I hope he's survived all this time." Davyn sighed.

"The house is cursed," Oddvar pointed out. "There must be some reason. Maybe this Dragon Knight is cursed to stay there till someone comes to ask him a favor?"

Davyn shrugged. It was as good a theory as any. He hoped this journey hadn't been an enormous waste of time. He wanted to trust Shemnara's vision, but the closer they got to Viranesh Keep, the worse he felt about it.

Oddvar led them around to the south side of the keep. The gardens and paths here were marred by several large sinkholes. Davyn shuddered as he wondered how many men had lost their lives when tons of dirt and rock had come tumbling down on them.

"This is it," Oddvar declared, stopping in front of a small hole in the ground.

There was no sign of any pursuit, but Set-ai remained confident that some would come eventually. Despite that, they were all tired and hungry and Davyn ordered a halt long enough to eat.

Hector, Set-ai, and Mudd got Hegga unhitched and began unloading the supplies while Jirah got a fire going. Rina took her bow and went looking for something fresh for them to eat. An hour later she was back with a hawk and two rabbits.

Oddvar and Davyn spent the time examining the hole and the short passage beyond it. The passage was cut from the solid rock the keep sat on and was so short Davyn had to stoop.

"This is a sewer drain?" Davyn asked. "Why isn't it just a little pipe?"

"Because it's hard to crawl through a little pipe to clear a blockage," Oddvar said, leading the way into the dark opening. "You always have to consider maintenance when you build."

After traveling about a dozen yards toward the keep, they encountered a solid wall of rock and debris. After a few minutes of examining it, Oddvar declared that they wouldn't be able to dig their way through as he'd planned.

"Then there's no hope," Davyn said.

"Not so fast, boy," Oddvar chuckled. "Never tell a dwarf there's no hope where tunnels are concerned."

They crawled back out and Oddvar led Davyn up toward the keep until they found another small sinkhole.

"Ahh, that'll do," the dwarf said, dropping into the hole and examining the ground. "Get me a shovel."

Davyn went back to the wagon and returned with the shovel. He thought Oddvar intended to dig, but instead the dwarf was moving around the edge of the hole, tapping at the rock with the shovel's metal tip. After two trips around the edge, Oddvar finally stopped in one place.

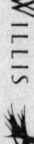

"You hear that?" he asked, tapping away with the shovel.

"No," Davyn admitted, not having the faintest idea what the dwarf was up to.

Oddvar sighed.

"I forget how inept you humans are when it comes to excavation." He tapped his shovel on the ground again and then immediately tapped in a different place. "Hear the difference?"

There had been a slightly higher pitch to the tapping in the first place, so Davyn nodded.

"That means it's hollow here," Oddvar said. "If we dig away carefully at the debris here, we can expose the tunnel underneath."

"And that gets us past the cave in," Davyn smiled, finally understanding. Since they couldn't dig through the blockage, they'd go around it.

"I'll get started," the dwarf said eagerly.

Davyn could smell the scent of breakfast and suggested that they stop to eat, but Oddvar seemed too excited by his find. Davyn left him to it and returned to the fire. Jirah and Mudd had cooked Rina's catch and the smell was making Davyn's stomach rumble. Before he could even ask for something to eat, however, his gut tightened and he forgot all about food.

Davyn could see dozens of shapes moving over the hills to the east.

"Smother that fire," he ordered, kicking dirt into the flames.

Mudd and Hector started complaining that Davyn had kicked dirt in their food but Set-ai waved them silent. Davyn pointed off in the distance and Set-ai squinted in the darkness.

"We don't have much time," he said.

"Pack up as much as you can carry," Davyn told them, darting off toward the spot where he'd left Oddvar. "Leave the wagon, just get the food and the important stuff."

A mad scramble erupted behind him as Davyn charged across the uneven ground, his sore ankle forgotten.

"What's going on?" Oddvar asked at the sight of Davyn, wild-eyed and out of breath.

"Your friends from town are here," he said. "We've got to get inside now."

Oddvar didn't need to be told twice. He'd already dug a fair-sized hole and Davyn could see a patch of inky blackness where the dwarf had broken through into the sewer drain below.

"Pull some of this dirt out," Oddvar demanded as he tried to cut the hole bigger with the edge of the shovel. "Use your hands."

Davyn dropped to his knees and dug out as much as he could. In a few minutes the hole was big enough for Hector.

"Are you ready?" Rina's voice came from behind him. "They saw the fire. They're heading straight for us."

Oddvar directed Hector down into the hole, where the gnome's quick lamps became very handy. Once he was down and the light was in place, Davyn and Rina passed him all the gear they'd packed up while Oddvar carefully enlarged the hole.

"Your turn," Davyn said to Jirah once the gear was down.

Jirah slipped easily down the hole, followed by Rina, who had trouble getting her hips through.

"Hurry up, lad," Set-ai said. "They're almost here."

Davyn could hear people shouting in the distance. He tore at the ground with his hands, pulling out rocks and chunks of earth to enlarge the hole. Finally it was big enough for the rest of them. Mudd went down first, followed by Set-ai.

"You next," Davyn told Oddvar.

The dwarf balked. "I'm not going back in there."

"If you want to stay here and take your chances with the angry mob, be my guest," Davyn said.

After a moment's hesitation, the dwarf dived, head first, into the hole. Davyn scrambled down after him just as the mob reached the remains of their camp.

"Move down the passage," Davyn hissed, bending over in the low tunnel. "We've got to keep them from seeing the light."

There was a mad rush as everyone hurried forward in the semidarkness. A shout behind them told Davyn that someone had found the hole.

Before he even had time to worry about it, however, there was a thunderous roar and a blast of air drove Davyn to his knees.

When he got up, the light from Hector's lamp revealed a wall of rock and debris behind him, blocking their way out.

Like so many who had come before, Davyn and his friends were trapped.

CHAPTER 12

BLADES IN THE DARK

Dust swirled around Davyn and he covered his face with the hem of his cloak. The sound of the passage collapsing behind them seemed to echo forever in the tunnel. After what seemed like an eternity, the dust and the noise subsided and Davyn emerged from under his cloak.

The flickering glow of Hector's quick lamp wasn't much, but it illuminated everyone's faces well enough. Everyone seemed to be all right but they were all looking expectantly at Davyn.

"Well, boss," Rina said, coughing. "What now?"

"I've still got the shovel," Mudd declared, picking up the tool. "We can dig our way out."

"Not until we get what we came for," Davyn said, getting to his feet. The low passage forced him to lean over and, in the dust-shrouded darkness, it seemed very tight indeed. "Besides, I don't want to be down here if that mob decides to start digging."

"He's right," Oddvar spoke up. "They'd be more than likely to bring the roof down on us."

"Well," said Set-ai from his stooped-over position. "Let's get going and find a place where I can stand up straight."

"You go first, Hector," Davyn said.

"No." Oddvar's voice stopped everyone. "If he goes first, that light will ruin our vision. I'll go first. My eyes are used to darkness."

Since only Hector and Oddvar could stand straight in the low passage, Davyn motioned for Hector to pass his lamp to Jirah. "Hector, get behind Oddvar and cover him with your crossbow."

The gnome gave a mock salute and then hustled off after Oddvar. Everyone else moved cautiously behind them. The sewer main was low and narrow and that only added to the oppressive feeling of the darkness. The light from the lamp wasn't bright, but it was enough to ruin Davyn's night vision.

As he crept along, Davyn couldn't see past the glowing ball of light. He heard his boots tread into water, but could barely see the little trickle running along the floor. Suddenly, he ran into Jirah.

"Sorry," he muttered, blushing furiously.

"What's the holdup?" Rina called from behind him.

"We may be stuck," Oddvar called back. "The passage is blocked up here."

Davyn squeezed past Jirah and Mudd up to where Oddvar had stopped. This time the sewer main was blocked not by a cave-in, but by a stone pillar that let water dribble out either side. It was too small for anyone but Hector to crawl past.

"Why is this here?" Davyn said.

"To keep people from doing what we're trying to do," Oddvar said, "get in through the sewer system."

"Now what?" Davyn asked.

Oddvar shrugged. "This place is riddled with pipes."

"So do we dig?" Jirah asked.

Davyn was about to respond when Hector began kicking at the trickle of water running past his boots. "I've been thinking," he said. "There are two rules to plumbing." He held up two fingers in the light and began ticking them off. "First, all boilers explode."

Davyn scoffed. "So?"

But Hector didn't seem to hear him. "And second," he continued, "water runs downhill."

"What exactly is your point?" Set-ai called from beyond the light. Being hunched over was obviously getting to him.

"Well," Hector replied, "I was just thinking that since the sewer is designed to let water run away from the keep and since the ground was dry where we came in . . ."

Hector just let his sentence trail off.

"The water must be going someplace." Oddvar grinned. "Back up and find where the water's draining out."

"I found it," Rina called from the darkness. She was somewhere behind Set-ai. "There's a little hole in the wall back here."

Davyn jostled his way back to the back, barely managing to squeeze past Set-ai. The hole turned out to be a little arched opening with a rusted metal grate over it. Davyn grabbed the grate but before he could even pull, it came off in his hands.

Casting the grate aside, Davyn knelt down and peered into the blackness beyond. A round pipe ran away from the main and slightly down.

"Hector!" he called. A moment later the gnome appeared at his side. "Take your light and go down this as far as you can," Davyn instructed, pulling a length of rope from his pack. "If you get in trouble, yell and we'll pull you back."

Davyn tied the end of his rope around Hector's waist as Jirah passed the lamp back to them. If the gnome felt uncomfortable about shinnying down the wet hole, he gave no sign of it. He took the glowing lamp, got down on his back, and pushed his way through the passage with his feet. In moments, the only light was the faint shaft of brightness emerging from the side passage.

"Whoa!" Hector's voice floated up the shaft.

"Are you all right?" Davyn yelled, tightening his grip on the rope.

"I'm fine," Hector said. "This shaft is pretty short, and it ends in a big room. I think I'm inside the keep."

"Why would a sewer main have a side passage that ends in a room?" Davyn asked.

"I think the pipe is broken," Hector called up the shaft. "It comes out of a damaged wall."

"How big is the pipe?" Mudd called.

"Big enough for you," Hector said.

Mudd looked up hopefully at Davyn, who shrugged and said, "Give it a try."

Mudd scrambled down the hole. Since he wasn't much bigger around than Hector, he fit just fine.

"I don't think I can fit through there, lad," Set-ai said as Davyn motioned for Jirah to go next.

"We can't stay here," Davyn said.

"Take your armor off," Rina suggested.

Set-ai reached around for the buckles holding his armor, but bent over as he was, he could barely reach any of them. "Easy for you to say," he grumbled.

"Hold still," Oddvar said as he began tugging at the buckles.

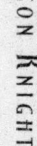

While the dwarf helped Set-ai out of his armor, Jirah slipped down the slimy hole. Rina went after Jirah. She didn't have any trouble either, so Davyn tried it next. The shaft was incredibly close and he couldn't raise his knees. Thankfully the water had made the bottom slippery and he was able to inch himself along with his heels. At last, his head emerged from the shaft into an open space. Rina and Jirah grabbed his shoulders and pulled him out like a greased pig.

"I don't think Set-ai or Oddvar are going to have enough leverage to push themselves down," Davyn said after he got to his feet.

"Have Hector take the rope back to them," Rina suggested. "They can hold onto it and we'll pull them through."

"Good idea," Davyn said. "Hector!"

The gnome was pacing the large chamber they'd emerged into. The light from Hector's lamp showed an elaborate tiled floor and what appeared to be a stone pedestal. "Can't you see I'm busy exploring here?"

Davyn sighed. "There'll be plenty of time for that in a moment. Right now we need you to go back up the shaft." He handed the rope to Hector. "Take this to Set-ai and Oddvar. Tell them to tie their gear on and we'll pull it through. Then tell them to use some oil from one of your lamps and oil themselves up good."

"Okay," Hector said, taking the rope. "But if they use up another of my lamps, that's only going to leave me with two more."

Davyn shrugged. "It can't be helped," he said. "We'll have to hope that's enough."

Hector hurried back up the passage. Set-ai sent Oddvar down first. The dwarf managed to wedge his bulk into the shaft and Davyn, Rina, Mudd, and Jirah hauled him through. As Oddvar put his armor back on, grumbling about the indignity of it all, Hector went back up to take the rope to Set-ai.

"I don't think this is goin' to work, lad," Set-ai called as Hector scrambled back down the shaft.

"What choice do we have?" Davyn asked.

"I'm thinkin' that, even if you get me down there, you'll never get me back up again."

"And if something happens to us down here, you could starve to death up there," Davyn pointed out.

Set-ai agreed there was nothing to do but try it. It took him ten full minutes to wedge his shoulders into the hole. From the sound of it, he was having trouble breathing.

"Pull," Davyn said and everyone pulled together.

There was a cry of pain from the hole and suddenly the rope came free. Davyn held the lamp up to the hole. Set-ai was still wedged tightly at the top of the shaft. "My arm!" he grunted. Davyn remembered his axe wound. The friction must have torn it open and forced Set-ai to drop the rope.

Davyn grabbed the end of the rope and quickly made a slip ring on the end. Set-ai was gasping for breath. The walls of the shaft wouldn't let his lungs expand. He was suffocating.

"Hector!" Davyn shouted. "Take this and put it around Set-ai's wrists, then pull it tight."

Hector took the line and scrambled up into the shaft.

"Hurry!" Davyn urged, though he couldn't see what Hector was doing.

Hector slid out of the shaft and nodded to Davyn. Together everyone pulled on the line. Davyn put his foot against the wall to give him leverage. He knew the tension must be tearing at Set-ai's wound, but the man didn't have enough air to cry out.

At last, the rope moved. A second later, they were pulling Set-ai free of the pipe. He gasped, breathing in great gulps of air, then collapsed in a fit of coughing.

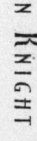

"Thank you, friends," he said, once he'd gotten his breathing under control. "I thought I was a goner for sure."

"Rina," Davyn said. "Have a look at Set-ai's arm."

Rina started moving, but Set-ai waved her away. "It's fine, lad," he told Davyn.

"Let's see it anyway," Davyn insisted.

While Oddvar put his armor back on, Rina peeled the bloody sleeve off Set-ai's arm. Leaving her to take care of things, Davyn took a torch from his pack. He peeled off the oilcloth wrapper and caught the heavy scent of pine pitch. Clutching the torch under his arm, he put his worn piece of flint against it and used the top of his knife to scrape a spark into it. The torch flared and a thick puff of smoke rolled up to the ceiling.

Davyn held the torch up and its ruddy light pushed back the darkness of the room. It was large with a low, vaulted ceiling. Four wooden support posts appeared to have been added later to help hold the ceiling up. Even so, the ceiling didn't seem secure and it made Davyn nervous.

In the center of the room were two large stone coffins. Davyn could see them plainly in the brightness of the torch. Each one was elaborately decorated with the figure of a reclining man on the top. Around the sides marched relief carvings of soldiers, horses, and dragons. The figures on top were rendered in ornate plate armor, painted black with a bronze dragon on the chest. Each clutched a carved sword over his chest.

Behind the tombs at the far end of the room, Davyn saw a large, black object. As Hector and Mudd moved over to have a look at the coffins, Davyn walked to the far wall, holding his torch high. The object behind the tombs was a statue. It had probably once been bronze, but now the corruption of ages had coated the metal black. Davyn held the torch closer and saw the heads of dragons rearing out of the sides, snarling in all directions. In the center, two huge claws held a shield that appeared to be separate from the statue itself.

The shield was not nearly as tarnished as the statue, though it was in pretty bad shape. There was a highly stylized dragon mounted to the front of the shield with its claws sticking up above the top on either side.

"It's not surprising that this is the home of the Dragon Knight." Jirah's voice seemed loud in the quiet of the room, and she had come up behind Davyn so quietly that he jumped.

"What?"

"There are dragons everywhere," she continued in a softer voice, "on the tombs, the statue, this shield."

As Jirah pointed out the dragons, Davyn examined the shield. There was a dirty round object protruding from the dragon's left claw. A closer look revealed it to be the hilt of a sword. Carefully, Davyn took hold of the hilt and pulled.

Nothing happened at first. Then, with a crack, the sword popped free. Whatever Davyn was expecting, this sword wasn't it.

It was short and broad with a sharply pointed tip and a round weight at the pommel end. The blade was free of rust but it appeared to be made of some very poor steel. The hilt was bronze with a round dragon emblem stamped into it and the leather of the grip creaked as Davyn held it up. One experimental swing was all Davyn needed to find out all he needed to know about the sword.

It was junk.

The balance was seriously off, with the tip being heavier than the pommel. Davyn replaced the sword in the dragon's claw and patted his own trusty sword. He'd stick with it.

"Davyn?"

Rina's voice cut Davyn's exploration of the crypt short. "You'd better have a look at this."

Davyn crossed to where Rina was bandaging Set-ai's arm. He held the torch overhead as Rina held up Set-ai's arm for his inspection.

"T'ain't nothin'," Set-ai blustered, but Rina wouldn't let go of his arm.

Davyn bent down, holding the torch close as he examined the wound. It looked much as he'd seen it before but this time there was dark blood at the edges of the wound and what looked like bruising all around.

"I'm not much of a healer," Rina said, "but this looks bad."

Davyn was forced to agree. If Set-ai wasn't careful, gangrene would set in and then they'd be in real trouble.

"There's nothing we can do about it now," Davyn said, trying to hide his worry. "See if Oddvar has some dwarf spirits to clean it, then wrap it up tight with a fresh bandage."

That was all that could be done, Davyn knew. He wished Shemnara were here. She could purge the wound and heal it easily. Set-ai ground his teeth and grunted in pain as Rina poured Oddvar's dwarf spirits over his wound. Davyn wondered who was in more pain, as Oddvar winced at the sight of his best drink pouring all over the floor.

Once Set-ai's wound was wrapped, Mudd and Jirah helped him get back into his armor. Davyn used the time to finish exploring the rest of the crypt room. Apart from the dragon statue at the head end of the crypt, and two freestanding fire pots, the room was empty. The thing that was strangely absent was a door.

"It's over there," Hector said.

Davyn jumped. The gnome had come up behind him so quietly Davyn hadn't heard him.

"Don't do that," Davyn said, trying to get his heart to slow down. "*What's* over there?"

"The door," Hector said, pointing to the wall to the right of the statue. "That was what you were looking for, wasn't it? Oddvar found it. He's really good at spotting stuff like that."

Davyn and Hector crossed over to where Oddvar stood looking at the wall. The plaster on the wall there had fallen away and Davyn could see the bricks behind it. The shape was rectangular, like it should be a door, but Davyn could see no evidence that it actually was a door.

"It's been sealed up from the other side," Oddvar said. "Look how some of the plaster has seeped through the joints."

As Davyn examined it closely, he could see that Oddvar was right.

"Is this the only way out?" Davyn wondered.

"There's the way we came in," Rina drawled, abandoning her inspection of the dragon statue.

"Thanks." Davyn turned back to Oddvar.

"This looks like it," the dwarf said, fishing around in his pack for a moment. When he emerged, he held up a short hammer and a crowbar. "Let's knock it down."

Davyn took the crowbar and together he and Oddvar managed to knock a small hole in the wall. To Davyn, it seemed as though the crypt echoed strangely every time the hammer hit the bricks. The sound was reverberating off the bronze statue like thunder. Finally, after half an hour of hammering and levering, they had a hole big enough to climb through.

The room beyond was pitch black and Davyn called for a torch. Before anyone could move to hand him one, however, light flooded into the room beyond the hole. Caught by surprise, Davyn blinked and covered his eyes.

When he could see again, he found himself staring at five or six ragged men armed with hammers and clubs.

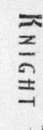

Their clothing was tattered, hanging in rags, and they wore necklaces of bones. The man closest to Davyn had a battered warhammer that he'd decorated with a human skull. The men stood in an open doorway a dozen feet away. Light from a hallway beyond was streaming in.

There was an awkward moment as each group stared at the other. Then, without any sign or warning, the ragged men gave an insane cry and charged.

"Get back!" Davyn pulled his torch back through the hole and tossed it to Jirah.

The man with the skull-hammer leaped through the hole without stopping and rushed Davyn.

He was screaming something incoherent and waving his hammer. Davyn jerked his sword free of its scabbard and attempted to hold the raving man off.

The rest of the ragged men flooded into the room, brandishing their weapons and screaming like demons.

Rina drew her fighting knives just in time to fend off a crazed man with a club.

A one-eyed man with an evil-looking axe took off after Mudd. The youth dodged around one of the coffins and jumped up on the top just as Hector shot One-Eye in the leg with his crossbow. One-Eye staggered and slammed into one of the support posts, bringing it down with a crash.

Davyn tried to parry the heavy hammer, but the blow pinned his sword against another one of the support posts. His sword snapped in two.

"You broke my sword!" he cried. He discarded the useless pieces and darted back to the statue.

The ornamental sword nestled in the statue's claw was junk, but it was the only weapon available. He jerked it out. The point was too heavy, and as Davyn slashed at

Hammer-Man to force him back, the weapon almost flew out of his hand.

"Time to go," Oddvar shouted, leaping through the hole they'd made in the wall.

A deep groaning sound filled the chamber and debris rained down from the part of the ceiling that was no longer supported by the wooden post. The ceiling was about to come down.

"Everyone out!" Davyn shouted, giving one last slash at Hammer-Man, then running for the hole in the wall.

Davyn paused just long enough to let Rina and Jirah dive through before going himself. It turned out to be a moment too long.

Hammer-Man slammed his weapon into Davyn's shoulder. Staggering under the force of the blow, Davyn lurched through the hole into the room beyond and fell to the floor.

The groaning turned into a roar of tortured stone. Someone flew over Davyn and landed heavily on the floor beyond.

Dust and smoke filled the room, blocking out the light from the still open hallway door. When it finally cleared, Davyn got painfully to his feet.

"Is everyone all right?" he asked, coughing.

"Not quite everyone," Set-ai said in a quiet voice.

From his position on the floor Davyn could tell that Set-ai had been the one who flew over his head at the last minute.

"I tried to get 'em out, but I was too late," Set-ai continued, his voice full of pain.

There was a sudden sinking feeling in Davyn's stomach. A quick check of the room revealed them to be two friends short: Mudd and Hector were missing.

Davyn turned to look at the rubble-filled hole in the wall. It was completely choked with debris. He launched himself at the pile.

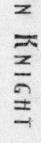

"Give me a hand," he yelled. "We've got to get them out."

Davyn had only moved three bricks when a shower of fresh debris rained down from the top of the pile.

"Mudd!" Davyn yelled. "Hector! We're coming! Hold on!"

Davyn reached for another brick when a hand seized his arm. He turned to find Oddvar looking sternly at him.

"It's no use," Oddvar said. "All you're going to do is bring the rest of the ceiling down on us."

"They could still be alive in there!" Davyn yelled, tearing his arm from the dwarf's grip. "I won't abandon them. Now get in here and help."

There was a long silence. No one moved, and no one would meet Davyn's gaze. Finally Set-ai looked up.

"The dwarf's right, lad," he said. "It's no use. I'm sorry."

Davyn's chest tightened. His stomach felt as if it were sinking and he wanted to throw up. Mudd and Hector had trusted him. He wanted to scream and beat the rubble down with his fists but his strength had left him. All he could do was slump down on the rubble.

"Stand right where you are," a sneering voice demanded.

Davyn gripped his sword so tightly that his knuckles were white. He turned and found himself facing a man in full plate armor standing just inside the door. As Davyn watched, five more armored men rushed in, swords drawn.

CHAPTER 13

HEIR TO THE HOUSE OF VIRANESH

The dust in the air was settling, but Davyn didn't notice. His entire attention was focused on the six fully armored knights facing him across the little room. He'd seen Set-ai take on eight armed men all by himself, but they hadn't been battle-trained knights. Set-ai's injured arm meant he wasn't up to his usual fighting skill. Davyn and his friends still might win a battle with the knights, but not without losing some people. His mind flashed to the dreams of Elidor and Rina lying dead. Mudd and Hector were already gone—he couldn't face any more death.

Davyn let the clumsy, ornamental sword clatter to the floor. After a brief pause, the others dropped their weapons as well.

The leader of the knights grinned. "Surprisingly lucid of you," he said. He gestured and two of his knights began gathering up the weapons on the floor.

"I am Karnac," the leader said, "first sword of the house Viranesh, and you are my prisoners."

Karnac was short for a knight, barely taller than Jirah, but he was broad and powerfully built. He had a mop of brown hair and bushy eyebrows, the left one split in two by a long scar that ran down onto his cheek. His face was pale and haggard, as if he had been sick recently, and his armor was dull and scarred from many battles. The only bright parts of the man were his unusually blue eyes.

"Please come with—" Karnac began.

"Karnac," one of the knights suddenly yelled. He had been gathering up the weapons but stopped when he got to Jirah. "Look," he said, an awed tone in his voice.

Davyn couldn't figure out what the man was going on about. Jirah was obviously a girl, but so was Rina, and the man had passed right by her. As he looked closer, Davyn saw that the knight wasn't staring at Jirah, but at the sling bag tucked under her arm.

"They've got gear," the knight gasped.

With an animal howl, he lunged at Jirah. He grabbed the bag and jerked it so hard it sent Jirah tumbling across the floor. As soon as the other knights saw the bag they forgot their prisoners and rushed forward.

"Hold your ground!"

Karnac's voice snapped the knights out of their frenzy and they retreated back to their positions. The knight who had torn off Jirah's bag had turned it over and began spilling the girl's extra clothes and gear on the floor.

"Put that back!" Karnac ordered the knight before turning his attention to Davyn.

"Are you the leader of this group?" he asked.

Davyn nodded.

Karnac looked them over with an appraising eye before continuing. His sardonic grin never faded.

"How did you get past the looters so well equipped?"

"I'm sorry." Davyn shook his head. "I don't know what you mean."

Karnac suddenly rushed forward, grabbing Davyn by the shoulders and pinning him to the wall. Gone was the easy smile, replaced by a wild-eyed look.

"Don't trifle with me, boy!" The mad knight screamed, so loudly Davyn's ears rang. "The looters control the upper floors, especially the area by the door. You could never have gotten down here without fighting them."

Davyn didn't know what to say. Karnac was raving like a man possessed. Worse, Karnac's knights didn't seem to find his behavior unusual. Some of them even sounded like they were giggling.

When Davyn didn't answer, Karnac drew a broad-bladed hunting knife with a broken tip. He pressed the knife to Davyn's throat and leaned in so they were nose to nose.

"I asked you a question, boy," he hissed. "How did you get past . . ."

The question just seemed to dribble away. Karnac's eyes suddenly widened and he stepped away from Davyn.

Davyn breathed a sigh of relief as the knife was taken away from his throat. Karnac was staring past Davyn at the debris-choked hole in the wall. This time, Davyn was watching the knight closely. The wild look in Karnac's eyes faded like water running out of a basin.

Whatever it was that Karnac saw, the other knights saw too. They gasped and one of them even dropped his sword. The clang of the weapon on the stone floor seemed to shock Karnac back to reality. He approached Davyn slowly, the knife still in his hand.

"You didn't come past the looters, did you?" he asked in a disturbingly quiet voice.

"No," Davyn admitted. He wasn't sure who or what the looters were, but he wanted to keep the unbalanced Karnac talking.

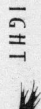

"You have a dwarf with you," Karnac accused. "Did you dig your way in?"

"Sort of," Davyn said.

Before Davyn could elaborate, Karnac lunged at him, pressing the knife into his throat again.

"Tell me how you came here, boy," he growled, the madness back in his eyes. "I've been in this room a hundred times and there's never been a hole in the wall before."

"We came in through a sewer drain," Davyn explained, trying to keep the mad knight calm. "It led into that room." Davyn moved his head as far as he dared in the direction of the hole.

"I told you there was no room there!" Karnac shouted.

"The door was sealed up from the inside," Rina said. "There was nothing in there but an old statue and a couple of coffins."

The knights gasped. The one who had dropped his sword before dropped it again. As the man bent to recover it, Karnac pulled the knife away from Davyn's throat and stepped back. His look wavered between madness and relief.

"Give the girl back her things," he told the knight that had taken Jirah's bag.

"But—" the knight began to protest.

"Do it!" Karnac gave the knight a dangerous look and he quickly handed the bag to Jirah.

"We'll take you to Gurgut," Karnac said, slipping his broken knife back in its sheath. "He is the last surviving heir of the house Viranesh and the master of this place. I suggest you tell him the truth of how you came here and what's in that room. Unlike us, Gurgut has no patience for fools and liars."

Karnac turned and walked out the open door into the lit hall. The knight who kept dropping his sword motioned for

Davyn and the others to follow. Davyn noticed the knights' scarred armor. Some of them had replaced broken or cut leather straps with bits of cord or what appeared to be belts. Several of the steel plates were punctured but the holes hadn't been patched.

The more he examined the ragged knights, the more convinced he became that they had been trapped in the house for a very long time. That might explain Karnac's emotional instability. Davyn wondered about Karnac's leader, Gurgut. If Karnac was right about him, Davyn would have to be very careful about what he said to the man. The way his luck was going, Gurgut was probably even more insane than Karnac.

The hallway through which Karnac led them was wide enough for two men to walk abreast. The walls were made from cut stone. The ceiling was arched, no doubt for extra support since they were underground. A series of smoky torches lit the hall, hanging in rings and wall sockets at regular intervals. As they passed, Davyn wondered how the knights could afford to keep so many torches burning when they had no way to get new ones.

Karnac led the group in silence for what seemed like half an hour. As they went along, they passed many side passages and closed doors. Sometimes Karnac would turn and lead them down a new hallway, but each one looked just like the others, with the result that Davyn was soon completely lost. He knew that dwarves were supposed to be especially good at navigating underground. He hoped that Oddvar could find their way back—if ever they got the chance to go back.

Just when Davyn began to suspect that Karnac was leading them in circles, the knight rounded a corner and stopped. This hallway was different from the others. It was wider and taller and ended a short way down in a set of double doors. In front of these doors, a knight stood at attention. As soon as he saw Karnac and the others, he drew his sword and challenged them.

"Halt! Who goes there?" the knight said.

"It's me, you great ninny," Karnac said. "Tell Gurgut I've brought guests."

"His lordship is feeling melancholy today," the knight replied, still holding his sword up. "He is not to be disturbed."

Davyn expected Karnac to get angry like he had with Davyn, but the little knight just sighed.

"Randor," he said, addressing the door guardian. "I have important news for Gurgut. If you make me wait here any longer, I'll see to it that you don't get any pudding with dinner."

The big knight looked hurt and sheathed his sword.

"You don't have to get nasty about it." Randor sulked, stepping aside so Karnac could pass.

Davyn wondered just how long these knights had been trapped in Viranesh Keep.

The room beyond Randor's door was large and round with a vaulted ceiling and a raised dais on the far side. Thick carpets covered the floor, except for a bare spot in front of the dais, and tapestries hung from the walls. Torches and firepots lit the room brightly and warded off the underground chill.

Despite the room's opulence, it was littered with trash. Bits of food and broken furniture were everywhere. Half a dozen knights were sitting around the room looking thoroughly bored; none of them paid Karnac and his charges the slightest bit of attention. The only person who did seem to notice Karnac's entrance was an enormously fat man who sat on a wooden throne atop the dais. He was dressed in black chain mail, like the rest of the knights, though his breastplate had obviously been hammered out to accommodate his gut. Over his armor he wore a ratty green robe that appeared to be the kind of thing a nobleman might wear to bed. His face was red, his hair had once been black but was now streaked with gray, and his dark eyes glittered like onyx in the firelight. At the fat knight's feet sat two bored-looking women. One was dressed in armor, the other in peasant clothes.

"What is this, Karnac?" the fat man bellowed, shocking the others in the room to attention. "Have the looters *elected* a new captain?"

Davyn surmised from the way the fat man emphasized the word "elected" that looter leadership and succession were bloody affairs. Since the fat man seemed to be in charge, Davyn assumed that this was Gurgut.

"Are these trespassers?" Gurgut continued. "You know how I hate trespassers. Better have their heads off."

The knights who had been sitting around bored suddenly leaped to their feet. The prospect of a beheading or two seemed to give them almost childlike glee.

Jirah squeaked in fear and Davyn quickly stepped in front of her. He felt Set-ai and Rina close ranks beside him as he watched the knights begin to draw their swords.

"I'm sure that would be a wise course of action for trespassers." Karnac nodded. "But these are not trespassers in our domain. I found them in the chapel. They had just tunneled their way in."

The palpable silence this statement brought was broken only by the sound of Butterfingers dropping his sword.

Gurgut rose to his feet, which was no small accomplishment. His enormous belly wagged from side to side as he lurched off the platform to where Karnac stood.

"Is there a passage, then?" he asked, grabbing Karnac by the shoulders.

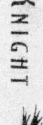

"No, my lord," Karnac said. He was about to continue when Gurgut shoved him so hard he fell down.

"Well, what are you wasting my time for?" Gurgut roared. "First you say these creatures tunneled in, then you say there's no tunnel."

Gurgut turned to go back to his throne. "I should eat your pudding for this."

Karnac clamped onto Davyn's arm and pulled him forward. "Perhaps you should ask their leader what happened."

"Well?" Gurgut demanded of Davyn. "What happened?"

"The tunnel we used emptied into a room with two stone tombs in it," Davyn explained. "Before we could leave, we were attacked by some wild men and one of them broke a support column. The ceiling came down and blocked the tunnel."

Gurgut had stopped listening about halfway through Davyn's explanation. Now he seemed to be struggling to speak and his face was turning blue.

"Remember to breathe, my lord," Karnac said.

Gurgut gasped and inhaled an enormous breath, then grabbed Davyn by the shoulders.

"This room," he said, "with the tombs. Was there a statue?"

Davyn nodded. "A group of dragons holding a shield."

Gurgut threw back his head and let out a howl like an animal. Before Davyn could even try to break free, Gurgut released him and began dancing around the room like a madman.

"That's it!" he cried. "After twenty long years, the sword is nearly mine!"

"What sword?" Jirah blurted out.

Gurgut froze in mid-dance.

"What sword indeed," he said, fixing his bloodshot eyes on Jirah. "You wouldn't have come here if you didn't know about the sword. The magic sword of my ancestor, Captain Viranesh, handed down through generations of Viraneshes to my great-uncle, the last known Viranesh to carry the sword."

Davyn had no idea what Gurgut was talking about, and neither did Jirah from the look on her face.

"Don't think you can deceive me, you silly cow!" Gurgut screamed. He reached out and slapped Jirah so hard he knocked her off her feet.

Davyn felt his fists balling up but before he could move, a sword was pressed into his back.

"It's mine!" Gurgut raged, towering over the frightened Jirah. "I'll kill anyone who says it isn't."

"We didn't come for a sword," Davyn yelled, trying to get Gurgut's attention. "We came to find the Dragon Knight."

Butterfingers dropped his sword again and Davyn assumed he'd said something important. Gurgut stopped in mid-rant and his face turned from purple back to its usual red.

"You did?" he asked, the delight plain in his voice. "Well, why didn't you say so?" Gurgut skipped quickly back to his throne. "I am Gurgut Viranesh," he said, sitting with a great flourish. "I am heir to this house, owner of all its treasures, and bearer of all its titles. I am the Dragon Knight."

Davyn was horrified.

"Why have you braved the cursed house of Viranesh to seek my aid?" Gurgut's voice was full of pleasure.

Davyn started to tell Gurgut the story of Nearra and Asvoria, but Gurgut got bored and waved him silent.

"I'm sure I will be more than happy to help you on your noble errand." He yawned. "But first, I must recover my great-uncle's sword from the crypt. Only then will the curse on this house be broken. Only then can we leave."

"There was a sword in the room," Davyn spoke up. "It was hanging behind a shield on the dragon statue."

"That must be it!" Gurgut exclaimed, leaping from his throne again, his fat swaying madly. "We must go at once and retrieve it."

Davyn was about to explain when Karnac cut him off.

"The room is blocked by a cave-in, my lord."

"What?" Gurgut's face turned purple again. "Who's responsible for that?" he raved. He waddled off the dais and stuck his finger in Davyn's face. "Was it you?" he demanded. "By the dark goddess herself, I'll have you gutted like a fish for losing my sword."

"The men that attacked us knocked the ceiling down," Set-ai said. "Your quarrel is with them."

Gurgut whirled on Karnac.

"Well? Where are these men?" Gurgut said. "I want them gutted like fish right now."

"The roof crushed them when it fell," Davyn said.

Gurgut seemed to relax.

"Oh," he said, a smile returning to his face. "That was a very good punishment. I'm glad I thought of it."

Gurgut turned a circle in the center of the room. It seemed to Davyn as if the knight were lost.

"Where was I?" Gurgut asked Karnac after completing three circles.

Karnac sighed. "Your uncle's sword," he said.

Gurgut's face turned purple again.

"How could you have let the ceiling fall on my great-uncle's sword?" he demanded of Davyn.

This time Davyn was smiling. He finally felt as if he might get on the good side of this lunatic.

"I took the precaution of bringing it with me," Davyn said,

almost glad his own sword had been broken. "Your men have it among the weapons they took from us."

Gurgut looked as if he'd stopped breathing again. One of the knights brought the bag of confiscated weapons forward but, before Karnac could open it, Gurgut knocked him away.

"It's mine," he cried, spilling the contents of the bag all over the floor. "No one but me must touch it."

Gurgut quickly found the ornamental blade among the pile of other weapons. He held the sword up with a look of rapture on his face and his knights took an involuntary step forward for a better look.

Davyn still didn't see anything special about the sword. It was point-heavy and stained with years of corrosion. Gurgut, however, was holding it as if it were made of precious platinum. At least, Davyn thought, now that he has what he wants, he'll probably let us go.

Gurgut took an experimental swing with the sword and the smile evaporated from his face. With the point being too heavy, the sword was seriously out of balance and the fat knight wasn't ready for that. The moment Gurgut swung it, the unusual weight pulled the sword right out of his hand and sent it skittering across the floor.

"That's not my sword," Gurgut howled.

Davyn felt a knot in his stomach as Gurgut's bloodshot eyes focused on him.

"You tried to trick me," he accused.

"That sword came from the crypt," Davyn said defensively.

"You want the sword for yourself," Gurgut raged. "Kill them all!" he screamed, jumping up and down like a toddler denied a treat.

The knights drew their swords as one and the sword at Davyn's back clanged to the floor as Butterfingers dropped it.

"Wait," Karnac called.

Davyn was shocked when the knights obeyed.

"I want them dead," Gurgut shouted.

"They're more use to us alive," Karnac said. "We need someone to dig out the crypt so we can recover the real sword."

"What do these fools know of digging?" Gurgut demanded.

"They got in," Karnac pointed out, "and they have a dwarf with them."

The statement seemed to hang in the air. Davyn tried to look relaxed but all his muscles were tight. If Gurgut ordered them killed, Davyn might be able to rush the Dragon Knight—but it was a long shot.

"Fine," Gurgut relented at last. "I suppose it's better for them to dig than to risk any of our own."

"A wise decision as always," Karnac said.

"I still want them punished, though," Gurgut said, an evil grin on his face. "Let them spend the night resting up in the pit. They've got a big day ahead of them tomorrow."

Gurgut began humming to himself and climbed back to his throne. With swords drawn, Karnac and his men ushered Davyn and his friends out of the audience chamber. The last sounds Davyn heard were Gurgut's tuneless humming and the sound of Butterfingers dropping his sword.

CHAPTER 14

THE PIT

Karnac and his knights marched Davyn and his friends through another endless series of hallways and down a flight of stairs to a round stone room. A circular iron grate lay in the center of the floor with a hinge on one side and a latch on the other. As soon as they entered, the knights hoisted the heavy grate off the hole beneath.

The pit was full of black water, almost to the top. It was so foul that Davyn couldn't see the bottom.

"In you get," Karnac said, prodding Davyn with the tip of his sword.

"How deep is that?" Davyn asked, trying not to jump in until he knew what he was getting into.

Karnac chuckled. "Deep enough."

The sword prodded Davyn again and he stepped off into the pit. The water was ice cold and hit Davyn like a punch to his stomach. It was barely deeper than Davyn was tall. He was forced to tread water. As soon as the grate was closed, he'd be able to hold himself up—at least until his strength gave out.

"You next, pointy ears." Karnac pointed his sword at Rina.

"Wait," Davyn gasped, trying to keep his head above water. "If you put them in here they will drown."

Karnac shrugged. "So?"

"So who's going to dig out the crypt if everyone drowns?" Davyn sputtered.

"We might lose a few of you," Karnac said, smiling, "but that's just the way it is. Gurgut's ordered you in the pit and I'm not going to argue with him right before pudding night."

Without warning he shoved Rina in beside Davyn. Jirah and Set-ai followed. Set-ai was just tall enough to stand with his face out of the water so he let Jirah cling to him.

"You can't afford to lose the dwarf," Davyn said as Karnac moved to put Oddvar in. Davyn knew dwarves didn't swim well and the water would be well over Oddvar's head.

"That's a risk I'll just have to take." Karnac grinned, shoving Oddvar on top of Davyn.

Davyn came up sputtering as the heavy grate fell with a clang. He grabbed the bars of the grate and held his head out of the water. Oddvar surfaced a moment later, cursing and flailing. Davyn grabbed the collar of his tunic with his free hand and hauled the dwarf up until he managed to grab the grate.

"I'll be back for you in the morning." Karnac grinned down from above. "There's water if you get thirsty." Then he leaned down and put his hand over his mouth as if he didn't want the other knights to hear. "I wouldn't drink any if I were you," he whispered loudly, "that water hasn't been changed in a long time."

The knights all laughed and Davyn could hear them tromping out of the room. They left a single torch that barely cast enough light into the pit to see. So far his friends were managing all right, holding themselves out of the water by clinging to the grate. Davyn wondered how long they could hold out against the icy cold of the water and the numbing power of fatigue.

"Now what, boss?" Rina's voice came from his left.

"We hang on," Oddvar growled. "I can do this all night if I have to. I won't give that bunch of armored loonies the pleasure of drowning me."

"I don't think the rest of us can hang on that long," Davyn said. He could already hear Jirah's teeth chattering. "Anyone have any ideas?"

There was a clanking sound before anyone could speak and all eyes turned to Jirah. Davyn could barely see her in the dim light, but she seemed to be threading something through the bars.

"Use your belts," she gasped, pulling the leather strap back through the bars and buckling it. She slipped one end over her head and arm and tentatively let go of the grate. The belt groaned in protest, but held.

Davyn tried to unbuckle his belt with one hand but couldn't get it. Finally he took a deep breath, let go of the grate, and sank under the water. With both hands free, his belt came off easily and he bobbed back to the surface. Shivering in the cool air, he threaded the belt through the iron bars and buckled it. Getting his head and arm through it without hanging himself, however, turned out to be more of a challenge. The loop was almost too small and by the time he had managed it, he was panting and exhausted.

Once Davyn was safely suspended above the water, he surveyed his companions to see how they were doing. Rina had managed the sling with ease and had spent the rest of the time watching Davyn with an amused look on her face. Oddvar's belt was plenty big enough, owing to the dwarf's stout girth, and he swung with his head completely out of the water. Set-ai, however, was still standing on the bottom of the pit with his face just out of the water.

"You too, Set-ai," Davyn said, his teeth beginning to chatter.

"It's no use, lad," Set-ai replied. "My belt won't be long enough to get around my shoulders. I'll just have to stand here all night."

"In this cold, your muscles will start cramping up in an hour or so," Oddvar said. "Then you'll have to hang on to the grate."

"He's only got one good arm," Jirah said. "Davyn, do something."

"Everybody calm down," Set-ai said. "I'll be all right."

Davyn shook his head. "Oddvar's right. We've got to get you tied to the grate."

"I'm open to any suggestions," Set-ai said.

"What about boot laces?" Rina suggested.

Davyn remembered the elf's high boots laced up the front. He shook his head.

"That's long enough but it won't hold my weight," Set-ai said.

"I've got it!" Davyn said, pointing at Set-ai's chest. "Your baldric!"

Set-ai looked down and grabbed hold of the big leather strap which he sometimes used to carry weapons. It went over the big man's shoulder and across his chest. It was plenty big enough for Set-ai and strong enough too.

"Good thinkin', lad," the woodsman said, grinning as he tugged the baldric over his shoulders and threaded it through the bars.

"Now that's settled," Oddvar said, "what are we going to do about Gurgut and his nutcases?"

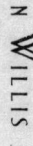

"Are they all crazy?" Jirah asked.

"Probably," Set-ai said. "I've heard tell of men that went mad in prison, from the isolation and the boredom."

"Gurgut said they've been down here twenty years," Rina added. "That's a lot of boredom."

"So what do we do?" Jirah asked. "How do you reason with crazy people?"

"I don't know," Davyn admitted. "How could Shemnara have sent us to this cursed place?" He was starting to get angry. "How is a crazy knight going to help Nearra?"

"Maybe he's not really the Dragon Knight," Rina said.

There was a long silence as everyone considered this.

"Who else could it be?" Jirah asked at last.

"Karnac said looters control the upper floors," Set-ai said. "And there was that group of crazies who attacked us. There must be many more people trapped in the house."

Davyn shook his head. As much as he wanted to believe it, it didn't make sense. "Gurgut's obviously insane, but he knows too much. He must be the Dragon Knight." Davyn sighed. "We have to get out of here."

"There's an idea," Oddvar sneered. "Why didn't I think of that?"

Jirah laughed. Davyn was very grateful it was dark and no one could see him blushing.

"What I mean," he said with exaggerated patience, "is that we need a plan."

"Which brings us back to the girl's question," Oddvar said. "How do we reason with a crazy man?"

Davyn didn't have any good answers, but before he could say so, Rina spoke.

"They all remind me of spoiled children," she said. "They want what they want and they get mad if they don't get it."

"You're sayin' we should humor them," Set-ai said. "It might work. If we keep tellin' them what they want to hear, they might give us a chance to escape."

"What about our weapons?" Oddvar said. "If there are more madmen running around this place we won't get far without them."

"We don't even know where they took our weapons," Rina pointed out.

Davyn was too tired to pay much attention. The fact was that there wasn't much they could do until they had more information about Viranesh Keep and its inhabitants. He'd just have to try to keep them all alive long enough to learn what they needed to know.

The thought of keeping his friends alive made Davyn's stomach hurt. He hadn't given a thought to poor Mudd or Hector since they'd been killed and he was ashamed. He hoped they hadn't suffered when the ceiling fell on them. Mudd had become like a kid brother to Davyn, always asking questions and getting into trouble. The more Davyn thought about the boy's loss, the sicker he got. He hadn't really known Hector that long, but the gnome had already proved himself a good companion and a fearless fighter.

Suddenly Davyn's mind snapped back to the present. Rina and Oddvar were yelling at each other about what to do next, with Set-ai and Jirah trying to calm them down.

"Stop it!" Davyn shouted with all the energy he could muster. "Our lives depend on our ability to work together and stay alert, and all you want to do is yell at each other. Mudd and Hector are dead! And if you aren't careful you'll be dead too."

Davyn could hear Jirah crying softly and Set-ai was rubbing his eyes.

"I'm sorry," Rina said at last, breaking the silence. "I didn't mean . . ."

Davyn cut her off. "Let's drop it," he said. "We're tired and we're cold and our friends are gone. Let's just get some sleep. We'll need all our strength tomorrow if we want to escape from Gurgut. There'll be time to grieve later."

Reluctantly, everyone agreed and a long silence settled in. Despite his weariness, Davyn found that he couldn't sleep. The cold of the water made his teeth chatter, and the harness kept making his arm fall asleep. He could hear Set-ai snoring and what sounded like regular breathing from the others, so at least they were getting some rest.

As quietly as he could, Davyn slipped out of his harness. He thought he might have better luck with his other arm. With a few minutes' effort and some whispered curses, he managed to work his way back into the harness. Almost immediately his arm began to fall asleep again.

"Comfy?" Oddvar said.

"You should be asleep." Davyn yawned.

"Dwarves don't need much sleep," he said. "I was just thinking about something."

Davyn was cold, wet, and tired and he really didn't care what was going through the dwarf's mind, but it was something to do.

"What's that?" he asked.

"After they threw you in here, you tried to stop them from throwing me in after you."

"Dwarves usually don't swim," Davyn said. "I was afraid you'd drown."

"I understand why you did it," Oddvar admitted. "I just can't fathom why you'd care. After all I did working with your father—"

"He's not my father," Davyn said, a bit louder than he'd intended.

"Whatever," Oddvar continued. "The way I figure it, you've got a right to want me dead, and you don't need me to get you into the keep anymore. So why did you try to help me?"

Davyn sighed. He wasn't sure exactly why he had done it. Trying to keep Oddvar out of the pit had just been a natural impulse, like trying to keep Rina and Jirah out.

"For better or worse," Davyn said, "I've been put in charge of this group. That means I'm responsible for everyone, even you. There was a time I didn't understand what that meant—and people died."

Oddvar nodded. "The elf boy."

"And Nearra," Davyn said. "As long as Asvoria has a hold over her."

"That still doesn't explain me," Oddvar pressed.

"These people are my friends," Davyn said, waving his tingling arm at the others. "They're going to have to trust me if we're going to get out of here alive. What would they think if I let Gurgut or Karnac kill you? How could they trust me with their lives if I sold yours cheap?"

There was a long silence, and then Oddvar chuckled.

"You humans are more complex than I gave you credit for," he said. "I think I'll get some sleep now." Within moments, the dwarf was snoring.

Davyn was so emotionally drained that he felt sleep pulling on him. Before he could succumb, however, Rina's voice whispered to him.

"He's right, you know," she said. "You humans are very complex."

"Hurray for us," Davyn yawned. "Did you want something? Because I really need some sleep."

"You asked me why I wanted to come with you," Rina said.

"And you said you wanted to know what kind of man could entice an elf to become his blood brother."

Rina nodded.

"And have you figured it out?" Davyn pressed when she didn't elaborate.

"I think I have," she said. "As humans go, you're a very good person. You always try to do what's right and protect those who are dear to you. I dare say you'd have made a good knight."

Catriona's face flashed before Davyn's eyes and he shuddered. "Don't say that," he said.

"I'm serious," Rina chided.

"Well, I'm glad I meet with your approval," Davyn said, trying to find a good way to end the conversation and get to sleep.

"When I came to Arnal, I was looking for someone," she said, "Someone who I thought had injured my family."

"You mean your father?" Davyn said, curiosity pushing his weariness aside. Rina had mentioned earlier that her father was dead.

Rina shook her head, causing the makeshift sling to swing. "My half-brother. He was murdered."

"I'm sorry," Davyn said. In a way, he knew what it was like to lose a brother. "What happened?"

But Rina didn't answer him directly. "I thought this certain human was to blame. I traveled to Ravenscar, the town where the human was said to live, but he was gone. Instead I met this fool." Rina tilted her head at the snoring Oddvar. "He promised to help me find the human I so urgently sought. And wonder of wonders, he actually kept his promise. I found my brother's murderer, and I prepared to kill him." Rina took in a deep breath and let it out slowly. "Then something I never expected happened. I discovered that this human loved my brother almost as much as I did. I decided to let him live."

Davyn's mind was too foggy to get what Rina was driving at. "I'm not sure why you're telling me this."

Rina smiled. "My name is Rinalasha Lelaynar. Elidor was my brother."

CHAPTER 15

THE OTHERS

The stone pillar was cold and damp. Mudd gasped as he tried to squeeze through the narrow opening into the passage beyond. When the ceiling had collapsed in the crypt, it cut him off from his friends. The only way out was up through the broken wall into the pipe by which they had entered. Mudd had scrambled into it just as the rest of the ceiling came down.

He made it up into the sewer main without any trouble. Now the only way forward was past the stone pillar—a passage that was decidedly narrow, even for Mudd.

"Squeeze all the air out of your lungs!" Hector's voice called to him from the far side of the barrier.

Hector hadn't been as quick as Mudd when the ceiling came down. As the gnome scrambled up into the drainpipe, a falling rock had cut a nasty gash in his leg. Mudd had bandaged it like Shemnara had taught him, but the wound was deep. Mudd had done all he could for Hector. He just hoped it was enough.

Despite his limp, the gnome had wiggled past the stone column easily. Mudd tried to force all the air out of his lungs, then pushed with all his might. The stones tore at his back, gouging and cutting him, but finally they relented. With a popping sound that Mudd was sure was his ribcage collapsing, he wrenched free from the narrow gap and lay gasping for air.

"See?" Hector's cheerful face greeted him. "No problems."

Mudd rolled his eyes. He pulled his tunic on and felt it sting his back. The passage through the gap had left him scratched and bleeding. "Now what?"

The light from Hector's lamp illuminated the passage beyond the barrier. To Mudd, it looked exactly like the pipe on the other side. A narrow corridor of stone ran off beyond the lamplight. The ceiling was still too low for Mudd to stand up straight. He squinted off into the darkness, trying to see an end to the narrow sewer passage.

They were lucky to see anything at all, of course. Hector had put his pack back on before the ceiling fell so they had access to his gear. Mudd's pack, on the other hand, was buried under the rubble in the crypt.

"There's bound to be a way into the keep up here somewhere," Hector said, limping off into the darkness.

As they moved, Mudd gradually became aware of light filtering into the passage in the distance.

Hector grinned. "Looks like our way in."

"I hope it's wider than the last way in." Mudd rubbed his sore ribs.

It was, but not by much. The light was coming in from a square hole in the ceiling of the passage that was covered by a metal sheet with holes in it.

"Looks like a drain," Mudd said, sticking his finger up through one of the holes. He pushed but the metal sheet didn't move. "It's stuck," he said.

Mudd used both hands but he still couldn't make the plate move or bend.

"It must be cemented in," Hector said, scraping some white powdery stuff from the edge where the plate was resting. Hector held up his finger so Mudd could see the chalky substance. "It's mortar," he explained, setting down his pack. "It's usually pretty soft. If we chip enough of it away, we should be able to get that plate out."

Mudd squinted up at the plate. All around the sides he could see the mortar globbing out, like icing on a cake.

Hector pulled a short metal pipe out of his pack. Two round collars circled one end. One collar was welded to the pipe. The second collar moved freely up and down the shaft. The other end of the pipe was sharp and flat like a crowbar.

Hector held up his strange crowbar with a smile. "Every job has a perfect tool," he said.

"What's that?" Mudd asked.

"This is my Friendly Persuader," Hector said. "It's part crowbar, part hammer, and works better than both."

To demonstrate, Hector put the sharp end against the joint where the plate and the stone of the roof met. He grabbed the free-moving collar and slid it quickly up the bar, banging against the stationary collar attached to the bar. It didn't seem to be doing much, other than making a lot of noise, but a steady stream of dust rained down. After a minute or two of this, Mudd moved the Persuader to the other side of the opening and repeated the process.

"That ought to do it," Hector said. "Try moving it now."

Mudd stepped back under the plate, put both hands against it and pushed. To his great surprise, it moved a little. He opened his mouth to tell Hector, when suddenly there was a booming sound from up above the plate.

"What was—" Hector began.

"I swear I heard bangin' in here," a strange voice declared.

Mudd quickly pulled his fingers out of the holes in the metal plate and backed against the wall of the sewer passage. Through the holes, he could see a torch moving around in the room above. Hector snapped the silver cap on his lamp shut.

"I don't see no one," a second voice said. "You must be hearing things."

"Check around just the same," the first voice said. "The boss'll have our skins if looters get in here."

"Just how do you think looters'll be gettin' in here?" the second man asked. "There's only one way in."

"Don't be so smart. This place is riddled with secret passages, in'it? All it would take is for one of those scruffy thieves to break in here and steal our pudding and that'd be it for us."

The second man grumbled and Mudd could hear boxes scraping against the floor. After a couple of minutes, both voices agreed that no one was there and they retreated back to where they had come from, shutting the door behind them.

"Who were those guys?" Hector whispered after a few seconds.

"Does it matter?" Mudd asked, trying to peer through the holes to see if the men were really gone.

"They didn't seem like the ones who attacked us," Hector said. "These guys were calm, almost bored."

"How many people could survive in here?"

Hector shrugged. "I guess that depends on how much food they have."

Mudd's stomach rumbled.

Mudd reached up and grasped the metal plate. He pushed it gently, not wanting to make any noise. There was a sharp cracking sound, and the plate lifted upward. Gasping with the effort, Mudd shoved the plate aside and slumped down against the side of the passage.

"I'll go up first, then?" Hector pulled himself up easily and disappeared into the room beyond.

As soon as Mudd could breathe easily again, he followed.

The hole was narrow—not as narrow as the gap between the pillar and the sewer passage had been, but close enough to make passing difficult. Mudd had to put his arms above his head, then wiggle his shoulders through. Eventually he managed it, but not without saying some of the words Set-ai wouldn't let him use.

He emerged into a long, vaulted room stacked with boxes and barrels. Mudd hadn't noticed it from below, but the entire room was permeated with the most wonderful smell of food. Mudd looked around but didn't see a fireplace, oven, or any other place set up for cooking.

"Where is that smell coming from?" Mudd wondered. He sniffed the air, but the smell of food was so heavy in the room that it was impossible to track.

"Over here!" Hector called from behind a row of crates.

Hector pointed to a row of shelves with large copper pots sitting on them. As Mudd and Hector drew near, Mudd could feel heat radiating from the kettles. He reached out and pulled the lid off the nearest one. Mudd's stomach grumbled at the sight.

"Is that roast chicken?" Hector gasped.

Mudd nodded and put the lid down, moving to another one.

"This one has potatoes in it," he reported.

"I've got biscuits over here," Hector said.

The other pots held similar delicacies: cornbread and sausages, stewed greens and ham, and every kind of sauce imaginable. Without even bothering to look for plates, Hector and Mudd dived in with their bare hands. They sliced bits off the chicken and the ham with their knives and used the pot lids to hold potatoes and greens. It was the most wonderful meal either of them had ever tasted.

"How did this stuff get here?" Hector asked, belching contentedly.

"I don't know and I don't care," Mudd sighed.

"I haven't eaten like that since my dear, departed mom used to cook for us," Hector said.

"I didn't know your mom died," Mudd said. "I'm sorry."

"She didn't die," Hector said. "She just departed."

Mudd chuckled, but Hector didn't crack a smile. Instead, he sat up. "I think we'd better get out of here."

"Do you hear something?"

Hector scrambled up and began putting the lids back on the pots. "No," he said. "But whoever cooked this food must have left it here mere minutes before we got here. And they're going to be coming back for it."

Mudd scanned the room for an exit. There was only one door.

"What if the men we saw are standing watch outside?" Mudd asked.

Hector's response was to begin pumping up his crossbow. Mudd slowly drew his short sword and held it loose in his hand.

"Ready?" he asked Hector once the gnome finished pumping.

Hector nodded and Mudd twisted the latch.

"What's the matter?" Hector asked, when Mudd didn't open the door.

"Locked," Mudd reported. He sheathed his sword and took off his right glove, slipping open the hidden pocket in the lining.

"You want me to use the Persuader?" Hector grinned.

Mudd shook his head and withdrew two slender metal rods from the hidden pocket. "Watch this." He slipped the tools into the lock. With a few deft twists, Mudd found the lock pin and snapped it open.

"Impressive," Hector said as Mudd returned the rods to the pocket in his glove. "I wonder if I could make a device to do that?"

Mudd tried to imagine such a thing with arms and gears and a crank somewhere. It would weigh as much as Hector. "I'll stick to doing it the old-fashioned way."

Now that the door was unlocked, Mudd opened it easily. Outside the door was a carpeted hallway. To the right, the hall ran down a dozen yards and ended in a large, ornate door. To the left, the hall made a right turn after a few feet. Since there was no one in sight, Mudd motioned Hector out the door and he closed it quietly behind them. The carpeted floor muffled their footsteps as they crept to the corner. Mudd was just about to peek around, when someone walked right into him. Two men in ragged clothes had just turned the corner.

"Hey," one of them shouted. "Where'd you come from?"

Mudd and Hector scrambled back down the hallway.

"Come back here, you," the second one yelled, breaking into a run.

Hector stopped long enough to shoot the man in the leg. The bolt just grazed the man, but he howled in pain and went down.

"Where to now?" Hector called, sending another bolt wide of the first man.

"The big door's our only chance," Mudd called, grabbing the knob and yanking it open. Hector limped inside as quickly as he could and Mudd followed.

The room they had entered was a large dining hall with an enormous table in the center and carved chairs all around. An ornate iron chandelier hung from the ceiling with hundreds of candles gleaming in it. What made Hector stop, however, was not the table or the chairs or the hundreds of candles. The room was occupied by about a dozen people.

Right in front of them, a man in an orange silk shirt and dark breeches drew a long, thin sword from his belt.

"Well, well." He smiled easily as he regarded the newcomers. "What have we here?"

CHAPTER 16

EXHUMING THE CRYPT

Davyn was numb. His entire body seemed to hurt. Every joint ached, and he couldn't seem to drag his unconscious mind back to full awareness. He had been dreaming—dreaming of attacking Asvoria—until someone called his name.

The voice came again. It seemed to come from a long way off.

"Wake up, blast you," the voice cried. Water splashed into Davyn's face.

Spluttering and coughing, Davyn finally managed to open his eyes. He hung from his belt, his head just above the foul water of the pit, just as he had been when he finally drifted off to sleep.

"It's about time you woke up," Rina whispered to him. "Someone's coming."

Davyn cast a quick look around. Everyone seemed to be all right—at least, they were still above the water. "Thank the gods," he said, his teeth chattering. "I'm almost frozen."

"They'll be here in a couple of minutes," Rina continued. "We've got to get everyone up before they get here."

"Why?" Davyn asked. "And how do you know someone's coming if they're still minutes away?"

Rina shot him an exasperated look. "Because there are two men in the next room and they've stopped to use the privy," she said.

Davyn listened for a moment but didn't hear anything. He was about to ask if Rina was sure but she cut him off.

"I have very good hearing," she said. "Now, we've got to get our belts back around our waists before they get here. If they see that we've used our belts to stay alive, they might take them away from us when they put us in here again."

Davyn nodded and unbuckled his belt. He dropped below the water and scrambled to put it on before he ran out of air. Finally he bobbed back to the surface with a gasp. By the time he was finished, Rina was moving to wake up Jirah.

Davyn woke up Oddvar and Set-ai while Rina helped Jirah get her belt back on. Davyn had just hooked his arm back over the grate when the door opened and Butterfingers entered along with another knight.

"You're all still here, I see." Butterfingers grinned. He turned to his companion, holding out his hand. "Pay up."

The second knight grumbled as he counted coins out of a purse into Butterfingers's hand. Davyn silently cursed them as his aching muscles strained to keep his head above water.

"All right, you lot," Butterfingers said, "let go of the grate and we'll get you out of there.

Davyn didn't have the strength to tread water so he was forced to sink to the bottom and then bob to the surface for air. It took Butterfingers and the other knight a few moments to lift and secure the heavy grate.

The knights pulled him up onto the cold stone floor. Davyn tried to rise and stand but his arms wouldn't even move to lift him. It was a full five minutes before he was even able to sit up.

"Now, we don't want any trouble and you don't want to be dead," Butterfingers said once everyone had managed to sit up. "So, if you'll behave yourselves, we'll take you to a nice hot breakfast."

The mention of the food gave Davyn the energy to stagger to his feet.

Butterfingers and the other knight, whom Davyn named Scar on account of the long scar across his forehead, led them out of the pit room, down the hallway, and into a small, snug room with a plain wooden table. Despite his fatigue, Davyn nearly ran to the table. It was loaded with fruit and eggs and bacon and bread and butter. Davyn had never seen anything look so good. Gradually Davyn began to warm up, despite the fact that his clothes and armor were still dripping wet. Butterfingers and Scar just watched.

"Where do you get fresh eggs from?" Rina spoke up.

"Every morning the larders are full," Scar explained. "The house provides for us. It just won't let us leave."

Now Davyn understood how the knights could afford to use so many torches. The house replenished them every day.

"Have you really been down here for twenty years?" Jirah asked.

Butterfingers nodded. "Twenty miserable years," he growled. "We followed Gurgut down here and now we're stuck."

Butterfingers sounded more than a little resentful of his commander. Davyn decided to fish for information.

"Why did Gurgut lead you down here in the first place?"

Butterfingers laughed.

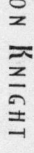

"He's the Dragon Knight's heir," Butterfingers explained. "Heir to the Viranesh family. All he has to do is claim his uncle's sword and the curse is broken and the house is ours."

Oddvar chuckled. "I take it that didn't work out."

Butterfingers's face went from sarcastic to angry and he grabbed the hilt of his sword.

"Do you mock me, dwarf?"

Oddvar held up his hands. "I'm just making conversation."

"Gurgut was convinced the curse wouldn't affect him," Scar said. "He was very angry when he couldn't find the Dragon Knight's tomb and we couldn't get out."

"So the sword is buried in one of the tombs in the room we came through," Davyn said. "And once Gurgut claims it?"

"He becomes the next Dragon Knight, the curse is broken, and we can all go home," Butterfingers said, a longing look in his eye. "All we have to do now is dig out that room."

"Which is where you come in," Scar said with an evil grin.

"Speaking of that," Butterfingers said. "We'd better go get your escorts. We'll bar the door, so don't bother trying to escape."

The two knights moved to the door. As Butterfingers left, Scar turned back to them. "You'd better eat hearty," he said, "you've got a big day ahead of you."

Davyn heard the scrape of a heavy bar being dropped into place outside and the clank of the knight's armor as they moved off.

"This might not be so bad after all," Set-ai said between mouthfuls of bacon.

"How do you figure that?" Jirah asked, still shivering from the cold.

"If them fellers are right about the curse being being broken when the Dragon Knight's sword is found, all we have to do is get it and we're free."

"Won't Gurgut just kill us when he gets his hands on it?" Rina said.

Set-ai grinned at her and shook his head. "Think about it, lass," he said. "If you'd been trapped in here for twenty years and suddenly you could escape, what would you do?"

"I'd drop everything and run for the exit," Rina admitted.

Jirah shivered. "But will Gurgut help us once he gets the sword?"

"Maybe it's not Gurgut's help we need," Set-ai said.

"What do you mean?" Davyn asked. "He's the true Dragon Knight—"

"Not yet he isn't. Not until he claims the sword." Set-ai lowered his voice conspiratorially. "That's why you need to get the sword first, lad."

"Are you cracked? Besides the fact that we'll probably be guarded by a dozen armed knights, how will the sword do anything for me?"

"Think on it, lad," Set-ai said. "Remember when Gurgut thought that sword you grabbed off the statue was it? He didn't want anyone to touch it but him. Why do you think that was?"

Oddvar's face split into a wide grin. "He didn't want anyone else to claim the sword first."

"So how do we get Davyn to claim it?" Jirah said.

"We'll just have to make sure we open those coffins as soon as they're free of the rubble," Set-ai said.

"And be prepared for trouble when we do," Oddvar added.

Davyn wanted to ask the dwarf exactly how they should prepare for trouble but at that moment Butterfingers and Scar came back with Karnac and a half dozen other knights.

"I hope you're all well fed," Karnac said easily. "There's lots of work to do today."

"I've been thinking about that," Oddvar spoke up before Karnac could go on. "If you want us to get to those tombs, we're going to need some tools and supplies."

Karnac's left eye twitched. "What kind of supplies?"

Oddvar began ticking off items on his fingers. "Hammers, chisels, shovels, a pickaxe, and timbers to brace the ceiling."

"I think you'll do just fine with your bare hands," Karnac said. "I have no intention of arming you."

"You wouldn't be afraid of little old us, would you?" Oddvar favored Karnac with an amused look.

Davyn almost gasped. The dwarf was risking Karnac's murderous temper.

Karnac's hand dropped to the hilt of his broken dagger. "Are you calling me a coward?" he asked in a measured voice.

Oddvar smiled as if nothing were wrong. "Not I," he said. "I'm just trying to point out that if we start moving rocks in there without tools, you won't be out of here until next year."

Karnac's expression grew sour.

"And, of course," Oddvar went on, "if we don't have timbers to brace the ceiling, we'll all be crushed to death before we've gone five yards. Who do you think Gurgut will send in once we're dead?"

Davyn had always wondered how the surly Oddvar had managed to avoid Maddoc's wrath for so long. Now that he saw the dwarf in action, he understood. Oddvar was a master manipulator, not to mention a first-class weasel.

The dwarf's abilities weren't wasted on Karnac. The knight knew very well that if Davyn and his friends were killed, he and his knights would be the next ones into the crypt. He made his decision quickly.

"Very well," he said, turning to Scar and Butterfingers. "Go to the supply room and get what they need."

Karnac seemed completely at ease as he beckoned for everyone to follow him. As Jirah moved, however, he seized her and held his broken knife up against her face.

"I don't want you even thinking of challenging me," Karnac said, tracing the broken tip of his knife across Jirah's face and over her throat. Jirah was pale with terror and didn't dare to move.

"If you try anything—anything at all," Karnac continued, "I'll kill this pretty little one. Very slowly."

Karnac shoved Jirah back at her friends and Davyn grabbed her. Jirah was shaking uncontrollably.

The knights led them back through the twisting hallways to the chapel room. The hole in the wall was choked with debris, exactly as it had been the night before. Davyn wondered how they would ever manage to get through the mass of shattered brick, timber, and soil to reach the tombs.

"We can do it," Oddvar said, once he'd looked the situation over. He motioned for Davyn to climb up on top of the pile of debris that choked the doorway. "See back there?" He pointed through a gap.

Davyn squinted in the torchlight. He could barely make out the massive dragon statue. "So?"

"There's a pocket back there where the ceiling didn't fall," the dwarf explained. "All we have to do is dig back to that and see where we are."

Once the tools arrived, the work began in earnest. Davyn, Oddvar, and Set-ai moved the larger bits while Rina and Jirah broke up rocks with the hammers. After several hours, they had managed to clear the hole in the wall completely and move several feet into the crypt.

Davyn dropped a head-sized rock on the growing pile in the chapel room. He was about to go back into the hole for more when Oddvar grabbed his arm.

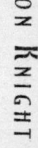

"We're getting in too far for the ceiling to hold," the dwarf said, picking up one of the timbers the knights had supplied. "Help me with this and we'll brace the ceiling."

The wood had been cut to the height of the ceilings, which were fairly uniform in all the rooms Davyn had seen. On one end a wooden frame had been attached, making the timber look as if it had a flat "foot." Davyn helped Oddvar carry the timber into the gap.

"Bang on the bottom until the post is straight," Oddvar said, once they'd wedged the timber against the ceiling.

"We'll have to do this every couple of feet," Oddvar said, as Davyn pounded with the hammer, "but we shouldn't have to worry about the ceiling falling on us."

Exactly as Oddvar had predicted, once they were inside there was a pocket of open floor. The rubble was concentrated mostly in the far corner near the drainpipe they'd used to get in. Davyn was secretly thankful that they wouldn't need to dig over there since he was sure they would find the bodies of Mudd and Hector there.

Karnac and his men watched their every move from the safety of the chapel room. At last, they managed to clear the debris off one of the tombs. Davyn grabbed a pry bar but before he could approach the coffin, Karnac stopped him.

"Wait," the knight said. "Everyone out until Gurgut arrives."

Davyn and the others moved out into the chapel room while Butterfingers went to get the Dragon Knight. The fat leader of the knights must have run the entire way from his throne room, for he arrived red-faced and panting. At the sight of the tomb Gurgut squealed like a child and Davyn could swear he saw drool on the man's lips.

"Get it open," he gasped, carefully wedging his bulk into the crypt.

"You heard him," Karnac said to Davyn.

Davyn moved to the tomb. There wasn't much room and he wondered if he dared to reach in for the sword before Gurgut. If he was fast, he might get it before Karnac could stab him in the back.

The stone lid was far too thick for Davyn and the others to lift. They took up positions on the far side and pushed the lid off. Little by little, the stone ground its way across the coffin. Gurgut hovered by the head.

With one final heave, Davyn and the others pushed the lid off onto the floor with a thundering crash that shook the whole room. Dirt rained down from the ceiling but the braces held.

As the dust settled, Davyn could see the body within the tomb. Whoever it was had been buried there a long time. All that remained were bones and the corroded fragments of what had at one time been a magnificent suit of plate armor. A sword lay across the warrior's armored chest, but time had eaten it away, pitting the blade with rust.

"This isn't it," Gurgut roared, his excitement turned to rage. "Where is my uncle's tomb? Where is the sword of the Dragon Knight?"

"My lord—" Karnac began.

"You know where it is," Gurgut accused Davyn. "You're trying to keep it from me."

Davyn backed up. "I don't—"

"Kill them," Gurgut roared. "No one shall have my uncle's sword but me."

"There's another tomb over there," Jirah shouted, pointing at the corner of the second coffin that was just visible under the rubble. "If this isn't the right tomb then that one's bound to be."

Gurgut stopped ranting and his eyes fixed greedily on the tomb.

"What are you waiting for?" he roared at Davyn. "Dig it out."

"Honored Dragon Knight," Davyn began. "It will take another full day of work to uncover that tomb. We need food and rest before we attempt it."

Gurgut's face turned purple. "You still try to deny me my birthright. You'll learn not to defy me."

Gurgut turned to Karnac. "These creatures shall have no food or rest. Throw them back in the pit until they learn obedience."

Karnac and his knights drew their weapons and Davyn allowed himself to be led back into the hallway. He was so weary from his first night in the pit and then digging all day that he could barely walk. At least we still have our belts, he thought, blessing Rina's foresight.

The cold water of the pit hit Davyn's body like a hammer. He just let the weight of his armor and clothes pull him to the bottom. He stayed there until his body's demand for air roused him enough to surface. As soon as the knights left, he clawed his belt off and strung it through the bars.

"Is everyone all right?" he croaked once he'd managed to secure himself.

"We've got to find a way out of here, lad," Set-ai's voice murmured from the semidarkness. "Jirah's barely conscious. She's too weary to last much longer."

Davyn summoned all his strength and pulled himself up as far as he could. He could see the latch that held the grate closed. If he could just release it, they could push the grate open and be free. Try as he might, however, the latch was just out of reach.

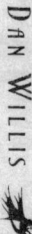

"Someone's coming," Rina hissed.

Davyn yanked his hand back as a soft grinding noise filled the pit room. Rina, Set-ai, and Oddvar scrambled to get out of their belts, but they were tired and stiff and not making much headway. Davyn couldn't see anything but when the grinding stopped he could hear soft footfalls. Suddenly a face loomed above Davyn in the torchlight. Without even thinking, Davyn grabbed through the bars, trying to seize whomever it was and make them open the grate.

"Whoa," a familiar voice said as Davyn grabbed empty air. "Take it easy, boss."

Davyn stared in shock as Mudd's face hovered back over the grate. "Unhook yourselves," he said, pulling the latch open. "I'll have you out of there in a jiff."

CHAPTER 17

REUNION

"Mudd!" Set-ai shouted, grabbing the young man's arm through the bars. "You're not dead." Davyn could swear he saw tears in Set-ai's eyes.

Mudd wasn't strong enough to lift the grate by himself. In the end, Davyn had to climb up on Oddvar's shoulders to get enough leverage to heave the grate open. Davyn switched places with the dwarf so he could scramble out of the pit, then Oddvar and Mudd helped Davyn and Rina out.

Set-ai had been holding the barely conscious Jirah the whole time. Together, the others lifted her out onto the cold stone floor.

"Will she be all right?" Mudd asked.

"She just needs something to eat and a warm place to rest," Davyn said. He hoped he was right.

After pulling out Set-ai, Davyn and Mudd carefully lowered the grate back into place and latched it. Davyn was about to ask Mudd how he got past the knights when he saw a large section missing from the stone wall of the room.

"It's a secret passage," said Mudd. "This place is full of them."

"Is that how you escaped the cave-in?" Rina asked.

Mudd shook his head. "I'll tell you all about it, but first we need to get out of here and get your weapons back."

Set-ai tried to pick up Jirah, but he winced as his wounded arm gave out.

"Let me." Davyn hoisted her unceremoniously over his shoulder like a sack of grain. She was small and light, but after the full day of hard work, Davyn's strength was all but gone. His knees wobbled as he followed Mudd into the opening in the wall.

The narrow stone hallway smelled of mildew and stale air. Once everyone was inside, Mudd pushed the stone door back in place, then led them along past several side passages to another stone door. This one stood open and light flooded through it. The room beyond appeared to be a storeroom, and a small figure was busily stuffing their weapons and gear into a sack.

"Hector!" Davyn nearly dropped Jirah on recognizing the gnome.

The gnome grinned. "Bet you never thought you'd see us again."

Davyn felt an enormous weight lift from his conscience.

"Save it for later," Rina hissed. "Someone's coming."

A moment later the sound of clanking armor could be heard outside the storeroom's door.

"Back into the passage," Mudd instructed.

Hector tried to lift the bag of weapons but it was too heavy for him. Before Davyn could do anything, Oddvar grabbed the bag and the gnome and darted back into the passage. Mudd and Rina pushed the stone door closed just as the door to the storeroom opened. Davyn unconsciously held his breath. He wondered if the theft of the weapons and packs would be noticed. A few seconds later there was a shout of alarm and

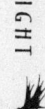

Davyn couldn't help but grin as he recognized the sound of a sword dropping to the stone floor.

Mudd rushed by Davyn carrying one of Hector's glass lamps.

"Let's go," he said, urgency in his voice. "We've got to get out of this passage before they raise the alarm."

With the glass lamp bobbing brightly ahead, everyone hurried along the passage as fast as they dared.

The secret hallway ended abruptly at a blank wall. Mudd deftly opened another hidden door, revealing a lit corridor beyond. Davyn recognized it as one of the passageways Gurgut's men had led them through on the way to the pit. As Davyn moved out into the hall, he could hear shouts and the clanking of running knights in the distance.

Mudd shut the secret door and directed the group down the hall and around a corner into another hallway. With Hector's limp and Davyn gasping under Jirah's dead weight, their progress was slow. Davyn could hear the knights gaining on them as the clanking of their armor grew louder.

Just when Davyn thought the knights would surely catch them, Mudd reached a heavy door on the side of the hall. He opened it quickly and ushered everyone through. The room beyond was a small bedroom with a dusty bed, a desk, and a wardrobe.

As soon as everyone had crowded into the little bedroom, Mudd softly shut the door. A moment later, they heard the shouts of the knights and the clank of feet racing by. With a conspiratorial wink, Mudd opened the wardrobe and reached inside. There was a click and the back of the wardrobe swung inward revealing another passage.

Davyn stepped up into the wardrobe. "H-how do you know about all this?"

"While you were playing with Gurgut, we found some friends." Mudd grinned. "They showed us how to rescue you."

Davyn wasn't sure he liked that idea. According to Gurgut, the only other residents of the keep were the crazed men who had attacked them in the crypt. He hoped Mudd wasn't leading them from one madman to another.

"How—much—farther," Davyn puffed. Jirah wasn't heavy by any means, but Davyn had been carrying her for a good quarter hour, and he was exhausted.

"This is it," Mudd called back from the front of the line.

There was a click and light flooded the narrow passage. Davyn stumbled out into a comfortable sitting room with couches and great stuffed chairs and a fire burning cheerfully in a great hearth. Without even slowing down, Davyn flopped Jirah's unconscious body onto one of the couches and collapsed onto the carpeted floor. The room was wonderfully warm and the carpet was soft. Davyn slipped into sleep almost immediately.

When he awoke, Davyn was surprised to find that he was not on the floor. Someone had taken the trouble of removing his armor and moving him to one of the sitting room's couches. He sat up and immediately wished he hadn't. His head was aching as if someone had smacked him with a warhammer, and every muscle in his body was sore from the intense work in the crypt.

Groaning, Davyn forced himself to his feet. Set-ai was sleeping under a thick blanket on one of the room's other couches but there was no sign of anyone else. Davyn's muscle pain was instantly forgotten when he realized that the couch where he'd left Jirah was empty.

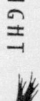

"Oh, you're awake."

Davyn turned a bit more quickly than he should have and the muscles in his back tightened painfully. Jirah stood framed in one of the room's several doorways. She wore a clean blue dress and she had obviously washed. Her hair was brushed and it shone inky black against the lightness of her skin.

Davyn sighed as relief and weariness flooded through him. He had worried that Jirah's strength was so tapped that she wouldn't be able to recover. Seeing her standing there, smiling at him as if nothing were wrong, lifted yet another weight off his conscience.

Jirah grinned. "We were beginning to think you'd never wake up."

"How long have I been asleep?" Davyn said, still trying to clear the fog from his brain.

"Half a day," Jirah said. "If you weren't awake by dinner time we were going to get you up anyway." Jirah crossed the room to a table that held a bowl of fruit. As she selected a golden apple, Davyn's stomach rumbled. He picked a red apple and bit into it with relish.

"Where are the others?" he asked once he'd stripped the apple to the core.

"Rina's cleaning her clothes and Oddvar's washing up," she said.

"Oddvar washing?" Davyn asked.

"Hector and Mudd are exploring the secret passages," Jirah continued. "They're two of a kind, both like kids in a sweetshop."

"So where are we?" Davyn asked, groaning as he stretched his back.

"Still in the underground part of the house. This side is controlled by a group called the freeholders. Their leader has invited us to dinner tonight."

"I hope it goes better than our meeting with Gurgut." Davyn grimaced.

Jirah smiled at him—it was the same smile Nearra had reserved for him. Davyn's heart skipped a beat.

"Mudd says he's a good man," she said. "A bit eccentric, but good."

"Eccentric?" Davyn sighed. "That's just a polite word for crazy."

Jirah shrugged. "He can't be too bad," she said. "He's the one who showed Mudd and Hector how to rescue us."

Jirah was right, as usual. Davyn started to pace around the room to work the kinks out of his muscles. He was probably just being paranoid. Of course after the year Davyn was having, he had a right to a certain amount of paranoia.

As if sensing Davyn's thoughts, Jirah put a hand on Davyn's arm to stop him. She looked up at him with her piercing blue eyes and smiled. "Don't worry," she said. "You'll find the Dragon Knight and get us out of here. I know you will."

That makes one of you, Davyn thought. But he returned her smile.

"Thanks," he said. Jirah put her head on Davyn's shoulder and he was suddenly very aware of how clean she smelled.

"I see you're finally awake." Rina's voice cut through the moment like a knife. Davyn took a step away from Jirah.

Rina leaned against the doorway, her arms crossed over her chest. "I came to tell you that the dwarf's out of the tub, but I can come back if you two need privacy. I didn't mean to interrupt."

Davyn felt himself blush to the roots of his hair. "You're not interrupting anything," he said quickly.

Jirah flashed an angry look at Rina. "Why don't you go back to washing clothes and I'll show Davyn to the washroom."

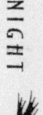

Davyn cleared his throat, his face still burning. "I can find it myself, thanks. Just point me in the right direction."

Rina jerked her thumb over her shoulder. "Back there."

Davyn stormed past Rina without giving Jirah a backward glance. The room beyond the door was a laundry, with washtubs and lines for holding clothes to dry. The washroom was visible through an open door on the far side of the room. Davyn hurried over the threshold and slammed the door shut.

The round, stone chamber seemed luxurious after all the rusty old inns he'd stayed in. Davyn filled the long wooden tub in the center of the room with warm water and sank into it. He chose not to imagine what might have been in the water from the pit but he was determined to get whatever it was off his skin and out of his hair. He scrubbed so hard that his skin stung. Once he decided he was clean, Davyn put on the cleanest of his dirty clothes and washed the rest. His armor had been stacked neatly in the washroom. Despite having been boiled to cure it, leather armor was not meant to soak for long periods. Davyn would have to oil it well over the next few weeks to keep it from deteriorating. Since he didn't have any oil, Davyn settled for wiping it clean with a damp rag.

"If you're finished, we could use you in here for a minute." Davyn looked up to find Rina watching him from the doorway. The mocking tone from before was gone and her eyes were serious.

Davyn sighed. "What now?"

Rina led him back into the spacious sitting room. Everyone was gathered around Set-ai on the couch.

"What's the trouble?" Davyn asked as he arrived.

"Nothin'," Set-ai growled. He seemed to be in a foul temper.

"Don't you say it's nothing," Jirah scolded. "Feel his head," she said, turning to Davyn.

Davyn pressed the back of his hand against Set-ai's forehead. The big warrior immediately pushed it away but not before Davyn felt the heat.

"He's burning up," Jirah said.

"It ain't nothin'," Set-ai insisted. "I just caught a chill from bein' in that cold water all night."

"How's his wound?" Davyn asked Rina.

"I cleaned it and put a new dressing on it," she said. "It doesn't look any worse, but it was soaking in that filthy water for who knows how long."

"It's fine," Set-ai grumbled.

"Mudd," Davyn said. "Do these freeholders have a healer?"

The boy shook his head. "I asked them to help fix up Hector's leg, but all they've got is a guy who knows less about healing than I do."

Davyn shook his head. "There's nothing we can do about it now. Let's go meet these freeholders. Maybe they can tell us about the Dragon Knight and if finding the sword will really break the curse."

Hector volunteered to lead the way to the freeholder's dining hall. Davyn decided against putting his armor on as a show of good faith, but he did wrap his belt around his waist. Someone had replaced the ornamental sword in the empty scabbard for him. Davyn was less than thrilled to see the unwieldy weapon, but since it was all he had, he took it.

The freeholder's dining room was down a short series of corridors that looked very much like the ones where Gurgut and his knights resided. Mudd led the group through a door onto the balcony ringing an incredible two-story library. Below them, shelves and shelves of books lined the walls and there were ornate desks and tables and overstuffed chairs.

At the far end of the library balcony was a large set of double doors. Each door had the head of a dragon carved into it and the handles were dragon claws. Hector pushed them open without stopping.

The room beyond was large and ornate, with an enormous oak table dominating its center. An iron chandelier hung above it and padded chairs stood around it. The outer walls of the room were curved to match the shape of the table. On one side were extra chairs; on the other was a vast oak sideboard, groaning under trays of food. The table had been set with porcelain dishes, linen napkins, silver utensils, and crystal goblets. At the far end of the room stood about twenty people. They seemed to be waiting patiently for the arrival of Davyn and his friends. Most of the men and women were dressed in worn clothing, though it looked clean and neat.

A tall man in a fancy orange shirt stepped forward with a wide smile.

"Ah, here you are," he said. "I was just going to send someone to fetch you. Welcome, friends, to the table of the freeholders. I am Cirill and I am your host."

He waved his hand toward the table.

"Sit everyone," he said. "First we eat, then we talk."

Davyn took the empty seat next to Cirill at the head of the table. Somewhere in the back of his mind the name Cirill resonated, but he wasn't sure where he'd heard it. Gurgut must have mentioned it.

The food was exquisite, easily the best Davyn had ever eaten. He decided, as he filled his empty stomach, that as prisons went, Viranesh Keep wasn't too bad. When, at last, Davyn had eaten his fill, he pushed his plate back and waited for the others to finish. As soon as he did, Cirill vaulted out of his chair and rang a small gong that stood by the head of the table. Immediately two of the freeholders got up and brought an iron kettle from the sideboard to the table.

"We welcome you all," Cirill said as the kettle was placed before him. "And to show you our faith and pledge of brotherhood, I present to you our rarest delicacy." With a great flourish he took the lid off the kettle and a gout of steam erupted from within. There was a murmur of anticipation from the other freeholders. "I give you the pudding."

Cirill reached into the kettle with a pair of tongs and brought out what looked like a lead ball about the size of a grapefruit. Belatedly Davyn recognized it as a plum pudding, a kind of steamed cake made with plums and currants. There was a cheer from the freeholders and everyone applauded. Davyn clapped too, not because he thought anything special had occurred but rather to avoid giving offense.

When the applause died down, Cirill continued. "To honor our guests, some freeholders, including myself, have graciously donated our portions to you."

Davyn wasn't sure what to make of this statement so he said a simple thank-you. One of Cirill's men began spooning out the soft pudding. Davyn noticed that he was being extremely careful to make each portion the same.

"Now it is time to talk," Cirill said, after everyone had gotten their portions of the small pudding. "We freeholders live here in this prison that is Viranesh Keep. Surely you know by now that escape is quite impossible and so, in order to survive, we must all work together. Gurgut and his crew, whom I believe you're acquainted with, would kill us and take all the pudding for their own if they could. Our cooperation and brotherhood is all that prevents that. Only by maintaining the most meticulous standards can we survive."

"I'm not sure what you mean," Davyn said.

"It's very simple." Cirill favored him with a warm smile. "If you and your friends can provide us with skills we need, if you're an asset to us, then you can remain in the freehold as one of us."

"And if not?" Rina asked.

"Anyone who cannot contribute to the success of the whole must leave," Cirill said sadly. "Exiled to the upper floors to become a looter and never to have pudding again."

"We don't have to worry about that," Mudd spoke up. "We can offer something you all desperately need. We can help you escape."

There was a round of laughter at the table but there was no joy in it.

"My dear boy," Cirill said in a kindly tone. "There is no escape from Viranesh Keep. The sooner you accept that, the better off you'll be."

"That's not true," Mudd continued, pointing to Oddvar. "He got out. Didn't you, Oddvar?"

Cirill looked at the dwarf and the color drained from his face. He gasped. "Oddvar?" It had been twenty years since Oddvar had been in Viranesh Keep, but those years apparently hadn't erased Cirill's memory.

Davyn looked down to the other end of the table where the dwarf sat with his hood up.

"Hello, Cirill," Oddvar said with no trace of a smile. "Long time, no see."

Cirill jumped to his feet, tipping his chair over backward with a bang. His hands were balled into fists and his face was even more purple than Gurgut's had been.

"You escaped!" he shouted. "And you didn't come back for us?"

Cirill was trembling with rage. He raised his hand and pointed at Oddvar.

"Kill him."

CHAPTER 18

The Escape Plan

Snatching a fork off the table, Davyn grabbed Cirill by the neck and held the fork to his throat.

Everyone froze.

"Stay where you are," Davyn yelled. "Just stay calm and nothing unpleasant will happen."

"Let me go, boy," Cirill said.

"You said that we could stay here if we could do something useful," Davyn said, keeping the fork against Cirill's throat. "Well, we can do something for you that no one else can."

Cirill laughed. "What can you do? Make pudding out of thin air?"

"No," Davyn said, raising his voice so all could hear, "but like Mudd said, we know a way out of the keep."

"Ridiculous!" Cirill yelled. "We've heard such claims before but they always turn out to be lies. There's only one way out of this place. Someone must claim the Dragon Knight's sword and break the curse."

"You're forgettin' about your dwarf friend here," Set-ai spoke up. He paused to pop an olive into his mouth before continuing. "He got out without breakin' the curse."

"He got out, and he abandoned his friends." Cirill twisted to face Oddvar. "You left us here to rot, you maggot!"

"I couldn't come back for you if I'd wanted to," Oddvar said. "After we got separated, I escaped through one of the sewer drains. I had to dig my way to the surface. That eventually brought the roof down on me. I got out but the passage caved in behind me."

"You could've got back in through the front door," said Cirill.

"And do what?" Oddvar shrugged. "Be trapped in here with you all over again?"

"I don't care what you say, dwarf," Cirill hissed. "I will never forgive you for abandoning us—never."

"That's enough," Davyn said. "You said the only way out of here is to break the curse."

Cirill tried to twist his head to look at Davyn. "So?"

"So I know where the Dragon Knight's tomb is."

This time there were no gasps. Everyone in the room just sat in stunned silence.

"If you're lying to me, boy," Cirill said, "I'll make sure you suffer greatly before you die."

"My friends and I entered the keep by digging up one of the sewer passages," Davyn said, still keeping the fork at Cirill's throat. "It caved in behind us and we ended up in a room containing two stone coffins. The door had been sealed up so we had to break our way out and that led us into the keep."

Now there were gasps. A woman with graying hair gave Cirill a meaningful look and nodded.

"All right," Cirill said. "If you can prove what you say no harm will come to any of you."

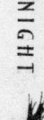

Davyn didn't release Cirill right away. "Including Oddvar?"

Cirill nodded. "Him too."

Davyn wasn't sure that he could trust Cirill. He was saner than Gurgut but that wasn't saying much. He would have to trust him at some point if he wanted to escape the keep. Davyn removed the fork from Cirill's throat and released him.

"You're pretty quick with the tableware," Cirill said after he picked up his chair and sat down. "I'd better keep an eye on you when the pudding comes around."

"That does it," Jirah said. "What is so special about pudding?"

Several of the freeholders looked at Jirah as though she were some kind of lunatic.

"My dear girl," Cirill explained, all thoughts of escape apparently forgotten. "The house provides for us, but it's always the same food every day. Pudding only happens once a week and, as you can see, it's a very small pudding. As such, pudding is highly prized." He took a small bite from the pudding on Davyn's plate and his face took on a look of rapture. "It's one of the only pleasures we have."

Davyn shivered. Cirill was just as crazy as Gurgut.

"Do you fight with Gurgut over pudding?" Jirah asked.

Cirill chuckled. "No. There are three places in the keep that create food. The larder here in our section, the kitchen on the main floor that is controlled by Gurgut, and a small pantry in the looter's territory."

"Who are these looters?" Mudd asked.

"A group of desperate wretches who haunt the upper floors of the keep. The pantry doesn't make enough food for all of them, so they survive by preying upon the poor souls who enter the keep looking for its treasure. Lately there haven't been many, so the looters have become more desperate."

Jirah asked, "How can they survive without enough food?"

"Some of them work for Gurgut in exchange for food," said the graying woman, whose name, Davyn later learned, was Carlotta. "The kitchen provides more food than he needs so he gives some to the looters if they bring him equipment or information."

"The men with the bone necklaces must have been looters," Mudd piped up.

Davyn remembered the raving madmen who rushed them when they first broke through the crypt wall into the keep proper. He wondered if it was hunger that had driven them into the underground.

"What if the looters don't bring Gurgut anything?" he asked.

Cirill shrugged. "Then they have to eat each other."

Davyn shivered and Jirah turned pale.

"That's monstrous," said Rina. "Why don't you do something about it?"

"We only have enough food for ourselves," Cirill said. "Besides, look around." He indicated his group with a sweeping motion. "Do we look like we could take on Gurgut and his knights?"

As Davyn looked around the table, he doubted it. The freeholders were more numerous than the knights, but most of them had no armor at all. They wouldn't last long against the knights.

"Gurgut leaves us alone because there are too many of us for a direct assault," Cirill explained. "We've fortified our position to prevent him from coming at us in force, so he ignores us."

"What do you know about the Dragon Knight?" Davyn asked, trying to pull the conversation back to escaping.

"He was the last owner of this house," Cirill replied. "When he died, the title was supposed to pass to his closest relative—Gurgut. Apparently the old boy disapproved of his great-nephew's career choice."

"He didn't like Gurgut serving Takhisis," Davyn guessed.

"Just so." Cirill nodded. "He called down a curse on the house and then hid the sword in the crypt that would be his final resting place. Only when a worthy successor came would the house let anyone leave."

"Does the successor have to be a blood relative?" Rina said.

Cirill shook his head. "Not at all," he said. "All someone has to do to become the Dragon Knight's heir is claim the warrior's sword and receive his blessing. But if someone claims it without receiving the Dragon Knight's blessing, the curse could go on . . . forever."

"How do you receive a dead man's blessing?" Hector wondered.

Before Cirill could answer, Davyn interrupted. "So if Gurgut finds the sword, the curse will never be broken?"

"That's right," Cirill said.

"Then we may have a problem," Davyn sighed. "Gurgut knows about the crypt."

Cirill slammed down his fork, sending bits of candied ham in all directions.

"You idiots!" he screamed. "How could you tell that maniac about it?"

"Easy, friend," Set-ai growled. "Gurgut captured us as soon as we arrived. We had no choice but to tell him."

Cirill stood up, careful not to knock his chair down again. "Don't you see? Now that Gurgut knows about the crypt, he's going to find the sword. And when he finds it, we'll all be doomed. The real Dragon Knight will never give his nephew his blessing. If he wanted Gurgut to have the sword, he'd never have cursed this place to begin with."

"Thurston." Cirill looked at a big man at the far end of the table. "Open the armory and get everyone ready. We've got to move against Gurgut before he gets that sword."

"Wait a minute," Rina said, standing up as well. "I thought you didn't have the manpower to take on Gurgut."

"We don't," Thurston said.

"But we can't sit here and let Gurgut get the sword," Cirill declared. "If that happens we'll all die here."

"There may be another option," Oddvar said, between bites of stewed potato. All eyes turned to the dwarf and he stood, reaching into the pocket of his jerkin. "Gurgut forced us to clean out the rubble in the crypt," he said. "I found this in the debris by that metal dragon statue." He held up what looked like a soggy bit of string.

Jirah wrinkled her nose. "What's that?"

"It's an earthworm. If there are earthworms in the dirt, then what's left of the ceiling couldn't be more than a dozen feet below the surface."

"What are you suggesting?" Davyn asked.

"All we have to do is wait for Gurgut to dig out the other tomb and get the sword," Oddvar said with a shrug. "Once he has it, he'll leave the crypt unguarded. Curse or no curse, if we pull down a small section of the ceiling, we can escape."

"What if we end up bringing the whole ceiling down?" Cirill said, sitting back down. "We've tried digging our way out before. All that happens is people get killed."

"You didn't have a dwarf with you then." Oddvar grinned. "I've done my share of tunneling. I know how it's done."

"It might work," Cirill said.

"It might," Carlotta said. "But Gurgut won't find the sword in the second tomb."

A dark suspicion began to grow in Davyn's mind. "How do you know Gurgut won't find the sword in the second tomb?" he asked.

"Yes," Cirill said, eyeing Carlotta. "How do you know that?"

Carlotta dabbed her lips with her napkin and stood up, setting the napkin on her plate. "If you'll come with me to the library, I'll explain everything."

Davyn and his friends stood and followed Carlotta and Cirill back into the library. Carlotta led them down a spiral iron staircase to the lower level, then across the floor to an intricately carved reading desk. There, she lay down on the floor and reached underneath the desk.

"When we first came here, Gurgut had his base here," Carlotta explained. "He abandoned it when he realized that the kitchen had a bigger food supply. Gurgut started here because he wanted to find out everything he could about his great-uncle." She pulled a large leather book from a compartment under the desk. "But he never found this."

On the cover of the book was a decorative bronze plate depicting the same dragon head that was on the crosspiece of the ornamental sword.

Cirill took in a quick breath.

"This is the journal of Heiro Viranesh, the last Dragon Knight." Carlotta placed the book on the desk.

"The guy's name was 'Hero'?" Mudd laughed. "His parents didn't expect much of him, did they?"

Cirill gripped Carlotta's shoulder. "Why did you never show me this before?"

Carlotta shrugged out of his grasp. "I didn't know it would be important until now."

"What's in the journal?" Davyn asked.

Carlotta smiled. "Heiro knew of the darkness in his great-nephew's soul," she said. "He hid his tomb well so that Gurgut would never find it, then he left this elaborate trap for anyone else who came seeking the Dragon Knight's power."

Davyn was about to ask where he did hide his tomb but Jirah spoke first.

"What powers does the Dragon Knight have?" she asked. "Why does Gurgut want to be him so badly?"

"The Dragon Knight is a warrior of destiny," Cirill answered for Carlotta. "He is drawn to momentous events and fate is his ally."

"Great," Set-ai scoffed. "A warrior who's always in trouble but has good luck."

"But you still haven't said how you know the Dragon Knight's sword isn't in the crypt," Davyn said.

"Heiro's sword was made of pure enchanted silver," Carlotta explained. "It's impossible to miss. To keep it hidden, Heiro had a special crypt made for himself."

"The crypt was walled off from the rest of the keep," Davyn said. "What makes you think it's not Heiro's crypt?"

Carlotta looked at Oddvar. "You mentioned a metal statue of a dragon," she explained. "According to the book, that's the *family* crypt, not the special crypt Heiro made for himself."

"So where is it?" Mudd was about ready to explode with curiosity.

Carlotta grinned and shrugged. "I don't know," she admitted. "I just know it isn't in the family crypt."

"When Gurgut doesn't find that sword, he's goin' to tear the crypt apart," Set-ai said.

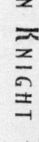

"Or he's going to think we took it after we escaped the pit," Hector added.

Cirill's face paled at that. "If he thinks you have it, he'll lead his men against us."

"All right," Davyn said, cutting off further conversation. "I don't care about the Dragon Knight anymore. Our first priority is to get out of here alive."

"We've got to get to the crypt then," Oddvar added. "It's the best place to tunnel out of here."

Cirill shook his head. "But now that Gurgut thinks the sword is there, he'll have all his forces guarding it. Especially with you on the loose."

Set-ai cleared his throat and sat down on one of the overstuffed chairs. "It sounds to me like what we need is a diversion," he said.

Cirill shook his head. "Nothing will draw him away from the sword."

"I know," Mudd said. "What if his food supply were threatened?"

"We can't get to the kitchen," Cirill said. "None of the secret passages go near there."

"That's not what I mean," Mudd went on excitedly. "You said the kitchen is on the ground level, right?"

Cirill nodded.

"Well," Mudd said, "the house might be made of stone, but the floors and the walls are made of wood. What if a fire started right over the kitchen?"

Oddvar grinned. "If it burned long enough, it would bring half the house down right on top of Gurgut's food source."

Davyn nodded—Mudd's plan had merit. Gurgut was crazy but he didn't appear stupid. He'd try to save his food no matter what the cost. Cirill, however, was shaking his head.

"The area above the kitchen is controlled by looters," he said. "You'd have to sneak past them."

"That shouldn't be too hard," Hector spoke up. "You humans are remarkably inattentive."

"Let's say this works," Davyn said, turning to Oddvar, "and Mudd is able to start a fire above the kitchen. Will that give us enough time to get out?"

Oddvar nodded. "All we have to do is pull down one of the braces and then pull down that part of the ceiling with a shovel," he said. "It won't take much time at all."

Davyn turned to Hector. "How many of your quick lamps do you have left?"

The gnome held up two fingers.

"That ought to be enough," Davyn said. "Mudd, do you think you and Hector can start the fire and get back here without getting caught?"

"Me?" Mudd's eyes bugged out.

"It was your idea," Davyn said. "Besides, you and Hector are more likely to get in and out without being seen."

"We can do it," Hector said, putting his arm around Mudd's neck. "After all, we got you guys out right under Gurgut's nose."

Mudd pushed Hector away with a playful grin but then his expression turned suddenly serious. "Is your leg okay?"

"It's still a bit sore," the gnome confessed. "But I can run if we have to."

"All right," Davyn said. "Cirill, your people will have to be ready to move and we'll need someone to show Mudd the layout of the keep. As soon as Mudd goes, we'll have to get as close to the crypt as possible and wait for Gurgut's men to leave."

"There's a map of the keep upstairs," Carlotta said, pointing up to the balcony that ran around the periphery of the room.

"Let's go then," Davyn said. "I have a feeling we're running out of time."

CHAPTER 19

FIRE IN THE HOUSE

Mudd leaned against the wall to catch his breath. He and Hector had run to the far side of freeholder territory. According to Cirill and Carlotta, the secret passage to the main floor was hidden behind a tapestry.

"This is it," Mudd said, pulling the tapestry aside.

Hector squinted at the bare wall behind the tapestry. The stone looked exactly like the rest of the wall.

"Are you sure?" he asked.

Mudd grinned and pushed a small stone. There was a click and a ragged edge became visible. The heavy stone door swung inward with a faint creak.

Hector grinned and shook his head. "I should never have doubted you."

Beyond the door was a spiral stone staircase going up. The passage was carved out of stone and it was so narrow that, as small as they were, Mudd and Hector still couldn't go up side by side. The sound of dripping water echoed down from the stairs and the passage was dank and humid.

Hector handed Mudd one of his quick lamps. "You go

first," he said, slipping his crossbow off his shoulder. "I'll cover you."

Mudd took the lamp and twisted the cap to light it. He moved into the secret passage and carefully up the stairs. It wasn't long until he discovered the source of the humidity. Water was running down the stairs in a slow trickle. About a dozen steps up, there was a crack in the wall into which the water was disappearing.

"Be careful," Mudd said, stepping cautiously onto the first of the wet steps. "It's slippery up here."

No sooner had Mudd said it than Hector slipped and almost fell.

"Thanks for the warning," he said once he'd regained his footing.

"Just don't shoot me in the back," Mudd said. He was glad to have Hector along with him. The gnome didn't have to come, but he had volunteered. Mudd was more than a little proud to have a friend like Hector. Since he'd lost his parents to the Beast, Mudd had made quite a few friends. They didn't make up for his loss, but they eased the burden. Sometimes he was amazed by how much his friends trusted him. The fact that Davyn was relying on him to create the diversion that would let them all escape was more than a little frightening.

Don't worry, Mudd, he told himself. All you've got to do is sneak into the room above the kitchen, start a fire big enough to draw away Gurgut and his knights, and get back to the secret passage, all without getting caught by the looters. Piece of cake, he thought to himself, or should that be pudding?

Somewhere up ahead, Mudd could see daylight reflecting off the stone walls of the stair. He snapped the silver cap on the quick lamp closed and its little light went out.

"I see light," he whispered back to Hector, passing the gnome his quick lamp.

"I'm ready," Hector replied, excitement in his voice.

Mudd climbed the last few steps and found the passage blocked by a stone door similar to the other secret passages. But this door had a large crack in it that let daylight in. A steady stream of water was seeping under it.

"Can you get it open?" Hector asked when Mudd didn't immediately open the door.

"I think so," Mudd said, checking the latch. "It looks like it opens in, though. If there's water behind the door, it will make a lot of noise going down the stairs."

"That's sure to bring the looters." Hector nodded. "Can you see anything through the crack?"

Mudd pressed his eye to the crack in the stone door. He knew the passage ended in the keep's great hall, but he didn't have any idea what that looked like. Beyond the door, he could see a sweeping staircase running along the far wall. The stair was easily wide enough to drive a wagon up, and it was covered in a ratty-looking carpet. The wood of the stair was chipped and broken and even burned in places. On the main floor, at the bottom of the stairs, Mudd could see stone statues. These were defaced and broken just like the stairs. A thick carpet covered the floor and the remains of tapestries hung on the walls. The light was streaming in from windows on the second floor. They appeared to be above the stairs, well out of reach of anyone trying to escape.

"I don't see anyone," Mudd reported. "Should we open the door?"

While Mudd had been looking through the crack, Hector had taken off his pack and was rummaging through it while trying to keep it off the wet floor. After another minute of searching, Hector withdrew a long tube and handed it to Mudd.

"Try this," he said.

Mudd took the tube and looked at it. There was a mirror mounted at an angle on the top and it was made up of two parts so the top could be turned.

"What is it?" Mudd asked.

"It's my Around-the-corner-looker." Hector grinned. "Push it through the crack and then look through it."

Mudd did as he was instructed and found himself looking up at the roof of the great hall. He could see an enormous iron chandelier that was fit for torches and a ceiling that had once been decorated with frescoes but was now blackened and stained. The effect of looking straight ahead and up at the same time made Mudd a little nauseous.

"Twist it," Hector whispered excitedly.

Mudd did as he was told and his view rotated down so he could see a second staircase on his side of the room and then the stone floor just beneath the door. As he had feared, the door to the secret passage appeared to open into a small fountain filled with rusty-colored water.

He passed back the Around-the-corner-looker. "There's water right in front of the door."

"What do we do?" the gnome asked.

"We don't have any choice," Mudd said, shrugging. "I guess we hope the looters are taking a nap."

Mudd took hold of the door latch and Hector shouldered his crossbow. The latch was rusty and squeaked as Mudd pulled it back. With a groan and a splash, the heavy door swung inward and snapped off its hinge with a bang. The water from the pool spilled in and ran noisily down the stairs. Mudd grabbed his sword as the sounds echoed through the great room. He waited, barely daring to breathe, but there were no shouts of alarm or sounds of running feet.

"Let's go," Hector urged.

Mudd stepped over the ledge of the now empty fountain and into the great hall. It was bigger than it had looked through the crack. The ceiling was four stories up with balconies running around the second, third, and fourth floors. Along the opposite wall was a bank of stained glass windows that started at the second floor and ran up the entire wall, filling the room with multicolored light. As Mudd looked around he saw broken furniture and bits of armor and what looked disturbingly like human bones littering the floor. There were more than a dozen passages entering the great room just on the main floor. One had been bricked up.

"That's the kitchen," Hector said, indicating the blocked door.

Mudd looked up above it. A closed door at the top of the nearest staircase seemed to lead into the room directly above the kitchen.

Motioning for Hector to follow, Mudd picked his way carefully across the floor and up the massive staircase. It creaked loudly, even under the minimal weight of Mudd and Hector.

The door at the top of the stairs was locked, but Mudd made short work of it with his picks. Beyond the door was a long room with wood paneling on the walls and carved oak pillars supporting the ceiling. The ruins of a table and chairs were piled in the corner and the carpet had been pulled up. Mudd could see several places where small holes had been gouged out of the floor.

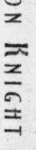

"Looks like the looters are stealing from Gurgut," Hector said, kneeling down to peek through one of the holes into the kitchen below. "This is perfect for fishing—all you'd need is a pole, a line, and a hook and you could get dinner."

"Let's hurry then," Mudd urged, "before someone comes looking for a bite."

Hector handed Mudd one of the remaining quick lamps and showed him how to open the oil reservoir. As Mudd poured the oil across the floor, Hector used the last quick lamp to make a trail of oil around the center posts and to the door. Mudd emptied his lamp and then traded the glass globe for a candle from his pack. Being careful to stand away from the oil on the floor, Mudd lit the candle and held it high.

"Ready?" he hissed.

The gnome grinned and nodded. Mudd picked his way across the floor, keeping his candle high. When he reached the door, he handed Hector the candle.

"You can do the honors," he said.

Hector touched the burning candle to the trail of oil. With a whooshing sound the fire raced across the floor, around the columns, and up the walls. In seconds, the room was a blazing inferno.

"Time to go," Hector said, tossing the candle into the room.

Mudd turned and headed for the stairs but stopped quickly at the top. A dozen ragged men were standing at the bottom of the stairs, a look of shock on their faces.

"Now what?" Hector asked, skidding to a stop beside Mudd.

With a howl of delight, the looters charged up the stairs. To Mudd's horror, he saw several of them break off and head for the stairs on the other side, effectively cutting off their escape route.

"Up!" Mudd shouted, pushing the gnome toward the third-floor staircase.

Together they charged up to the third floor landing with the looters in hot pursuit.

Davyn shuffled quietly from foot to foot to keep his muscles from stiffening up. A sliver of torchlight crossed the unused bedroom, emanating from the door, which was open just a crack. A few yards down the hall, Karnac was directing Gurgut's men in the removal of debris from the crypt. Davyn was close enough to hear the men complaining. For the fifth time in as many minutes, he pressed his eye to the crack in a vain effort to see something.

"This is not going to work." Oddvar's voice came out of the semidarkness.

"Well, it was your idea, dwarf," Rina said. "It had better work."

"Trying to roast ourselves alive by setting fire to our prison was *not* my idea," Oddvar said.

"Quiet," Davyn whispered.

Since Davyn wanted to get as close as possible to the crypt before the fire, it was decided that only he, Rina, and Oddvar would go. Set-ai and Cirill were waiting with everyone else a few hallways away, ready to move at a moment's notice. As soon as the fire drew the knights away, Davyn and Oddvar would start working on the roof and Rina would go get the others.

"Nothing's happening," Davyn grumbled, still trying to see anything through the tiny crack in the door.

"It's too soon," Rina assured him. "Don't worry. Mudd will come through. He takes after you that way."

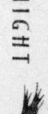

Rina was lounging on the room's dusty bed, absently checking her remaining arrows for loose fletchings in case there was trouble. Oddvar paced aimlessly around the room, walking softly so as not to make noise. When he noticed Davyn looking at him, he stopped.

"There's something I've been wanting to tell you," he said. He cast a suspicious glance at Rina, but the elf appeared to be absorbed in her arrow inspection and not paying attention to them.

"I wanted to thank you," the dwarf continued, "for saving my life again. If you hadn't grabbed Cirill when you did, he'd have gutted me."

"Don't mention it," Davyn said, still listening for any sound of a disturbance outside, "to anyone." He was only half-joking. Though he'd come to respect Oddvar, the dwarf was not his favorite person in the world.

"I'm serious," Oddvar said. "That's the third time this trip you've saved my life and I'm grateful. Mine hasn't been much of a life, but it's the only one I've got and I'm kind of attached to it."

Davyn shrugged. "We've been over this ground before. You put me in charge and that means I can't let some pudding-addled nutcase order you skewered."

Oddvar chuckled, looking genuinely amused. "You're pretty good for a human," he said. "I don't know how you managed it, growing up with Maddoc and all."

The mention of the wizard made Davyn's jaw tense up but he didn't say anything. After an awkward pause, Oddvar went on.

"Look," he said, seeming to fish for the right words. "There's something I want to tell you—in case we don't make it out, I mean."

He hadn't really asked a question so Davyn waited for him to continue.

"A long time ago, I did some things that got me into trouble," he began.

So far Davyn had no trouble believing the dwarf's story.

"When I was 'invited' to leave my homeland, my father came down specially to see me off. Now, he knew he'd never see me again, his only son. Do you know what he said to me?"

Davyn shook his head.

"He called me useless," the dwarf confessed. "He said I was worthless, a disgrace, and that I'd never amount to anything. Ever since then I've spent every waking moment trying to beg, borrow, or steal enough magic or steel or influence to prove my father wrong."

Davyn remembered his own struggles to win Maddoc's approval and he suddenly felt for Oddvar.

"Why are you telling me this?" Davyn asked.

"Because I see the way you are," Oddvar said. "The way people who barely know you try to help you. They trust you." The dwarf cast a sidelong glance at Rina. "Even those who by all rights should hate you, they trust you with their very lives. You always keep your goals in mind but at the same time, you make sure everyone's needs are met," he continued. "You're a born leader, make no mistake."

Davyn was beginning to feel a little embarrassed by all this praise.

"What's your point?"

"I think maybe I've been doing things all wrong," Oddvar confessed. "I've spent the last thirty years of my life trying to get enough power to go home and stick it to my father and those cowards who banished me," he said. "What has it got me? Nothing, that's what. I'm just thirty years older."

Davyn shrugged. "So change."

"You mean turn over a new leaf and do things differently

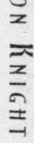

from now on?" Oddvar laughed. "It's never that easy."

"Then why tell me all this?" Davyn asked.

Oddvar took a deep breath and stood up to his full height. "May I be blessed with a son like you." Oddvar's face was stony and serious. "That's an old saying among my people," he said, somewhat formally. "It's a great compliment and is never said lightly."

Davyn was speechless. Oddvar looked away and quickly resumed his pacing. Davyn cast a sidelong glance at Rina. She was still busily examining every minute detail of her arrows, but her hair had been pulled back from her pointed ears. Davyn was sure she'd heard the entire exchange.

Just at that moment, Rina's head snapped up and she jumped off the bed.

"This is it," she whispered.

A moment later, Davyn heard the sounds of running and shouting in the corridor beyond. Gurgut roared out orders and a moment later the knights were charging down the hall, away from the crypt.

"Well, shave my beard and call me human," Oddvar exclaimed. "It worked."

"All right," Davyn said, pulling the door open. "Let's go."

Mudd rounded the corner of the fourth floor stairs and pounded up as fast as his legs would carry him. Hector was right behind him and somewhere behind the gnome were a dozen crazed looters. Smoke from the fire below was beginning to fill the great hall.

The fire was spreading fast.

Already tongues of flame had erupted from the dining room and were sweeping up the third-level stairs. The litter of furniture and ripped tapestries seemed to be feeding the fire, allowing it to race along walls and over the floor. Mudd could feel waves of heat rising up from below.

"What do we do now?" Mudd coughed as they reached the topmost balcony.

Thick smoke rising from below was slowing the looters and none of them had managed to reach the fourth floor stairs yet.

Hector grabbed Mudd's arm and pointed. A rickety wooden ladder ran up the back wall to a trapdoor that presumably led to the roof.

"We can't go up there," Mudd gasped as the smoke began to fill up the ceiling. "We'll be trapped with a fire under us."

"Maybe we could jump to the ground," Hector suggested.

"The curse won't let us out," Mudd yelled. "Even if it would, that's five stories up. We'd be killed."

"What about the chandelier?" Hector yelled back.

Mudd turned and looked at the great iron monstrosity. It was held up by a chain that ran through a hook in the ceiling, then wrapped around a giant wheel on the far side of the upper balcony.

"If we get on that and release the capstan," the gnome called, indicating the chain-wrapped wheel, "we can ride it to the bottom."

"That's crazy," Mudd said. "It's just like jumping off from here."

Hector shook his head. "The chain has to unwind," he said. "That will slow it down a little."

An incoherent yell from below told Mudd that the looters had found the fourth-level stairs. He made his decision quickly.

"I love this plan," he yelled. "Let's do it."

Mudd and Hector raced around the balcony to the capstan. All they would have to do is release the pin that held the chain in place and the chandelier would drop. The only problem was that the chandelier was a very long jump away.

"You go first," Hector yelled. "I can't jump that far. Once you're out there, start it swinging and I'll jump on when it's closer."

Mudd took three steps and hurled himself over the balcony railing. For an incredible moment he hung in the air, suspended over the smoke-filled hall like a feather on the wind. A moment later, he crashed into the chandelier, hitting the edge with his stomach. Stars swam before Mudd's eyes and he had the wind knocked out of him, but he grabbed the iron frame and held on.

Mudd scrambled up onto the chandelier. He was about to start it swinging when the first looters reached the top of the stairs. Smoke was rapidly filling up the top level but the looters saw Hector despite it. They staggered forward, coughing from the smoke. It would only be moments before they reached Hector.

Mudd looked at Hector and time seemed to stop. The gnome's face was calm, even serene. Before Mudd could do anything to stop him, Hector winked and pulled the capstan pin. Mudd felt a lurch in his stomach as the chandelier dropped from under him, plunging down through the rising smoke. The last thing Mudd saw was Hector scrambling up the ladder to the attic, the strange flaps on his pack waving in the updraft, with the looters right on his heels.

CHAPTER 20

REDEMPTION

From somewhere on the floors above came a thunderous boom. Davyn charged down the hall, skidding to a stop just short of the chapel room's open door. Gurgut might have left someone behind. With his back to the wall, he quickly stuck his head around the door to survey the room. The look revealed no remaining guards, but what Davyn did see stopped him cold.

The chapel room was almost unrecognizable. When they'd first arrived it had been stripped of everything, but now there were piles of rubble everywhere. The thing that grabbed Davyn's attention was a thick wooden support post that was dead center in the middle of the room. Apparently Gurgut's attempts at excavation had caused a minor cave-in. A long crack ran from the hole into the crypt all the way across the chapel ceiling. The wooden brace had been placed right under the crack to keep any more of the ceiling from coming down.

"Get a move on, boy," Oddvar said.

Davyn slipped around the door but stopped immediately, causing Oddvar to run into his back. Just inside the door was one of Gurgut's knights. He lay face down, like he was asleep, but his armor was battered and scarred as if many rocks had fallen on him. Davyn recognized the knight. It was Butterfingers. Davyn knew he would never wake up again.

"I guess he went home after all," Davyn said, moving carefully around the body.

"What's that fool done?" Oddvar growled, finally entering the room. He didn't give Butterfingers's body a second look but was staring instead at the chapel room's single support post. "We'd better warn everyone to stay away from this," he said. "I'm afraid if someone bumps it the whole room will fall down on us."

Davyn scooped up a shovel and, being careful to avoid the support post, stepped through the hole into the crypt. Gurgut's men had been busy. The second tomb had been exhumed and broken open; its contents were strewn about the room. Several new support posts had been added to hold up the newly exposed ceiling but none of them looked very solid.

"Those fools have done our work for us," Oddvar said, mirroring Davyn's thoughts. "If we pull down those three supports," he went on, indicating the new posts, "it'll weaken that whole section. We'll be able to pull it down, no problem."

Davyn and the dwarf carefully removed first one support post, then another. By the time they were ready to pull the last one, Rina and Cirill arrived with the others.

"Careful of that post," Oddvar called, pointing to the support post in the chapel room.

Rina began directing people around the dangerous post. Davyn was about to pull out the third support when he caught sight of Jirah's face. She was leading Set-ai by his good arm and he was unusually pale.

"Davyn," she said, directing Set-ai to sit on a pile of rubble. "I need you."

"Rina," Davyn called as the last of the freeholders shuffled into the crypt. "Help Oddvar."

Rina moved to help the dwarf, and Davyn picked his way past the huddled freeholders to where Set-ai was sitting.

"This isn't a good time, Jirah," Davyn began, but she cut him off.

"Set-ai's wound has soured," she said. "Rina has no idea what she's doing. Her so-called healing has only made him worse."

"Tain't nothin'," Set-ai muttered. "I've had . . . worse than this." Set-ai seemed to be having trouble getting his thoughts together. He looked terrible. His skin was white and pasty and he was drenched with sweat.

"He's delirious," Jirah declared. "If we don't get him to a real healer soon, he could die."

"If we don't get the ceiling opened up before Gurgut and his knights get back, we might all die," Davyn snapped back.

He wasn't mad at Jirah, but there wasn't time for this discussion. He hoped Jirah knew that. He hoped Set-ai did too. The thought of losing his friend tied Davyn's guts in knots. He pushed those thoughts out of his head. He had to concentrate on the task at hand. Everyone else's life was depending on him.

"Keep him warm," Davyn said. "That's all we can do right now." He turned to go, but then stopped. "Stay with him," he told Jirah. If the worst happened, he didn't want Set-ai to die alone.

"Someone's coming!" Rina's voice shocked Davyn back to the task at hand. She and Oddvar had removed the last support beam and the dwarf was prodding at the ceiling with the shovel.

Davyn waved Rina to him. "Cover the door," he told her. "Shoot anything that tries to come through."

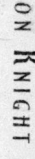

Davyn turned to help Oddvar but Rina grabbed his shoulder before he could go.

"It's Mudd," she gasped, relief plain in her voice.

A moment later, Mudd staggered into the room. His light leather armor was scorched and burned and he was cradling his right arm. His dirty face showed the tracks of tears and Davyn could see why—Mudd's arm was twisted quite unnaturally. It was obviously broken.

"Grab him," Davyn yelled as the lad staggered toward the unstable support post.

Rina darted through the hole into the chapel room with all the speed and grace her elf heritage granted her. She slipped her arm around Mudd's waist and steered him across the room and through the hole in the wall.

"Where's Hector?" Davyn demanded once Mudd was safely inside the crypt.

Rina eased Mudd down onto the floor. The boy's tear-stained face turned up and Davyn realized that he wasn't weeping from pain.

"Looters trapped us on the top floor," Mudd croaked. "Hector didn't have time to escape. The last I saw they were chasing him up into the attic."

"And you left him?" Rina was shocked.

Mudd shook his head. "I didn't have any choice. The fire is out of control. The whole upper house is burning."

Davyn felt an all-too-familiar knot in his stomach. If the fire was truly out of control, no one in the attic would survive.

"Maybe he can get out on the roof and jump for it," Rina said, reading the look on Davyn's face.

"It's too far," Davyn said. "Besides, the curse on the house wouldn't allow anyone to escape that way."

Rina said, "Maybe—"

At that moment, another crash shook the room. Dirt and debris rained down where Davyn and Oddvar had removed the supports.

"That was the roof," Mudd asked, "wasn't it?"

Davyn nodded, a tear in his own eye. "Good-bye, Hector."

There were tears in Rina's eyes too. "Maybe it got Gurgut, too," she said, struggling to control her emotions.

At the mention of Gurgut, Mudd suddenly sat up. An instant later he was wincing in pain from moving his broken arm too quickly.

"I almost forgot," he said. "I saw Gurgut and his knights in the great room."

"Did he see you?" Davyn asked.

Mudd nodded. "Yeah, but I was on the other side of the fire from him."

Davyn's mind raced. Gurgut had never seen Mudd, but he had to know that Davyn had help escaping the pit. If Gurgut saw Mudd, the first thing he would think to do is protect his treasure. Almost on cue he heard shouts and the sounds of clanking armor from the hall.

Rina was already moving, having heard the sounds of the approaching knights an instant before Davyn. She nocked an arrow and positioned herself by the hole in the wall.

"Here they come," Davyn shouted. "Oddvar, we need that ceiling down now."

The dwarf was swinging the shovel at the ceiling but he couldn't reach it.

"I'm too blasted short," he yelled. "Get over here and give me a hand."

Davyn started to move, but Gurgut's voice from the hall cut him off.

"They're after my sword," Gurgut screamed. "Get in there after them. Kill them all."

Davyn didn't have to look out in the corridor to know what was happening. Over a dozen armed and armored knights were charging down the hall as fast as they could go. Rina might be able to shoot one, but then the knights would be on them. Cirill and his roughly two dozen people were armed with swords. Unlike the knights, however, they had no armor or military training. Davyn's best warrior was delirious with fever and Mudd had a broken arm.

Gurgut would lose most of his men in the coming fight, but he would still win. Davyn had only seconds to do something to stop the knights. He looked at Oddvar and their eyes met. It was clear the dwarf was doing the same mental math—and reaching the same grim conclusion. There was only one thing that could be done.

Without a second thought or a moment of hesitation, Davyn turned. He leaped forward toward the hole in the wall but something caught his feet and he fell on his face. Oddvar had tripped him with the shovel.

"Not so fast, boy," the dwarf said, leaping over Davyn's prone form. "These people still need you."

Oddvar jumped through the hole and into the chapel room. Gurgut and his men arrived at exactly the same moment. Without a pause, Oddvar hurled himself smack into the room's lone support post. The post was already quivering under the strain of holding up the ceiling and it snapped in two with the force of Oddvar's blow. The dwarf and the remains of the post collapsed to the floor.

Gurgut roared with rage as the ceiling began to crumble. He dashed through the chapel room and hurtled through the hole in the wall. A moment later his knights charged after him, but they were too late. With a deafening roar, the ceiling in the chapel room collapsed. Hundreds of tons of earth descended, burying the knights and Oddvar in a tomb of rock.

Davyn scrambled to his feet, but there was nothing he could do. Oddvar was gone.

He'd spent a good portion of his life hating the dwarf, but that was forgotten. Oddvar had done the very thing Davyn had intended to do: he gave his life to save his friends.

In the shock of the aftermath, Davyn suddenly felt empty. When he'd started this journey, he'd have been happy to push Oddvar under a falling ceiling himself. Now he felt as if he'd lost not just a team member, but a friend.

"He died a hero's death," Davyn said, more to himself than anyone. "Maybe that will give his soul some peace."

The sound of cursing and the scrape of armor against rock snapped Davyn out of his trance. Gurgut had made it through the hole before the ceiling had fallen and was now levering his considerable bulk off the floor. He grabbed for his sword, but Davyn moved quickly. Drawing the heavy, ornamental sword, Davyn swatted Gurgut's sword from his hand. It skittered across the floor and came to rest at Rina's feet.

Gurgut lunged at Davyn with his bare hands. Davyn hit him in the face with the crosspiece of his sword and the fat knight staggered back against the wall. Davyn grabbed Gurgut by the front of his armor and pinned the knight to the wall.

"You miserable, posturing toad!" Davyn shouted at him. "Do you have any idea what your stupid quest for your uncle's title has cost?"

"You want it for yourself," Gurgut screamed. He shoved Davyn away with more force than Davyn expected.

Davyn stumbled back into one of the crypt room's remaining

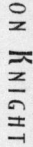

support posts. Gurgut lunged for his sword but before he could grab it a shudder ran through the room.

"Everybody get back," Davyn yelled.

There was a groaning sound and a small part of the ceiling collapsed. Much to Davyn's dismay, Gurgut was not buried. A large rock did hit him in the head and the fat knight collapsed in a heap.

As soon as the ground stopped shaking, Davyn moved toward Gurgut. He was angry enough to simply run the fallen man through but before he had to make that decision, a brilliant light dazzled him.

Squinting against the brightness, Davyn realized that it was the sun streaming in. There was a gasp from the freeholders. Carlotta was crying uncontrollably and Cirill had a look of rapture on his face.

"This is better than pudding," he said.

Gurgut forgotten, Davyn looked up. Above him, the ceiling had fallen in, exactly the way Oddvar had predicted. At the top of a mound of earth and rock there was a wide opening and a patch of inviting blue sky beyond. It was the most beautiful thing Davyn had seen in a month.

"Y-you did it, lad," Set-ai croaked from where he lay by the blocked door.

Jirah nodded next to him and Davyn could see tears in her eyes.

"Okay," Davyn said, slipping the ornamental sword back into his scabbard, "let's get everyone out of here. Rina, go first and make sure it's secure up there."

Rina grinned and gave him a mock salute. She scrambled easily up the mound of dirt and out through the hole.

"All clear up here," she reported.

"Mudd, you're next," Davyn said.

Jirah and Davyn helped the wounded youth up to where Rina could help pull him out, then Davyn sent Jirah up after him. Next came Cirill's people, climbing one by one into the freedom they hadn't known in twenty years. Finally, it was just Davyn, Set-ai, and Cirill.

"What have you done with my uncle's sword?"

Davyn had forgotten about Gurgut. The big knight had recovered himself and stood facing Davyn with a pickaxe. He swung it back over his head as Davyn scrambled to draw his sword. Davyn didn't have anything to worry about; Gurgut was standing by the bronze statue when he raised the pickaxe. The pickaxe struck the statue right in the center, and the statue broke into two halves and clattered to the floor. Gurgut dropped the pickaxe in his haste to get out of the way.

When the dust settled, Davyn strode over to where Gurgut had hurled himself and pushed the tip of his sword against the knight's throat.

"I should kill you right here," Davyn hissed, his rage boiling over at Gurgut. "I don't have your stupid sword and I don't want it. I just want to go home."

Davyn took his sword away from Gurgut's throat and started to turn. Gurgut let out a shout of glee and lunged to his feet. Davyn reacted, expecting an attack, but the knight ran right by him. What Gurgut had seen that Davyn had not was a gaping hole where the bronze statue had stood. As Gurgut hurled himself blindly through it, Davyn realized it must be the Dragon Knight's hidden crypt.

"Let's get out of here," Davyn said, slamming his sword back in its sheath, "before Gurgut finds his uncle's sword."

Cirill and Davyn each took one of Set-ai's arms and helped him up through the hole.

"I can't say I shall miss this place," Cirill said, giving the crypt one last look around. With a smile and a wink, he scrambled up the mound and out into the free air.

Davyn cast a backward look at the hole where the statue had been. Gurgut might get the sword, but Davyn was more sure than ever that he wouldn't get his dead uncle's blessing.

"Serves him right," Davyn growled as he climbed the earth mound, pulled himself up through the hole, and flopped down on the grass. Lying there with the sun on his face and a faint breeze stirring, Davyn decided he was more comfortable than he'd ever been.

The feeling didn't last. Davyn sat up suddenly, a worrying thought in his mind.

Set-ai was sitting on the grass just to the side of the hole. In the field beyond, the freeholders were running and playing and rolling in the grass like children. Mudd and Jirah were lying in the grass beside Set-ai, and Rina sat on the other side of Davyn with her bow at her feet.

Rina noticed the look on Davyn's face. "What is it?" she asked.

"Shemnara said that the only way to save Nearra is with the Dragon Knight's help," Davyn said. "I think I have to go back and get that sword."

"I'll go with you," Rina said, scooping her bow off the grass.

"No," Davyn said, sitting up. "We've lost too many people on this trip already. I'll go alone."

Davyn put his hand on the hilt of the ornamental sword to make sure it was still there, then he took a deep breath and dropped back down into the darkness of the crypt.

Chapter 21

Dragon Knight

Davyn slipped back into the crypt, landing softly on the balls of his feet. Sounds of metal striking stone echoed from the open hole where the bronze statue had been. Davyn guessed that Gurgut had found the Dragon Knight's tomb and was trying to open it with the pickaxe.

He was surprised how dark it seemed. Even a few brief minutes in the sun had been enough to ruin his night vision. He took a tentative step in the darkness of the room and bumped one of the support posts holding the ceiling up. A shower of dirt rained down but the post held.

"Be careful," Rina said, peering down from above.

"This whole place could collapse any minute," Davyn whispered. He hoped Gurgut was too busy searching for the sword to hear him. "Get everyone away from here in case the roof falls in."

Rina looked as if she would argue, then flashed him a dazzling smile.

"Try not to get killed," she said. With that, she was gone.

Davyn sighed. Gurgut wasn't likely to give up the Dragon Knight's sword without a fight. He probably won't give it up while he's got breath left in his body, Davyn thought ominously. The weight of the ornamental broadsword rested comfortably on Davyn's hip. He wished he had a better weapon, but all Gurgut had was the pickaxe, so Davyn felt he had some advantage.

Trying not to make any noise, Davyn drew the point-heavy sword and gripped it loosely. He crept carefully across the rubble-strewn floor toward the hole where the bronze statue had stood. The only noise was the sound of his own ragged breathing. Either Gurgut had gotten the Dragon Knight's tomb open, or the passage beyond the hole went farther than he'd thought. Davyn tried not to hurry, but he knew he had to get to Gurgut before the knight got a hold of his uncle's sword. Davyn was a fair swordsman, but Gurgut was a trained knight. He had no desire to face Gurgut with only the ornamental sword.

The hole past the statue was dark and Davyn's eyes hadn't fully readjusted to the dim light yet. All he could see was a few feet into the room beyond. The floor was rough, as if the room had been chiseled out of the rock in a hurry and never finished. An eerie silence had fallen over the room and Davyn held his breath, listening for any signs of Gurgut. After a moment, Davyn took a tentative step through the hole and into the room beyond. His eyes finally caught up with the darkness and he could see to the back of the room. It was long and narrow with rough-cut walls and support timbers like the ones Oddvar had them use in the crypt. At the far end of the chamber stood a massive marble coffin with a stone lid. The tomb was tall, at least up to Davyn's waist. Dragon heads had been carved at each corner, glaring out menacingly, and there were carvings of knights and dragons all around the side. On the top of the lid, Davyn could see the likeness of a reclining knight, no doubt the image of Captain Viranesh. Strangely, the tomb's lid was still in place and there was no sign of Gurgut.

Davyn moved forward. It was instinct that drove him. He didn't even know he was moving until he'd already taken two steps into the room and turned around with his guard up. With a ringing clang, the point of Gurgut's pickaxe slammed into the floor right where Davyn had stood.

Davyn raised his sword. "So much for chivalry," he said.

Gurgut jerked the pickaxe out of the ground and lunged. Davyn sidestepped the blow and brought the ornamental sword down hard on Gurgut's shoulder. He was aiming for the seam in the armor but he missed and the blow rebounded harmlessly away. Gurgut swung the pickaxe again as if nothing had happened.

Davyn danced back, trying to avoid the pickaxe and get in position to strike Gurgut's unprotected belly. Gurgut was sweating and even more red-faced than normal, but he kept coming, driving Davyn back. Davyn slashed at the knight's arms, trying to knock the pickaxe out of his hands, but Gurgut's grip never failed. The knight brought his weapon around, attempting to cave in Davyn's ribs, forcing him back again. When he leaped back, Davyn hit the tomb and it threw him off balance. With a cry of glee, Gurgut raised the pickaxe over his head and brought it down with all his force.

Davyn launched himself backward, rolling over the tomb and falling heavily to the rough floor beyond. Gurgut's blow slammed into the marble top of the coffin and punched straight through it. As Davyn scrambled to his feet, Gurgut tried to free his trapped weapon. With a cry of rage and a mighty heave, the knight yanked the pickaxe free, cracking the lid and sending pieces of marble flying. As Gurgut staggered back from the tomb under the weight of the pickaxe, the marble lid crumbled and fell away in slabs.

Inside the tomb, Davyn could see a skeletal knight in armor gripping a shiny sword. Both the sword and armor were bright and new with no signs of age. Mesmerized, Davyn reached out, intent on taking the sword. At that moment Gurgut slammed the pickaxe into the open tomb and Davyn almost lost his hand.

"I knew it," Gurgut snarled. "You came here to rob me, to steal what's mine."

The knight lashed out at Davyn, forcing him back away from the tomb. He tried to parry the next blow, but the pickaxe had too much mass. The ornamental sword went spinning out of his hand and landed with a ringing clatter by the entrance.

His fingers stinging, Davyn raced around the tomb. He ducked under a vicious sweeping blow and scooped up his sword.

"You can't win, Gurgut," Davyn said, turning back to face the knight. He'd expected Gurgut to go for the sword, but the knight's training wouldn't allow him to turn his back on an opponent.

Davyn stepped to the side so that one of the posts was between him and the knight.

"Even if you get the sword, you won't become the Dragon Knight. Only someone with your uncle's blessing can truly claim the sword."

"Liar!" Gurgut screamed and swung at Davyn. The pickaxe handle hit the support post and the old timber snapped in half and clattered to the floor.

Davyn was waiting for just such an attack. He stepped back out of range until the blow went by, then lunged in, attempting to skewer Gurgut. The fat knight was faster than he looked, however. As Davyn moved in, he brought the pickaxe down. The spike barely missed Davyn's arm but the handle slammed into his wrist with a sickening crack.

Pain exploded in Davyn's wrist as his sword went flying. He cradled his arm and dodged back behind the room's second support post.

"You see," Gurgut laughed. "It's my destiny to take the sword. You can't stop me, twenty years in here couldn't stop me, and now it's almost mine." Gurgut raised the pickaxe over his shoulder. "All I have to do first is kill you."

Gurgut swung and Davyn hurled himself out of the way, landing painfully only feet from his sword. Gurgut's blow missed Davyn but it connected solidly with the room's remaining support pillar. The force of the blow drove the spike all the way through the wood. As Davyn scrambled to recover his sword, Gurgut tried to wrench his weapon free. A shower of dirt from the ceiling rained down.

"Stop!" Davyn yelled, "you'll bring the roof down."

Mad though he was, Gurgut was no fool. He abandoned the pickaxe and ran to the tomb. Davyn scooped up his sword with his left hand, still holding his right hand against his chest. He couldn't fight with his left hand, but Gurgut didn't need to know that.

Gurgut reached into the tomb and pulled out the silver sword. A look of rapture washed across his face and the sword blazed with a pale light as if in response.

"At last," he cried, "it's mine. My birthright. You tried to deny me, Uncle," he went on, ranting at the corpse, "but I beat you."

Gurgut turned and looked at Davyn. Davyn tried to pretend he still had a chance.

"It turns out I didn't need to kill you to get this sword," Gurgut said, an evil grin spreading across his face. "It's just a bonus."

Davyn briefly thought of kicking the remaining post down and running for his life. Before he could move, however, a bony hand grabbed Gurgut's arm. A chill washed over Davyn, unlike anything he'd ever felt before, freezing him to the bone. He stood, rooted to the floor as if nailed there, though every instinct within him was screaming for him to run. Another skeletal hand emerged from the tomb and grabbed Gurgut's belt. Davyn knew what was coming but that didn't make it any less horrific. With a chilling creak, the Dragon Knight himself sat up out of his coffin and turned his sightless eyes toward Davyn.

Davyn was terrified. He'd felt the paralyzing effect of dragonfear before but this was unlike anything he had ever experienced. It was as if the very breath were being squeezed out of his lungs.

Gurgut was clearly frightened too, but his madness for the sword drove him to act.

"You won't deny me, Uncle," he shrieked, "not in life and not in death."

Gurgut brought the sword down on the bony arm that held him but before the blow connected, the Dragon Knight released Gurgut's arm and grabbed the sword. Absently Davyn wondered how a dead man could move so fast.

The Dragon Knight shoved Gurgut away from the tomb and the fat knight landed in a heap in the middle of the room. Creaking and snapping, the Dragon Knight climbed out of his coffin and stood before it. His head turned, bringing the empty eye sockets around to look at Davyn.

Davyn gasped. It was like a sudden weight was pressing down on him, threatening to bear him down to the floor and crush him. The cold of the grave assaulted him and he felt the blood freezing in his veins. Davyn would rather have faced a dozen dragons than stare at those empty eye sockets above that skeletal grin. Somehow he knew the next moments would be his last.

The Dragon Knight began to move. He raised his sword and, even though he was several yards away, Davyn felt the coming blow would be for him. He wanted to run but his body stood, frozen to the spot. Then something completely unexpected happened. The Dragon Knight raised his sword in a gesture of salute.

He was saluting Davyn.

"You can't give my sword to him," Gurgut said, heaving his bulk off the floor. "I won't let you. It's mine, you understand? Mine!"

Gurgut charged. Not at Davyn, or the Dragon Knight, but at the pickaxe still wedged in the wooden post. Driven by fear and madness, the knight jerked the weapon free, shattering the timber in the process.

Dirt and debris fell from the ceiling and a great crack appeared and spread across the room. Heedless of his peril, Gurgut raised the pickaxe and charged the Dragon Knight. He brought the axe down squarely in the middle of the Dragon Knight's forehead.

At that moment, everything seemed to happen at once. The pickaxe shattered as if it had been made of glass. Gurgut was thrown across the room by an unseen force. The ceiling began to collapse. And Davyn could move again.

As head-sized rocks crashed down around him, Davyn turned and raced for the opening back into the crypt room. He hurled himself through, landing hard on the tiled floor beyond, his wrist exploding in fresh pain. Davyn lurched to his feet as the rumble in the secret room turned into an angry roar. Through the debris Davyn could still see the light from the silver sword, raised in salute. A moment later it was gone as the whole ceiling came down and rock and dirt spilled out of the hole and across the floor of the crypt.

Davyn stood for a long minute staring at the ruins of the Dragon Knight's crypt. His breath steamed in the air and he was shivering and pale. He'd assumed the chilling effect of the undead knight's gaze was just in his head but the entire room seemed colder than winter in the mountains.

Trembling from the cold, Davyn staggered to the dirt mound that led to the surface. The sun was still streaming in and it warmed him enough so he could climb. When he reached the top, Rina and Jirah helped haul him up through the hole in the roof and onto the grass.

"Careful." Davyn winced as Rina pulled on his arm.

"He's freezing," Jirah said.

"Did you get the sword?" Rina demanded. "What happened?"

"J-just a m-m-minute," Davyn said, his teeth chattering.

Davyn lay back in the sun and closed his eyes. He hadn't gotten the sword and soon he'd have to tell Jirah that. They'd come an awful long way for nothing. All he had to show for the entire trip was a broken wrist and a point-heavy sword that wasn't good for anything but hanging on a wall. No, he corrected himself, the trip was worse than a waste. Oddvar and Hector were dead. And he didn't get the sword, so Nearra was probably dead too.

He was vaguely aware of Jirah and Rina talking but the words seemed to come from a long way away. Suddenly pain shot through his wrist and he sat up with a cry of pain.

"Hold still," Jirah scolded him, taking his arm a bit more gingerly than before.

"The sword is gone," he said. "Gurgut knocked out a support post and buried himself and the sword."

"You did what you could," Jirah said after a pause. "I couldn't ask any more."

"What do we do now?" Rina asked.

Davyn sighed. "I guess we go back to Potter's Mill and tell Shemnara that I failed. Maybe we can convince her to use some more of the liquid from the Dragon Well to try again, though I wouldn't blame her if she said no. Then someone's got to tell Bloody Bob about Hector."

"Look," Rina said, pulling Davyn's chin up until his eyes met hers. "I know things didn't exactly turn out the way you wanted, but you're not a failure." She pointed off to the east where Davyn could see Cirill's people running and laughing on the grass.

"There're over twenty people who would have died in that horrible prison if it weren't for you. If it hadn't been for you, we'd probably have joined them."

"If it wasn't for me, you'd never have been here," Davyn countered.

"And if it wasn't for me," Jirah said, "you wouldn't have been here either."

Davyn knew that arguing with Rina and Jirah was pointless, but he was angry. Before he could even take a breath, however, there was a low rumble and the ground started shaking.

"The house," Jirah gasped.

Davyn turned. Several hundred yards away, Viranesh Keep stood burning. The wind had been in Davyn's face so the smoke had been blown west, behind him. Now that Davyn looked at it, the smoke was a huge dark tower in an otherwise cloudless sky. The ground shook again and finally Davyn saw what Jirah had been looking at. The entire keep seemed to be leaning to one side. With a last, great shudder, the supporting walls fell and the entire structure collapsed in on itself.

The ground began to shake in earnest.

"Come on," Rina said, pulling Davyn painfully to his feet. "We've got to get out of here before everything collapses."

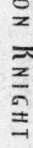

Davyn's muscles and joints were still stiff from the cold. As he stood, he saw holes opening up in the ground as more of the underground complex collapsed. That was all the motivation he needed. Together with Rina and Jirah, he raced across the remnants of the once beautiful gardens and walkways. Behind him, Davyn could hear more holes opening up. None of them stopped running until they reached the spot where Mudd and Set-ai were waiting—well outside the keep's grounds.

"I'm glad you're back," Mudd said before any of them could speak.

Jirah had tied Mudd's broken arm up with a splint and a sling, so the youth gestured with his other hand.

"I think Set-ai's really sick." There was worry in Mudd's voice and Davyn could see why. Set-ai was white as a sheet, drenched in sweat, and trembling.

"He went to sleep and now I can't wake him," Mudd said.

"It's his wound." Jirah's eyes narrowed as she looked at Rina pointedly. "It's not healing properly."

"What can we do?" Davyn asked.

"We've got to find a healer to purge the wound," Rina said.

Mudd gave them an ominous look. "What if we can't find a healer?"

Rina shuddered and tears welled up in her eyes. "We may have to amputate his arm."

"No," Davyn declared. "I'm not going to cut off Set-ai's arm."

"Someone will have to," Rina declared. "Otherwise he'll die."

CHAPTER 22

AFTERMATH

It was a six-hour march back to Kentrel under the best of conditions. Davyn wanted to shave off as much time as possible. Rina had done what she could for Mudd's arm and his own, but there was nothing she could do for Set-ai. His condition continued to deteriorate. After the first couple of hours, he wasn't able to walk by himself. Davyn had Cirill rig up a drag-sled, and the freeholders took turns pulling it.

"If you want, I can run ahead," Mudd volunteered as they walked along beside the drag-sled. "Maybe I can get help from Kentrel."

"You'd be defenseless if you ran into trouble," Rina said, indicating Mudd's broken arm. "I should be the one to go."

Davyn shook his head. "We need you here," he told the elf. "You're one of the only warriors we've got left."

"No," he said after a pause. "We're just going to have to stick together and hope for the best."

"He'll make it," Jirah said softly, mopping the sweat from Set-ai's forehead.

"It's all right," she said, looking up to meet Davyn's eyes.

Davyn looked away.

"You couldn't have done any more than you did," she continued. "If you'd gone back in to get the sword, you'd be buried under all that rock with Gurgut."

"So that's it?" Davyn asked. "We just give up?"

"I didn't say that," Jirah replied. "You said we should go back to Shemnara and see what she thinks. I think that's a good plan."

"Why did Shemnara send us here?" Davyn said to no one in particular. "What was the point of all this?"

"Maybe there was something here we had to learn?" Jirah suggested.

"Well, it's cost two lives already," Davyn said, scowling. "Whatever it was had better be important."

"What if we haven't learned it yet?" Jirah said. "What if our journey's not over?"

"So, what? The keep was just someplace to go while we were here?" Davyn tried to moderate his tone, but he was getting angry.

"I don't know," Jirah admitted. Her voice was quiet and her eyes were downcast.

Davyn felt like a jerk. He was mad about his own failures and he was taking it out on Jirah.

"I'm sorry," he said, walking beside her. "You've got to be worried sick about your sister."

"I haven't given up hope yet," she said. "If you didn't care about her, you wouldn't be so upset now."

Davyn hadn't thought about it that way, but it did make sense. Jirah looked up at him and smiled.

"At least I know you're as dedicated to saving Nearra as I am," she said. "That means I'm not alone."

Davyn put his good arm around Jirah and gave her a friendly

hug. "Keep an eye on Set-ai," he said, then walked up to the head of the group where Rina was leading.

"How are things with you and Jirah?" the elf asked once Davyn caught up to her.

Davyn wasn't sure exactly what Rina was getting at. "Okay, I guess," he said.

Rina cast him a withering look.

"What?" Davyn shrugged.

"Honestly," Rina sighed. "You're the only thing keeping that girl together," she said.

"Jirah's fine," Davyn protested. "She's holding up better than I am."

"That's because she still believes in you," Rina said. "If you keep telling her that we've failed, she's eventually going to believe it."

Davyn hadn't considered that. Maybe Jirah was so calm because she couldn't let herself believe that they'd failed. What would happen to her if she was forced to consider the idea that Nearra was forever beyond her reach—or that her family curse could not be broken?

"I see what you mean," Davyn said.

"So what will you do?" Rina always seemed to ask the most annoying questions.

"I'll tell her I believe Shemnara sent us here for a reason," he said. "I don't believe she sent us here to fail. All we have to do is go back to Potter's Mill and find out what to do next."

Rina nodded. "That will work if you believe it too."

Davyn was tired of this discussion so he changed the subject. "Where's Mudd?" he asked.

Rina laughed. "He kept bugging me so I sent him up to the top of that hill to look around."

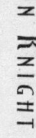

Davyn looked where Rina was pointing and saw Mudd running down a nearby hill at full speed.

"Something's up," he told Rina.

"There's someone up ahead," Mudd gasped once he'd reached them.

"How many?" Davyn asked, shooting Rina a worried look. Rina nocked an arrow in her bow.

"Looks like a whole bunch," Mudd said, "maybe fifty. They've got wagons and horses with them, too."

Davyn didn't want to face a force that large, but before he could get everyone off the road and into the bushes, he heard the thunder of approaching horses. Seven wretched nags emerged from the dust of the road and cantered up to where Davyn, Rina, and Mudd waited. As they drew near, Davyn recognized Miruel, the woman who owned the inn in Kentrel. The woman who had led the party of vigilantes that had chased them out of town.

"You," Miruel said when she recognized Davyn. She snapped her fingers and the men with her drew their swords.

"How did you escape the house?" she demanded. "Where's Oddvar?"

"He's dead," Davyn said, looking at the armed men with contempt. He knew Rina could probably shoot them all from their saddles before they could even move. "As for Viranesh Keep, it's gone."

One of the men turned to the woman. "That must have been the smoke we saw, Miruel."

"You destroyed the house?" Miruel shrieked.

"It was the only way to escape," Davyn said. Miruel was getting under his skin.

"Do you have any idea what you've done?" Miruel asked, tears beginning to stream down her face. "Years ago our friends and loved ones went into that cursed place and never came back. We stayed here in the hopes that someday they'd return. Now you've made that impossible."

"Most of the people who went in there died," Davyn said. He'd forgotten how closely tied these people were to Viranesh Keep.

"What of the rest?" Miruel yelled. "Did you leave them to burn?" She turned to her companions. "Tell the others to come and get these people," she spat. "They'll be our special guests tomorrow at a bonfire."

"Does that include me, Miruel?"

Davyn turned to find Cirill and his freeholders emerging from the underbrush beside the road. There were tears in Cirill's eyes and most of the freeholders were crying as well. Miruel gasped. She jumped off her horse and rushed by Davyn and into Cirill's arms.

"Daddy," she cried.

Cirill grabbed Miruel in a ferocious hug, kissing her hair as he wept.

"Where is your mother?" he asked after a moment.

"She died," Miruel said, "seven years after you left."

"And you've waited in Kentrel all this time?"

Miruel nodded. "I always knew you'd get out," she said. "No prison could hold an old thief like you."

"Actually," Cirill said, pushing Miruel out to arm's length. "If it hadn't been for Davyn and his friends, we never would have gotten out."

Miruel turned her tear-stained face to Davyn.

"Thank you," she sobbed.

Davyn felt a warmth in his heart that he hadn't felt in a long time. Rina had been right. Even though they didn't get the Dragon Knight's sword, their quest hadn't been a failure.

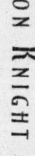

At least not for the freeholders and their relatives.

Others from the freeholders began to come forward to greet the men on the horses as brothers and sons. One of the young men, after hugging Carlotta so hard Davyn thought he'd break her, rode back to the oncoming townsfolk to spread the news.

"I hate to break up the reunion," Davyn said, "but is there a healer in your town?"

Miruel shook her head. "No self-respecting priest would stay in a town as poor as Kentrel," she said. "The closest thing we have is Nerik. He was a surgeon during the war."

Davyn exchanged worried looks with Rina.

"We need a wagon and a team of horses to take a sick man to him," Davyn said.

"I can do better than that," Miruel said, wiping the tears from her eyes. "He's with the others."

Miruel dispatched one of the mounted men to find Nerik. Davyn helped Jirah and the freeholders pull Set-ai out of the trees and onto the road.

Nerik turned out to be younger than Davyn had expected, twenty-five at the oldest. He was tall and thin, with straw-colored hair and a neat goatee. Davyn noticed Rina eyeing the man approvingly. For some reason, Davyn took an instant dislike to Nerik.

Despite his apparent youth, Nerik spoke with the confidence of experience.

"His arm has to come off," he said after examining Set-ai.

"Are you sure?" Davyn asked. Almost anything would be preferable to losing Set-ai's arm.

"I'm amazed he's lasted as long as he has," Nerik said. "His wound is sour, and it's poisoning his blood. If I take the arm now, he might still be strong enough to recover."

Set-ai was unconscious and likely to remain that way. All eyes turned to Davyn. The weight of the terrible decision pressed down on Davyn. After a moment, he realized there was nothing else to do. If Nerik didn't amputate, Set-ai would die.

"Do it," Davyn said.

Nerik unpacked his surgeon's kit. It was the most frightening and sickening collection of drills, saws, knives, and hooks Davyn had ever seen. Nerik took out a leather strap and instructed Davyn to put it in Set-ai's mouth to prevent him from biting off his tongue. Then he cut open Set-ai's shirt, exposing the arm.

"Hold him," Nerik said.

Davyn, Rina, Jirah, and Cirill grabbed Set-ai's unconscious form and held him down. Nerik went to work. Davyn didn't want to look, but he couldn't seem to look away. Set-ai cried out and thrashed, but didn't wake up. In a minute it was done, and Nerik was stitching up the wound.

"He'll need to rest for at least a week," Nerik said as he wiped the blood from his tools. "After that, he'll need to take it easy for a month or two."

"How soon can he travel?" Davyn asked.

"Not for at least a week," Nerik replied.

"You're welcome to stay with us," Miruel said. "No charge."

Davyn thanked her. He was grateful for her generosity and for Nerik's skill, and that he'd managed to get most of his friends out of Viranesh Keep alive. Despite all that, Davyn felt the weight of all the tragedy that had transpired pulling him down. He'd started this journey to atone for his past mistakes and all he'd gotten were more things to atone for.

They loaded Set-ai in the back of one of the wagons and brought him, slowly and carefully, to Kentrel. Davyn and the others stayed at Miruel's inn while they waited for Set-ai to recover. The citizens of Kentrel, meanwhile, had a weeklong celebration that seemed to be going on twenty-four hours a day. By the end of the week, Set-ai's fever had broken and he was able to traverse the inn's stairs to have his meals in the taproom.

For his part, Davyn had avoided the celebrations and his friends and especially Set-ai. He hadn't been there when the woodsman finally woke to find himself without his left arm but he could imagine how Set-ai felt. To take his mind off his troubles, Davyn went down to the docks to arrange for a barge to take them back upriver. Despite the celebration in town, Davyn wanted to be gone as soon as possible. After he'd arranged passage aboard a barge that would be leaving the following morning, Davyn walked to the end of the docks. He was surprised to find Mudd there, sitting with his feet over the side and looking absolutely miserable. Davyn didn't want to talk to anyone, but Mudd looked like he needed it. Davyn was becoming quite good at putting aside his personal feelings for the good of the team.

"How are you?" Davyn asked, plopping down beside Mudd.

Mudd looked up and Davyn realized he looked positively green.

"I ate the fish," he confessed.

Davyn shrugged. "So?"

"Shemnara told me not to," he explained. "I should've remembered." Mudd leaned forward and was noisily sick in the water.

"Feel better?" Davyn asked when Mudd finally came up for air.

"No," Mudd said, "but it's got nothing to do with my stomach."

"What is it, then?"

Mudd hung his head. "It's Hector."

"You miss him," Davyn said, "don't you?"

"Yes, but it's not that," Mudd said. "I was in charge of setting the fire. Hector came along because he was my friend and now he's dead."

Davyn knew what was coming so well he could have quoted it.

"It's my fault," Mudd said, with tears in his eyes.

Davyn put his arm around Mudd as the youth paused to throw up more fish.

"I'm going to tell you something that Set-ai tried to explain to me," Davyn said once Mudd was finished. "Sometimes, when you do the right thing, bad things happen. It doesn't make it any easier, but it's true."

"What do you mean?" Mudd asked, suppressing another bout of sickness.

"I mean someone had to start that fire," Davyn explained. "You and Hector risked your lives because if you hadn't no one would have escaped. Hector knew what he was getting into. He gave his life so the rest of us could escape."

Mudd nodded. "He let the chandelier loose so that I'd make it, even though he knew he'd be trapped."

"He was brave and heroic," Davyn said. "We should always remember that. We can mourn him, but we need to realize that he died doing what he thought was right."

"And he saved all of us," Mudd added.

Davyn agreed. He knew Mudd would never be free of the loss, but maybe he could let go of the guilt.

"Thanks, Davyn," Mudd said, standing up. "I feel a lot better now."

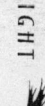

Mudd went back toward town and Davyn stayed to contemplate the river. Set-ai had given him the exact same advice on several occasions but he hadn't believed it till now. He sighed. He knew that Elidor, Hector, and Oddvar had died serving good and right, but that only made it marginally easier. Then there was Set-ai's arm. Now Davyn felt sick—and he hadn't been anywhere near the fish.

"I understand you're leaving us."

Davyn jumped. He turned to find Cirill regarding him from a few paces away.

"I'm sorry to startle you," he said, sitting down next to Davyn. He pulled a bundle from beneath his cloak, "I wanted to give you these."

Cirill handed Davyn a jingling purse and Davyn looked at it, somewhat confused.

"That's all the steel Miruel found in your strongbox after she chased you underground," Cirill explained. "Your mule and your cart are in the barn too, ready to go."

"Thanks," Davyn said, a smile coming back to his face. "I was wondering how I was going to get provisions to go back over the mountains."

"There is one more thing," Cirill said with a strange twinkle in his eye. He reached into his bag and withdrew a large, leather-bound book. When he turned it over, Davyn saw a bronze, stylized dragon head. It was the Dragon Knight's journal.

"I brought this along because I thought the bronze might be worth something," he confessed. "I think, however, that you might have more use for it. I know you didn't get what you came for," he said, "but the answers you need might still be in there somewhere."

"Thank you," Davyn said, accepting the book. "What about you, though? How will you and the freeholders survive?"

Cirill flashed Davyn the most devious smile Davyn had ever seen.

"Do you know why we went to Viranesh Keep in the first place?" he asked.

Davyn nodded. "The place was supposed to be absolutely stuffed with treasure. Too bad it wasn't true."

Cirill's grin grew wider, if that were possible. "Who said it wasn't?"

"I was there," Davyn stammered. "There wasn't anything valuable in the whole place."

Cirill pulled a pouch from his belt and opened it. It was stuffed full of steel coins and precious stones. There were rubies and emeralds and diamonds as big as quail eggs.

"You're absolutely right," Cirill said, his eyes flashing with mirth, "by the time you got there, there was nothing valuable to see."

Cirill let out a cackling laugh and stuffed the loot back in his pouch. He wished Davyn a good trip and then strode down the dock.

Davyn sat in the bow of the barge watching the tree-lined shore slip by. It was cold, but Davyn had his fur cloak on and the sun was warming him. His broken wrist was still a bit sore, but it was healing well enough. Normally, Davyn wouldn't sit outside in such weather, but he was still trying to avoid Set-ai. Set-ai's health had returned rapidly and now he was able to get up and move around a bit. This had forced Davyn to go further afield to avoid talking to him.

"There you are, lad," Set-ai's voice cut through Davyn's thoughts.

Davyn ground his teeth together. "Hello," he said.

"They tell me I owe you my life," Set-ai said, sitting down beside Davyn.

Davyn hung his head. He might have saved Set-ai's life, but he wasn't sure the cost was worth it.

"None of that, now," Set-ai chided him. "You did what you had to do to keep me alive. I'd have done the same in your place."

When Davyn didn't speak, Set-ai continued. "I know there are some men who'd rather be dead than lose an arm, but they're fools."

"I'm sorry," Davyn said at last.

Set-ai shrugged. "Don't be. It's not your fault. I came on my own. Shemnara wouldn't have sent us out here for no reason, lad. Neither would she send us to fail. You're supposed to take somethin' away from this, and you'd better figure out what before we get back. If you don't, Shemnara's goin' to be mighty disappointed in you."

With that, Set-ai got up and tromped back to the warmth of his cabin. Despite the chill in the air, Davyn felt warmed. He settled back to watch the scenery some more, but finally decided it was time for him to rejoin his friends. With his good arm, he pushed himself up and headed aft, toward the cabins.

CHAPTER 23

Heir to the Dragon

The town of Potter's Mill wasn't large or lavish. It had only one inn, of average quality, and four other businesses, three of which were devoted to farm supplies. All in all it was one of the most unremarkable places in the entire world.

As Davyn trudged over the last snow-covered hill and saw the lights of the town, however, he decided that no place had ever looked quite so wonderful.

As he crossed the cobblestones of Potter's Mill's town square, Davyn felt as if he'd like to stop and have a few drinks in Kirian's taproom. No matter how he turned the events at Viranesh Keep over in his mind, he couldn't escape the conclusion that his quest had been a failure. The only things he came away with from the cursed house were the ornamental sword and Dragon Knight's journal.

Contrary to Cirill's opinion, the journal hadn't been any help at all. Davyn had read it cover to cover on the barge trip—twice. The curse on the house of Viranesh was mentioned, as was the need to obtain the Dragon Knight's blessing, but there was precious little about the sword or what enchantments it might have. After reading the journal the only real conclusion that Davyn could draw about the Dragon Knight was that he'd lived a life of adventure. That was something Davyn didn't envy as he and his friends trudged through the snow to Shemnara's porch.

Davyn kicked the pole holding up the porch railing to dislodge the snow from his boots. He climbed the steps and was about to knock on the door when Shemnara herself opened it. She wore a simple blue robe with a green sash for a belt. Her white hair hung loose except for where it was caught by the bandage around her eyes.

"It's about time you got back," she scolded before Davyn could say anything. "I was expecting you weeks ago."

Davyn didn't know how Shemnara knew who it was at the door. She always seemed to know things without being able to actually see them.

"We had some trouble," Davyn said. He knew Shemnara was fond of Set-ai and he wasn't sure how to tell her about his arm.

Shemnara stepped back, holding the door open.

"You didn't expect it to be easy, did you?" she said as Davyn and the others came in. "Take off your boots and wet things and put them by the door."

Davyn did as he was told, hanging his fur cloak on a peg by the door and pulling off his soggy boots. The others followed suit, though Mudd stopped long enough to hug Shemnara first and tell her how glad he was to be back.

"I've had food prepared," Shemnara told them once everyone had shed their wet gear. "It's a little cold, I'm afraid, but it should still be fine."

She led the way through the narrow hall to the back of the house. Just opposite the healing room was a dining room that

Davyn had never been in. Like most things in Shemnara's house, it was simple and elegant at the same time. The dining room contained a sturdy table and padded chairs with a finely carved hutch at one end. The table was set and covered with dishes of ham, potatoes, rolls, and corn, and a few apples sat in the middle.

Just as Shemnara had predicted, the food was cold. No one seemed to care, however. After weeks of trail rations and cooking what they could hunt, this was as good as a feast. Shemnara sat at the end of the table with Davyn on her right and Set-ai on her left.

"I know you've endured many hardships," she said as they ate.

Davyn noticed that she reached out and found Set-ai's right hand when she said this and he wondered exactly how much the seeress knew.

"But I want you to save your tale for later," she went on. "First you need food and then we will go to my chamber and discuss your quest."

Davyn was just as happy to let the story of his failure wait, so he ate in silence. Too soon for his taste, however, the meal was over and Shemnara ushered them into her back room. When they all were seated, she took the padded cover off her stone basin. Mudd gasped when the light from the pearlescent liquid shone out. Davyn instantly saw what elicited that reaction—the liquid in the well was almost gone.

"You've been keepin' an eye on us," Set-ai scolded her. "You shouldn't have wasted your talents like that."

"Until now, the liquid from the Dragon Well has been mine to use as I see fit," she said.

"What do you mean, 'until now'?" Mudd demanded.

"I will explain everything," Shemnara said, "in time. First, however, I need to hear an account of your quest."

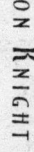

Davyn groaned inwardly. He didn't want to tell Shemnara how he'd failed, but he definitely didn't want anyone else to do it for him, so he recounted the whole tale. When he got to the part where Set-ai lost his arm, Shemnara reached out and clutched the man's good hand. From the mildness of her reaction, Davyn suspected that she'd already known about that.

"It sounds like you had a difficult trip," Shemnara said once Davyn was done with his story. "You've all done very well."

Davyn shook his head. "I don't see how we've done anything at all," he said. "We're no better off now than when we started."

"Aren't you?" Shemnara had a knowing smile on her face. "Tell me about the Dragon Knight."

"According to his journal," Davyn began, "the last Dragon Knight put the curse on Viranesh Keep because there wasn't a worthy successor for his title."

"And how would someone become the Dragon Knight's successor?" Shemnara prodded.

Davyn shrugged. This was the part that still didn't make much sense. "A person would have to get the Dragon Knight's sword and then receive his blessing—although I don't have the faintest idea how you get a dead man's blessing."

"Perhaps a gesture of approval," Shemnara said, that same knowing smirk on her face, "like a salute, perhaps?"

"What . . ." Davyn stopped cold, the image of the dead Dragon Knight holding up his sword fixed in his mind.

Mudd apparently had the same idea. He looked quickly from Davyn to Shemnara. "You don't mean . . . Davyn?" he said.

Shemnara nodded. "Why do you think the fire was able to finally destroy the house when others before it could not? Did you think that was the first time someone tried that?"

Davyn was speechless. He hadn't considered the fire but now that he thought about it, it only made sense. The only way the fire could have destroyed the house was if the curse had been broken.

Jirah leaned forward. "You mean that Davyn is the new Dragon Knight?"

Shemnara nodded.

"Wait," Davyn said, holding up his hand. "Wait just a minute. According to the journal, the Dragon Knight's heir has to have the Dragon Knight's sword. We didn't get that. It's buried under several tons of rock."

Shemnara held out her hand. "Give me your weapon," she said.

Davyn drew the ornamental sword from his sheath. For some reason he'd procrastinated replacing it with a more serviceable sword even though he'd purchased gear several times since their escape. He passed the ungainly weapon, hilt first, to Shemnara. She held the sword firmly, feeling its weight and balance.

"This is not your sword," she said.

"Mine was broken in a fight," Davyn said. "I picked this one up because it was convenient."

"And where did it come from?" Shemnara asked.

"He got it in the crypt," Mudd piped up, "in Viranesh Keep."

Rina let out an explosive laugh and slapped her knee.

"What's so funny?" Jirah asked.

Davyn was wondering the same thing.

"Don't you understand?" Rina said. "Everything in the keep belonged to its owner, the Dragon Knight. That sword *is* the Dragon Knight's sword—it belonged to him."

"I don't think that's what the journal means," Jirah said.

"Trust me, breaking curses requires a very specific set of conditions to be met."

Davyn nodded. He agreed with Jirah. There was no way the point-heavy, piece-of-junk weapon was the Dragon Knight's sword spoken of in the journal.

"You are quite correct," Shemnara told Jirah. "But the language of a curse can also be vague." She turned to Davyn. "Did the journal say that the Dragon Knight's heir had to get the silver sword?"

"No," Davyn admitted.

"Then any one of the Dragon Knight's swords will probably do," Rina said.

"There is no possible way that sword is what the Dragon Knight had in mind," Davyn said, indicating the ornamental blade.

Shemnara held the weapon up. "Whether or not you believe it, Davyn, this *is* the Dragon Knight's sword and you *are* his heir."

Davyn didn't know what to say. It seemed like Shemnara was saying his quest wasn't a failure after all, but he just couldn't believe it.

"You are right about one thing, however," Shemnara said, testing the sword's balance. "This weapon is insufficient to the tasks ahead of you."

"Does that mean Davyn can't help me then?" There was a note of distress in Jirah's voice.

Shemnara smiled. "Now it's time to tell you the adventures I had while you were gone," she said. "One night, I felt my basin calling me. When I came in, the Trinistyr was sitting on top of it, even though I did not remove it from its hiding place."

"What happened?" Mudd asked, instantly curious.

"A vision came over me," Shemnara explained. "It told me that, like all of you, I must make a sacrifice if Nearra is to be free."

"What kind of 'sacrifice'?" Set-ai asked. He clearly didn't like the sound of that.

"I must give up something precious to me," she said. "Davyn's sword can only be purified in the blood of an innocent. Only then can the Dragon Knight sever the bond that the Dragon Well created."

Davyn reached unconsciously for the sword. He wasn't sure where Shemnara intended to get the blood of an innocent, but he didn't want her doing anything desperate to herself.

Before he could reach the sword, however, Shemnara stood up. She pulled off her bandage, exposing her milky white eyes, then she turned the sword point down and plunged it into her stone basin.

There was a flare of light, so bright that Davyn had to cover his eyes. When it faded, Davyn could see the last remaining liquid from the Dragon Well soaking into the blade. Shemnara held the sword up before her face; it reminded Davyn of the skeletal Dragon Knight's salute.

Davyn thought Shemnara was finished, but she suddenly cried out in pain. He watched in horror as white mist was pulled from Shemnara's eyes into the blade. A moment later, the sword clattered into the basin and Shemnara slumped down in her chair.

The room erupted into pandemonium. As one, everyone rushed to check on the seeress. Davyn and Set-ai were seated on either side of her and got there first. Shemnara was only stunned. Just as Davyn reached her, she opened her eyes and looked right at him. He gasped. Instead of milky white, Shemnara's eyes were now a brilliant blue.

"What's happened?" Set-ai asked, as Shemnara sat back in her chair. "Are you all right?"

Shemnara turned to Set-ai, an amazed look on her face. She reached out and touched his craggy face, running her hand down to his neatly trimmed beard. Then she began to cry.

"Are you all right, Shemnara?" Mudd asked, concern and wonder in his voice.

"I'm fine," she said, looking around at them. "I should have guessed that Paladine would reward a sacrifice freely given."

"I don't understand," Jirah said.

Shemnara shooed them all back to their seats. Davyn had seen her look at people when her eyes were milky, but it was always clear that she wasn't actually seeing them. Now he was certain her eyes worked as well as his.

"You gave up your powers," Davyn said, aghast. "I mean, your ability to see the future."

Shemnara nodded. "Your sword could only be purified by the blood of an innocent—in this case, poor Theoran."

Davyn had all but forgotten the dragon whose blood was used to make the Dragon Well.

"The liquid in the Dragon Well was Theoran's blood," Shemnara said. "It gave me the power to see the future, and now it has blessed your sword."

Shemnara reached into the basin and withdrew the weapon. It looked exactly the same as it had. When Davyn took it from Shemnara, however, he could feel that it was different. The balance was no longer off and the edge seemed unusually keen. He wanted to examine it further, but this wasn't the time, so he slid the weapon back into its sheath.

"What will you do now?" Jirah asked. "I appreciate your sacrifice for my sister, but how will you make a living without your ability to see the future?"

Shemnara smiled and turned to Mudd. She paused for a moment, taking in the youth's features for the first time.

"My young friend has generously provided for that," she said.

"Mudd?" Davyn said, turning to the lad.

Mudd blushed and shifted in his seat, then he pulled a small pouch from around his neck.

"When I was exploring the keep, I found Cirill's treasure room," he confessed. "I didn't think he'd miss these."

Mudd tipped the bag up and a shower of jewels spilled into his hand. Davyn didn't know much about jewels but he could easily see that Mudd had selected the best jewels Cirill had possessed.

"I brought them for Shemnara," he said, putting the jewels back into the bag and passing it to her.

"You're a good lad," Set-ai said, nudging Mudd with his shoulder.

"Now," Shemnara said, tucking the bag into her belt, "it's time for me to tell you my final vision." She turned to Davyn. After regarding him for a moment, she continued. "You now have the power to sever the Dragon Well's bond and destroy Asvoria forever."

"But how can I do that?" Davyn asked.

Shemnara said, "You will know when the time is right."

"But how will I know?" he asked.

"When the time comes, you will know," she repeated. "Seek Asvoria out and enter her service. Give her no cause to doubt your loyalty. When the time comes, you will be ready."

Davyn stiffened. The very idea of working for Asvoria repelled him.

"It is the only way," Shemnara said, seeing his tension. "You will find her in the ruins of Valoria, a town not far from Trevska."

Davyn nodded grimly. "I know the place."

"What about the rest of us?" Rina said. "I've come this far. I don't want to sit this one out."

Shemnara nodded patiently. "Davyn's friends will be the keys to his success. Both new friends"—Shemnara cast a quick glance at Rina—"and old."

"Old friends?" Davyn said. "You mean—"

Shemnara nodded. "The warrior, the kender, and the wizard have not forgotten you. They walk a parallel path. You must return them to your side."

Davyn blushed at the memory of his last words to Catriona and Sindri. So much had changed since he had last seen his friends. He almost felt like a different person. But would they ever understand what he'd been going through? Would they forgive him?

Davyn shook his head. "The last time I saw them, they were on a ship bound for Southern Ergoth. I'll never find them."

"Not all journeys follow the path that one intends. You, of all people, should understand that." Shemnara looked deeply into Davyn's eyes. "Your friends failed in their quest so that they could succeed in another." Shemnara sat back in her chair. "The trail begins in Palanthas."

"But how—?"

Shemnara held up a hand. "No more questions. I think I've had quite enough for one day."

She got heavily to her feet. As she stood, Davyn noticed that it wasn't just her eyes that had changed. Her white hair was now a soft blond.

"I need some rest," Shemnara said. "I've told Kirian to save rooms for you at the inn."

CHAPTER 24

PATHS

Davyn was running.

He felt the despair washing over him as he pounded through the corridor. The dream was always the same: Asvoria would possess Nearra; Elidor would die. Regardless of the despair, Davyn continued his mad dash. Despite knowing the outcome, something always drove him onward.

The screaming reached its crescendo as the dais came into sight. His lungs puffing like a bellows, Davyn leaped up the stairs. He knew he was too late to save Elidor; what was done was done. Nearra, however, still had a chance. All he had to do was wait for the right moment to strike.

Davyn reached the top. He stepped around Elidor's body and confronted Asvoria with the Dragon Knight's sword. The sorceress just laughed at him. Her laughter became shrill and she seemed to tear away from Nearra, her ghostly form rising high into the air. In a flash, Asvoria became an immense black dragon. The dragon roared and dived at the platform.

Below Davyn, on the platform, Nearra slumped to the ground, back to herself. There were only moments left before

Asvoria would be on them, but still Davyn held his blow. The time wasn't right.

As the great dragon's mouth yawned open to consume Davyn and Nearra, something came out of the darkness and struck her. Mortally wounded, the dragon crashed to the ground.

"Davyn." Nearra stood, weakly. "Help me."

Davyn looked and saw Nearra's blue eyes turn violet again. Somehow Asvoria had survived the destruction of the dragon. Suddenly the Dragon Knight's sword blazed with silver light. Davyn didn't hesitate. He drove the sword into Nearra's chest up to the hilt. Asvoria's voice shrieked from Nearra's mouth. There was a tearing sound and the Dragon Knight's sword was jerked from Davyn's hand. As he watched, Nearra's body split in two. One half was the Nearra Davyn remembered. The other was a dark-haired woman with violet eyes. The sword did not split in two; it remained, driven to the hilt, in the dark-haired woman's chest.

With a crash, Asvoria's body fell to the platform. She let out a gurgling sigh and was finally dead. Nearra's eyes were full of tears as she rushed into Davyn's arms.

Davyn woke suddenly.

His room at Kirian's inn was dark. He was sweating heavily, despite the winter cold. The dream always affected him, but for the first time in a year, there was a glimmer of hope. The sword had told him when to strike, and he'd saved Nearra.

Davyn got up and pulled on his clothes. It was dark in the room but instead of lighting a candle, he took his sword down from a peg on the wall and drew it out of the scabbard. In the darkness he could see what the light usually kept hidden. The sword had a very faint silver glow.

"You'll tell me when to strike," Davyn said, holding the dimly glowing blade up. "That's what Shemnara meant."

He replaced the sword in its sheath and set it on the table. With only an hour or so left until dawn, it wasn't worth trying to go back to sleep. Davyn had to get an early start anyway. He washed his face at the basin, then set about gathering his gear.

In the two weeks he'd been in Potter's Mill, Davyn had kept busy. His armor was in desperate need of repair after soaking in Gurgut's pit. Davyn had oiled the parts that could be saved and the town's part-time armorer had replaced the rest. Mudd's armor wasn't as well made as Davyn's had been and it had to be completely replaced. Rina's only required minor repairs. Shemnara had graciously agreed to pay for the repairs and supplies they needed out of the jewels Mudd had brought her.

Davyn took his time putting his armor on. Since a good portion of it was new, it was stiff and a bit uncomfortable. Davyn knew that a few weeks on the road would break it in, but he wasn't looking forward to the blisters he'd get doing it.

Once he was fully armored, Davyn scooped up his pack and left the room, clomping down the stairs to the taproom. The cook had just arrived in the kitchen, but no one had been out to lay a fire in the taproom's hearth. Davyn could see his breath as he stepped off the stairs.

To his surprise, Davyn found he was not alone. A single figure sat at a table near the empty hearth.

"Good morning, Rina," he said, dumping his pack on the floor next to hers and sitting down.

"Hail, Dragon Knight." She grinned.

"Don't call me that," Davyn said.

Rina's grin grew even wider. "Well, I guess I could go back to calling you 'boss.'"

"Dragon Knight it is." Davyn laughed in spite of himself.

"You don't have to do this, you know," he said, turning serious.

Rina nodded. "I know," she said. "But Elidor was your brother and mine. I figure I owe it to him to look out for you."

"I guess that kind of makes you my sister." Davyn laughed.

"I don't think I want to be your sister." Rina winked and shook her head, then she put her hand on top of Davyn's. "There are certain rules in elf society about what's appropriate between brothers and sisters."

Despite the cold, Davyn was suddenly very warm. He was torn between removing his hand, or turning it over so Rina could clasp it.

"Here you are."

Jirah's voice cut through Davyn like a knife and he jerked his hand away from Rina's. He was glad there was only a single candle on the table as he felt himself blushing furiously.

"I looked in your room and you weren't there," Jirah continued.

"And why were you visiting his room at this hour?" There was a strange edge in Rina's voice.

"I-I couldn't sleep," Jirah stammered. "Davyn said he wanted to get an early start, so I went to see if he was ready."

"Uh-huh." Rina didn't sound convinced.

Jirah shivered in the cold air. She pulled out the chair on the other side of Davyn and sat down. As she did so, Davyn noticed that she scooted it right up against his.

"Are you cold, dear?" Rina asked Jirah, a false sweetness in her voice.

"Why, yes," Jirah admitted, huddling close to Davyn.

Davyn suddenly had the feeling that this was a very bad place to be.

"Why don't I get a fire going?" he said, standing up so quickly he knocked over his chair.

Davyn almost ran out to the woodshed. By the time he got back with an armload of wood the room actually seemed colder. Rina and Jirah were looking daggers at each other in silence. Once Davyn got the fire going, he took a chair on the far side of the table. He was very grateful a moment later when Mudd arrived.

"Here you all are," he said. "I thought you'd left without me. Are we all ready, then?"

"Let's eat first," Davyn said, feeling eagerness well up within him. Something about Mudd's energy was infectious. "We've got a long day ahead of us."

"And a long voyage after that," Jirah said, grimacing. "I really don't like sailing."

Mudd grinned. "At least we don't have to go back over the mountains."

Davyn's stomach tightened. He would have to tell them.

"I'm not—" he began. But just then, the cook arrived with breakfast: hot porridge with honey and warm bread.

"Where do we go first?" Rina asked as she chewed thoughtfully on a hunk of bread.

Davyn stirred a swirl of honey into his bowl of porridge, trying hard not to meet Rina's eyes. "Witdel. It's about two days west of here. There should be a ship bound for Palanthas from there." He lifted a spoonful of porridge to his mouth. The warm mush melted on his tongue and he savored the sweet taste for as long as possible. He knew it would be the last solid meal he'd have for a long time to come.

"Are you sure we'll be able to pick up your friends' trail?" Jirah asked. "Palanthas is a big city. Even if Shemnara's right—"

"Don't you know by now that Shemnara's always right?" Mudd asked.

Jirah wrinkled her nose, as Mudd, Rina, and Davyn all laughed.

Davyn ripped a chunk of bread off the loaf. "If I know Sindri and Catriona, they'll have left quite an impression on people. They shouldn't be hard for you to find."

"What?" Jirah held a spoonful of porridge halfway to her lips. "What do you mean, hard for *us* to find? What about you?"

Davyn finished chewing. "I'm not going with you."

"What? We can't go alone!" Mudd shouted.

"We need you!" Jirah gripped his arm. "You need us! Shemnara said so!"

Rina slumped back in her chair, her arms crossed.

"Shemnara also said I shouldn't give Asvoria any reason to doubt my loyalty." He pushed back his empty bowl. "I can't very well walk into her manor with a bunch of friends by my side. She would never trust me. Besides, there's no time to search for Catriona and Sindri while we leave Asvoria alone and unguarded. I need to watch her so I'll be able to gauge her plans, and wait for the right time to strike." Davyn sighed as he glanced at his friends' worried faces. "Trust me. This is something I have to do on my own. And soon, before Nearra . . . before we lose Nearra for good." He turned toward Jirah and stared deeply into her eyes. "It's like you said. It's time for me to stop running."

They sat there for a moment, not speaking, until Jirah released her grip with a sigh. "But how will we find you again?"

"We'll meet in Valoria. I've made a map." Davyn pulled out a scroll. "And I've written detailed directions." Davyn pressed the loosely bound parchment into Mudd's hands. He grinned and made his voice low, in imitation of Set-ai's gruff brogue. "I'm countin' on you, boy-o, to keep 'em safe and lead 'em true."

Mudd nodded, the glint of a tear in his eyes.

Rina uncrossed her arms and smiled. "Don't worry, boss. You can count on us."

"I know I can." Davyn pushed back his chair and stood up. "Now, who's ready to end this thing, once and for all?"

Chapter 25

City of the Dead

Davyn pushed through the undergrowth of vines that choked the walls of the ruined town. In the centuries since its destruction, massive trees had grown up and now rope-like vines hung down into the streets and alleys and ruined houses. The early spring air was warm and already some of the vines had begun to flower, and green moss was flourishing in the humid air. It would have been pretty if the stink of evil didn't hang in the air.

Davyn moved cautiously. He hadn't drawn his sword, but his hand rested on the hilt.

Long-abandoned houses stuck up from the ground like so many broken teeth. Years of weather and moss had cracked the once-solid stone, and piles of rubble littered the ground. Almost nothing remained intact, but there were enough standing ruins to prevent Davyn from seeing very far.

Not that he needed or wanted to see what inhabited the town.

Ever since he'd entered the festering ruin, Davyn had been aware of being watched. Shadows moved in the distance, scuttling between the broken walls, always just out of sight. Worse, Davyn could hear something sloshing along, parallel to his course. Whatever it was, it sounded big. It must have been aware of Davyn's presence, but it made no attempt to intercept him. Davyn took that as a good sign.

Since he didn't know exactly where he was going, Davyn just kept moving. Finally, he saw a cluster of trees, choked with thick nets of vines and forming a more or less complete structure. Davyn knew he'd reached his destination. He took a deep breath to steady his nerves. His hand was itching to draw his sword but he resisted the impulse. A sword would do him no good here.

There seemed to be a path leading to an area where vines hung down between two trees like a curtain. Davyn didn't even have to kneel down to see signs of many footprints going and coming.

Davyn took a deep breath and reached for the vine curtain.

Before his hand even touched the vines, a familiar voice called out from inside.

"Come in," the voice said. "I've been waiting for you."

Davyn pushed the vines aside and stepped through the opening. The inside of the mass of trees, rubble, and vines was warmer than Davyn would have thought. At the far end of the space stood a squat willow tree with a small spring bubbling up beneath its roots.

The sorceress was seated on a throne of sorts, made where one of the roots of the giant trees jutted out to reach the pool. Davyn's heart skipped a beat. She was exactly as he remembered her. Only the violet eyes were different.

She'd covered the root with a thick cloth to give the impression of a chair. Asvoria herself was clothed in a green dress, with her blonde hair spilling over her shoulders like water.

"I always knew you'd come back," Asvoria purred.

"I had to," Davyn said.

Asvoria smiled at the hardness in Davyn's voice.

"Have you come to fight me?"

Davyn kept his emotions in check.

"No," he said, kneeling before her. "I've come to serve you."

Will Davyn and his friends be able to stop Asvoria?

Don't miss the final battle in . . .

DRAGON SPELL

by Jeff Sampson

Asvoria sets her ultimate plan in motion: to transform herself into a dragon. It has never been done before . . . until now. With her newfound power, she hopes to rule the dragons of Krynn, with all other races as her servants, willingly or not.

But Catriona, Sindri, Maddoc, and Davyn are determined to stop her. With renewed hope and reunited forces, the companions prepare for the battle of their lives. If they succeed, Krynn will be saved from Asvoria's tyranny. If they fail, Nearra's soul will be lost . . . forever.

DRAGONLANCE
THE NEW ADVENTURES

THE DRAGON QUARTET

The companions continue their quest to save Nearra.

DRAGON SWORD
Ree Soesbee

It's a race against time as the companions seek to prevent Asvoria from reclaiming her most treacherous weapon.

DRAGON DAY
Stan Brown

As Dragon Day draws near, Catriona and Sindri stand as enemies, on opposing sides of a feud between the most powerful wizards and clerics in Solamnia.

DRAGON KNIGHT
Dan Willis

With old friends and new allies by his side, Davyn must enlist the help of the dreaded Dragon Knight.

DRAGON SPELL
Jeff Sampson

The companions reunite in their final battle with Asvoria to reclaim Nearra's soul.

Ask for Dragonlance: the New Adventures books at your favorite bookstore!
For ages ten and up.
For more information visit www.mirrorstonebooks.com

DRAGONLANCE and its logo are trademarks of Wizards of the Coast, Inc. in the U.S.A. and other countries. © 2005 Wizards of the Coast.

DragonLance

THE NEW ADVENTURES

JOIN A GROUP OF FRIENDS AS THEY UNLOCK MYSTERIES OF THE DRAGONLANCE® WORLD!

TEMPLE OF THE DRAGONSLAYER
Tim Waggoner

Nearra has lost all memory of who she is. With newfound friends, she ventures to an ancient temple where she may uncover her past. Visions of magic haunt her thoughts. And someone is watching.

THE DYING KINGDOM
Stephen D. Sullivan

In a near-forgotten kingdom, an ancient evil lurks. As Nearra's dark visions grow stronger, her friends must fight for their lives.

THE DRAGON WELL
Dan Willis

Battling a group of bandits, the heroes unleash the mystic power of a dragon well. And none of them will ever be the same.

RETURN OF THE SORCERESS
Tim Waggoner

When Nearra and her friends confront the wizard who stole her memory, their faith in each other is put to the ultimate test.

For ages 10 and up

DRAGONLANCE and its logo are trademarks of Wizards of the Coast, Inc. in the U.S.A. and other countries. ©2004 Wizards.

DRAGONLANCE

WANT TO KNOW HOW IT ALL BEGAN?

WANT TO KNOW MORE ABOUT THE DRAGONLANCE® WORLD?

FIND OUT IN THIS NEW BOXED SET OF THE FIRST DRAGONLANCE TITLES!

A RUMOR OF DRAGONS
Volume 1

NIGHT OF THE DRAGONS
Volume 2

THE NIGHTMARE LANDS
Volume 3

TO THE GATES OF PALANTHAS
Volume 4

HOPE'S FLAME
Volume 5

A DAWN OF DRAGONS
Volume 6

Gift Set Available
By Margaret Weis & Tracy Hickman
For ages 10 and up

DRAGONLANCE and its logo are trademarks of Wizards of the Coast, Inc. in the U.S.A. and other countries. ©2004 Wizards.